UPROOTED

Hycea 34 Book 1

Kennedy Rhodes

Cover design by InstaLove Graphics
ISBN: 979-8-218-67768-8
First Edition: 2025
Printed in USA

For Brandon—always my #1.

01

Elowen

It's possible I have underestimated my ability to deceive. I don't think of myself as a fraud, but there is no other explanation. I have somehow managed to fool my boss into believing I deserve to be here. I search everyone's faces, looking for any sign that they know the truth: I don't belong here.

The ballroom is stifling, and it's taking every ounce of self-control to not fidget with the itchy neckline of my gown. So long as I stay focused on the gray-haired man behind the lectern, I can fight the temptation to scratch at my suffocating black dress. He's been rambling about the significance of tonight way too long. I wince at his clumsy analogy to the 18th-century European expansion into North America. He drones on about the politics and bureaucracy that led to the new alliance between Earth and Hycea 34. Sparing no detail. *Yes, this is exactly what people like to hear. Tell us more about the bureaucratic red tape.*

"The Apollo Treaty marks the beginning of a special relationship between Earth and j'Tilak," he says, butchering the pronunciation of the planet's name, saying "Jay-Tilak" instead of using the soft J. You'd think he would learn the right way to say zhuh-Tilak. "This mutually beneficial agreement will provide military support to our new allies while enabling us to research the most imperative environmental issues we face. The Earth Galactic Alliance has selected our botany department to lead the research that could help solve the pollinator crisis that has threatened a global famine for the last few centuries. Together with a team of geneticists, they hold our future in the palm of their capable hands."

No. Pressure. I shift my weight back and forth to give each foot a break from my pinching shoes. I can't be the only one who wants this to wrap up. The monotonous hum of his speech pauses and everyone turns in my direction.

Oh shit. What did he say? I zoned out there for a second. I smile at the applause directed toward me and hope he doesn't call me up on stage. The six steps leading up taunt me.

Cedrik nudges the small of my back, putting some distance between me and those standing nearby. I stumble a little from his touch. He doesn't notice and enthusiastically adds to the applause.

"Congratulations, Elowen!" A stranger roughly pats me on the back and the champagne in my glass sloshes with the impact. I wish people would keep their hands to themselves. I'm going to end up face down on the floor if they keep this up.

"Dr. Andi Kahn and Ms. Elowen Carson, please come up and say a few words!" My stomach drops. This is a nightmare. My vision narrows and I numbly climb the stairs, clinging to the handrail for dear life. By some small miracle I reach the stage without falling or fainting, or both. I'm saved by my boss. She takes center stage and thanks the EGA and the University for the honor of being sent on this important mission.

I hold my smile and swallow down the stage fright that has creeped up. The bright lights on the stage blind me from seeing far. It's a small comfort. At least I can't see anyone's judgmental faces. I'm sure they are asking themselves why I'm up here. Dr. Kahn is a world-renowned botanist who has dedicated her life to addressing food scarcity. She's the youngest program director at the University. At 33, she's built the botany department into something so impressive we were selected for this task. Standing next to her, it's hard not to feel like a total loser. I'm only six years younger than her and I'm just finishing up my postdoc.

Dr. Kahn steps back from the lectern to make room for the wretched man who called us up here. "You don't mind that I did the talking? It's not too late to say a few words," she says quietly through a clenched smile.

"Nope, I'm staying right here." My cheek twitches from holding my fake smile so long.

"And finally, I want to thank the representatives from all five noble houses of j'Til… Hycea 34 for coming to celebrate this momentous occasion. Your incredible courage and leadership have made this all possible. We commit to being good allies and working to win the trust of those who are skeptical." He gave up on the planet's name this time, opting for the universal registration instead.

The crowd turns and claps for the group of Tilaks at the far end of the room. They stand out in the ballroom with their various shades of blue skin and tall stature. In addition to their physical contrast to humans, their clothes make them stand out as well. They are all wearing the same light gray formfitting shirt. An asymmetrical seam runs from the high collar down to one side with cords draped across their chests indicating house and rank. Their black hair is styled differently. Some have it long and tied back, others keep their hair short. At nearly seven feet tall, they tower over everyone else in the room. And no species I've ever seen compares with their broad muscular bodies. The alien delegation is surrounded by fawning humans whose blatant attempts at getting their attention are giving me second-hand embarrassment.

"We're all counting on you!" a woman says, leaning uncomfortably close to my face the moment I descend the stairs. Cedrik comes back to my side as I step away from the close talker. I position myself to put his lean frame between me and the crowd. I wish he was just a little bit taller so I could fully hide behind him.

"I feel like I'm dating a celebrity." His intended compliment falls flat. I smile and pat his arm. Maybe once we've got all the research we need from Hycea 34, and we come back with a viable solution for pollination, then I'll be worth all this fuss.

I spot my dad at the other end of the room and make my way toward him with Cedrik following closely behind. Dad's easy to find in a crowd. Just look for the middle-aged man in the middle of a cluster of people hanging on his every word. I catch his eye as I approach, and he acknowledges me with a wink. He's enjoyed every moment of notoriety his job has brought him. He's one of those people that was born to command attention. His career has been equal parts hard work and luck. His expertise in water conveyance systems combined with the political issues that inevitably arise during a drought have catapulted him into being the most famous hydrologist in the universe.

"Dad's holding court, per usual," my mom says, intercepting me on my way. She moves with ease in her long dress. She has a lot of practice with events like this.

"I wonder which story he's telling this time," I whisper in her ear. He's got the greatest hits, but every once in a while he'll surprise us.

"I bet it's… flash flood on Tarune," she says.

"Good guess!" I reply, countering with, "I'm going to say Draconis 5".

We join the crowd surrounding him just in time to find out. "Believe it or not, there was not a single casualty." We suppress our laughter when they reward him with a polite applause.

"You owe me five credits," she whispers. I can probably tell Tarune's story better than he could at this point.

"There she is! The woman of the hour!" He directs everyone's attention to me with dramatic flourish.

"Dr. Carson, you must be so proud," a finely dressed stranger tells him.

"I couldn't be prouder of my baby girl. She is the greatest botanist of her generation. Did you know Dr. Kahn handpicked Elowen for the team?"

"Dad." I scold him for outright bragging.

"Don't be modest, sweetie. This is a big deal," Mom says, taking his side. *Traitor.* I give her the same look. Silently begging her to stop.

"It's an amazing opportunity. I'm just grateful to be selected," I tell the crowd. Hopefully that is enough to redirect their attention back to my dad.

"There's no one better for the job." He puffs up with pride.

"If only you weren't retired," an eager fan of my dad says. I'm not offended by her obvious preference. She probably thinks I'm a nepo baby.

"Oh no—my exploration days are over. Time for me to pass the torch to the next generation," Dad says graciously.

The crowd seems to sense that the storytelling portion of the evening is over as they wander away to fill drinks and talk to others in the crowded ballroom. My eyes linger on the group of Tilaks. One smiles back and raises a glass. Embarrassed at being caught staring, I look back to my mom who is now talking to Cedrik, my soon-to-be-ex-boyfriend.

My dad hands her a fresh glass of champagne with a charming smile. She lights up from his attention. Over thirty years of marriage and they still look at each other with googly eyes. It's gross. And annoying. And a little bit sweet.

Certainly something I don't anticipate having with Cedrik. He's a nice guy. Emphasis on nice. We met in the lab and fell easily into a comfortable relationship. He was always around. We could spend hours in the lab in a companionable silence.

However, the decision has been made. I'm going to break it off with him before I leave. I've put it off for too long. I considered doing it before tonight, but he was just so excited about coming. This was my little act of kindness, postponing the inevitable.

Our relationship is more casual than my mom would like. Over the last few years, her gentle prodding about my love life has gotten less subtle. I'm looking forward to the temporary reprieve from her well-meaning meddling. She can save up all her hints about future grandchildren for when I get back.

"There's Dr. Napier. I'm going to introduce myself," Cedrik tells us and heads towards his target. He's been hoping for the opportunity to speak with the department head of Agricultural Science.

"He's a nice boy," Mom says once we're alone.

I look around to make sure we aren't within earshot of anyone. "I'm going to break it off tonight," I tell her reluctantly.

"Are you sure? I get the feeling he would wait for you," she suggests, squeezing her eyebrows together.

"It's better this way. I could be gone for a long time, and I just want to focus on my research with no distractions. And after that, I might not even stay on Earth."

"I never minded moving around. Maybe Cedrik would want to as well," she says.

"It's way too early to suggest something like that. A clean break is better for both of us." Our conversation is cut short when Cedrik returns.

"How did it go?" I ask.

"He told me to stop by his office to discuss the fellowship!"

I look over to her with my best "I told you so" face. Maybe now she sees Cedrik has his own career aspirations that don't include following me around from planet to planet.

"That's great!" I'm genuinely happy for him. Even though I'm calling it off between us, I still want the best for him.

With all the speeches done, I think I've found my opportunity to sneak out unnoticed. I lean closer to my mom and whisper, "How much longer do I need to stay?"

She'll know if I can get out of here without accidentally offending someone. I'd hate to trigger an interplanetary outrage over something as simple as me wanting to get back to my sweatpants.

"Have you spoken with Chancellor Mietner yet?" she asks as she scans the room for notable figures I am obligated to talk to.

"Yes, right when I got here."

"Dr. Brunell?"

"Done."

"Mrs. Gates?"

"Yep."

"Then you are free to go, my girl." With a quick kiss goodbye and a promise to talk tomorrow we part ways.

"Want to share a porter?" Cedrik asks, oblivious to what's coming next.

"Let's walk. It will give us a chance to talk." The streetlights reflect off the wet pavement. I dodge the puddles trying to keep my feet and the hem of my dress dry.

"What's on your mind, Babe?"

I've told him repeatedly over the last year that I hate being called Babe. No point correcting him now.

"I've been thinking about this a lot… I think it's for the best if we go our separate ways. I'm leaving and you'll be here. It would be too hard to try and make it work long distance." I take a deep breath and wait for his response. I can't bring myself to look up from my feet. I count our steps until he finally breaks the silence.

Cedrik lets the news sink in and says slowly, "Wow, okay. I'd be fine with waiting for you to get back. It's not like you're leaving forever."

"Trust me, you don't want to wait."

It's been effortless and easy with him from the beginning. We got along just fine, and in the year we've been together we never argued once. If I weren't leaving Earth in a few days, there wouldn't be a need to break up. I'm fully aware that it's more effort to break up with him than to stay together. But I can't find it within myself to fully commit to someone at this point in my life. For better or worse.

"Well, then I guess that's it. I hope it all works out for you," he says with a bitter smile. "I should have asked you for an autograph back there. Now it would just be weird," he jokes. I appreciate his attempt at lightening the mood.

"You don't hate me?" It's not fair of me to ask, but I do it anyway to ease my guilt.

"We're good."

"You can get that autograph when I get back." Cedrik is a class act. He's let me off the hook so easily. I probably deserve to be cursed at or at least be called heartless. He deserves someone a lot nicer than me.

02

Elowen

I stare down the pile of mangled and rusted pollinator bots. I toss the worthless ones aside and pick through the rest that might have salvage-able parts. Towards the bottom of the pile I find one with potential. Its rotator joint appears to be in working order. I volunteered to come out to the field today and show the new incoming class how to operate the polibots, a decision I now regret. I trudge back out to the field with my replacement part. It's hot out today, and it's not much cooler in the storage shed. Sweat stings my eyes. I use the cleanest part of my dirty coveralls to wipe my face.

Three freshman botany students wait for me. They look out of place in their crisp, out-of-the-pack coveralls. I drop the spare bot at their feet, kicking up a cloud of red dust onto their brand-new work boots.

I pry open the external panel and rip through frayed wires and rusty components quickly, not bothering to explain the steps to my audience. They'll figure it out eventually. No one ever showed me how to fix them, I had to figure it out on my own. I take more care the closer I get to the necessary replacement part.

"Don't bother repairing that polibot. They're going to be obsolete soon," Dr. Kahn says, peering over my shoulder. She's dressed for field work today, her pants tucked into tall boots, and a sunshield to protect her skin from the blazing sun. Her Senegalese twists are loosely gathered behind her.

"Worthless bucket of bolts," I say while trying to get the polibot's arm to rotate correctly.

The rusted components creak with every adjustment. I drop the broken bot and survey the damage left in its wake: the entire row of wheat ruined with each stalk bent awkwardly over at a ninety-degree angle. Its job is to gently disrupt the head of each stalk, pushing it over to pollinate the stalk next to it. This overzealous bot broke them instead.

"Go check the bots in Delta7," I tell my three new trainees. They scurry away, no doubt trying to impress the program director with their ability to follow orders.

"The polibots have always been a temporary solution. It's actually impressive that we've been able to get as far as we have with them," Dr. Kahn says.

"This one's salvageable. We only have twenty left, and they are dropping like flies." I tighten in the last screw. These bots have been the bane of my existence. For decades, humanity has been nursing along this out-of-date tech.

I remember my first day on this very field. A polibot malfunctioned and uprooted a long row of wheat. My lab partner and I meticulously disassembled the bot. We found the broken component, fixed it, polished the old metal, and sent the bot back into the fields. I was gentler back then.

"Dr. Kahn, I never thanked you for picking me." I flip the toggle on. The polibot sputters before lurching forward and continuing down the row, this time not breaking off the stalks as it moves.

"You were the obvious choice," she says with a kind smile.

"I appreciate the chance. And I won't let you down." I rub the dirt off my hands and try to brush the debris off my pants.

She gives me a curious look. "Won't let me down? Why would you say that?" she asks with so much kindness in her voice it makes my throat clench up.

"I don't want you to worry that I won't work hard while I'm there. I want you to know you chose the right person."

"I have no doubt that you will put that brilliant mind to work and help us find a solution to this mess," she says and waves over the ruined rows of wheat.

"I guess I am freaking out a little," I admit.

"Where is that confidence I saw during your interviews? The Elowen who showed up prepared and put everyone else to shame?"

"I don't know. I've been feeling the pressure set in. Every time someone congratulates me, I just feel this pit in my stomach."

"It feels different when it's your own expectations versus someone else's."

She nailed it and named the very thing I've been feeling for the last few weeks as we've been preparing to leave. Having the words to explain my mental state takes some of the pressure off.

"I think you're right."

"Everyone is going to react to those external expectations differently. For some, it's the fuel they need to achieve. For others it's paralyzing. Some will even rebel against any form of expectations internal or external."

"I think I fall into the second category," I say reluctantly.

"And there is absolutely nothing wrong with that. Just stay focused on the things that keep you motivated and focused. Ignore all the rest."

I grab a broken stalk and turn it between my fingers, letting her advice sink in. She's right. Now's the time to get focused, to let go of all the things that drain my energy.

"Thank you. I appreciate it," I tell her honestly. I have never been more grateful to have a mentor like Dr. Kahn. She has pushed me academically and helped me grow as a person. We aren't that far apart in age, but I look up to her.

"Good. Leave that rusty robot there, and let's have our last cup of good coffee before we leave."

I take a final look at the sprawling wheat field, hoping it's the last time I'll see a field being tended by polibots. I kick the leftover heap of metal as I turn and follow her.

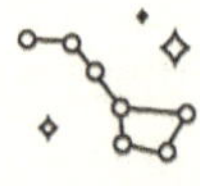

I savor the smell of the freshly brewed coffee before I test the temperature on my lips. Dr. Kahn is right about a lot of stuff. She's absolutely right about this being one of the last cups of decent coffee we will get. The synthetic coffee they try to pass off at research centers doesn't come close to the real thing.

"I'm going to miss this place," she says and scans the coffee shop. It's the heartbeat of the University. It's on the corner of campus that leads to the rest of New Boston. The seats are well worn, the tables nicked and ring-stained. It's not trendy or glamorous.

"I am too."

"Maybe they will put a plaque on one of the tables. 'Here sat the illustrious Elowen Carson,'" she says. My mood lightens from her gentle teasing.

"I've always dreamed of coffee spilled on my name."

"Young college students will make a pilgrimage here. They'll flock to see where you got your last cup of coffee before you saved humanity."

"And what about the great Dr. Kahn? Where will students go to honor her part in ensuring our survival on Earth?" I turn it back on her.

"If I could pick, I would say, an empty field. A place where soil can sit and rest and replenish." Her beautiful words put a lump in my throat.

Industrial agriculture has destroyed much of the usable soil. Overcultivation is necessary now to account for the high rate of crop failures, but we are stuck in a vicious cycle. The majority of every crop withers before it can provide sustenance for our struggling planet.

"That's not fair. I get a sticky table and you get poetry."

She shrugs and lifts her cup in a toast, enjoying the last of her warm coffee.

03

Elowen

I take one last look around my empty apartment. This little shoebox of a place has been my home for the last rotation. On one hand, I'm sad to say goodbye. On the other, I've grown restless here and cannot wait for a new challenge. There will always be something bittersweet about closing a chapter and starting a new one. There were times when I was younger that all I wanted was to live on Earth, but reality didn't live up to expectations. I just never felt at home here.

This is a career-defining moment, a chance of a lifetime to make a real difference. When I heard that the University had been granted access to the research center, I became obsessed. Singularly focused on getting on the team. You name the gold star, I got it—great grades, peer-reviewed papers published, and my fair share of awards. Every interview, I showed up like I was defending my dissertation. Any qual-ification I made sure to exceed. As far as I was concerned, the position was mine for the taking. Had things not gone my way, I absolutely wasn't above begging.

I'm ready to get to j'Tilak and get to work. The seemingly end-less receptions and dinners and celebrations all feel empty when we don't have solutions. I'd prefer we save all the celebrating for when we return with answers. After that, I'll be the first to run up on stage. Maybe then all the attention will feel deserved.

The front door slides open when my parents arrive. My mom's eyes are already red and brimming with tears. She sniffles and plasters on a shaky smile. I've seen this look before. Every time we're separated from each other, she falls apart. I definitely inherited my independent streak from my dad, and I'm always the one to offer comfort in these situations.

"I know, I know, I'm being silly. You're not even going to be gone that long." I pull her into a tight hug and her body relaxes into mine. She's the closest friend I've got. But every once in a while, I feel like a third wheel. My parents are at a stage in their lives when a romantic dinner shouldn't include their grown daughter.

"I'll miss you too, Mom."

"No one will be missing anyone if we don't get going," Dad says as he picks up my luggage. Using my bags, he nudges us out and into the round, reflective porter waiting for us on the street.

Everything outside blurs as the porter reaches full speed. I turn my head away from my parents to the window, giving myself a moment to rein in my tears. My breath fogs against the cold plexi. The glass reflects my dark shoulder-length bob and well-defined eyebrows. My dark brown eyes stare back, lingering on the smattering of freckles across my nose which have always made me look a bit younger than I actually am. My freckles are my favorite thing about my face. My mom always teased that she could map out constellations on them.

It's not long before the astroport comes into view. In the distance I see the lander that will bring me to the shuttle where I'll spend the next 6EMs. The porter makes a quick stop at the entrance to the terminal. I step out and take the last breath of unrecycled air I will have for a long time. I wonder what the atmosphere will be like once I get to j'Tilak. I can't wait to breathe in the hydrogen-rich air.

My mom frets over my luggage, trying to hide her tears from me. My dad has a wistful look on his face, likely reliving his glory days.

We silently hug one last time. Right before I enter the terminal, I hear my dad call out, "Make us proud, Ellie!" I give one last smile and wave before I walk through the sliding doors and officially start the next chapter of my life.

I plunge into the moving crowd and weave my way through the bustling astroport. A group of Xandarans have gathered and blocked my path. I try to politely make my way though, uttering apologies when I brush up against their transparent jelly-like skin.

A Pyrrion couple cuts across my path as they chase after their toddler who's running full speed away from them. The father scoops up the small tentacled child and chides her in their garbled language. She sticks her tongue out and covers his face with spit.

I love the familiar feeling of being surrounded by so many different species and languages. Some things are so universal, like a group of tourists unaware of their surroundings, or a kid giving their parents a hard time. I never really got used to the homogeneous student population at the University. I've never felt fully "human" since I wasn't raised on Earth.

The crowd thins as I get to my boarding agent. We're separated by a transparent plexi with a bright yellow edge. Without waiting for instructions, I align my face with the hollow outline in the shape of a head to initiate the facial scan.

I can do this in my sleep. I remember my dad used to hoist me up for my facial scans when I was too little to reach. He'd tease me with a tickle under my arm to make me squirm and mess up the scan. Luckily, he was the one that would get the stern looks from the staff.

The agent helping me today stays focused on the screen, flipping through to verify all documentation is in order. She finally looks past the plexi and makes eye contact. I search for signs of humanity in her unnaturally symmetrical face. Sometimes it's hard to know if I'm talking to a living breathing person or if this is an upgraded AIBot. At some point in our history, beauty standards for humans started to mirror the immaculate expressionless faces of AIBots. It's a sort of "chicken and egg" situation. Which came first—the AIBot replicating the beautifully sculpted features of a human, or humans being inspired by the uniformity of bots?

"Thanks!" I wait for a response that doesn't come. She goes back to swiping at her screen. She's a bot—or a really tired and overworked human. Either possibility is just as likely. I'm still not entirely sure when I head towards my gate. My rule of thumb is to always assume human. They tend to take offense to being mistaken for a bot. Not a lesson I need to learn twice.

The sky bridge crowds as I make my way onto the lander. I follow the lights directing my way through the hallways to my assigned capsule. The flight crew is busy preparing for take-off. Every few feet they cluster around huge floor-to-ceiling monitors that are flush with the smooth white walls, furiously swiping and tapping away. I give them a wide berth and try my best to stay out of their way. We exchange polite smiles as I pass by and I decline their kind offers to help me board. I know my way around a shuttle, and they have far more important things to do.

A door frame lights up, indicating I've reached my room. I duck in and drop my bag on the ground. Not too bad. This will be just fine. It's nicer than other capsules I've been in. Sometimes it's a glorified cargo bay with hard steel seats and fraying harnesses. I get a whole room with my own hydrogel bed.

Most of my belongings were loaded and unpacked days ago. I check the drawers to make sure everything is ready to go.

I've got everything tucked away and I'm comfortable on the bed when the first liftoff warning chimes.

"Welcome aboard, Elowen. Are your accommodations to your satisfaction?" a cheerful robotic female voice asks.

"Everything's great." I'm giddy with anticipation. I give a little eek and kick my feet in the air.

"Please indicate when you are prepared for liftoff," she instructs.

"I'm ready." I close my eyes and feel a faint shift in the air around me. A cool mist fills the room, and a metallic taste hits the back of my throat as I drift effortlessly into stasis.

The tips of my fingers brush over soft, fluffy wheat stalks as I wander through endless fields. Bright green rows stripe across the fields. Soon they will turn golden and be ready for harvest. I'm alone out here. A strange feeling of isolation takes hold of me. I turn around trying to figure out where I am. In the distance I see a tall slender building. My subconscious tells me I'm familiar with it, but I've never seen it before.

I walk towards the building feeling like that is where I should be. No matter how long I walk, I never get any closer. I try going faster. I run towards my goal. My legs feel heavy and slow. The harder I push the more resistance I feel against my body.

My vision grays at the edges, and suddenly I'm looking up at the night sky. I see a meteor shoot across the sky. "On Earth, they used to call those shooting stars!" I point out and reach for the person next to me. My hand lands on soft, cold grass. An empty space where I had expected to find someone.

Everything fades to black and I settle into a deep sleep.

04

Aro

"You know what time it is?!" I yell over the crowded briefing room. I get a handful of grumbles at my enthusiastic start. "I said, do you know what time it is?!" I ask again, this time more aggressively.

"Respectfully, sir, it's too early for this shit," Tai says, pinching the bridge of his nose. He taps his bionic fingers on the desk impatiently. The silver zirconite makes a loud ting with every strike.

"It's time for post assignments, so if you'd like to do something other than stare at security streams, I'd suggest you fucking pay attention."

That gets the result I was hoping for. The slouchers sit up straight, the sleepy ones perk up, and those talking give me their undivided attention.

"We're going to try something a little different. I'm going to offer up the best post, and you all are going to try and convince me that you deserve it."

Most captains would just give out assignments and move on with their day. For some reason Commander Rialto lets me have a little fun here and there. And I can't pass up any opportunity to break up the monotony of the day.

"You can cut my hair." Bennet is the first to speak up.

"Bennet coming in hot, ready to give up his boyish good looks so he can sleep in. That's gonna be hard to beat. Who else?" I scan the room, looking for the next offer.

"I'll clean your bunk every morning and bring you breakfast," Viktor says.

"Oh, and here's Viktor going in the opposite direction, I'm not about to hinge my mornings on your culinary skills. I've seen what you eat for breakfast. Disqualified."

"You can have half of my overtime credits!" I hear from the back of the room.

"Paying for a post? That is called a bribe. You're out. I'm leaning towards Bennet. Anyone else out there willing to sacrifice their dignity? Tai? You look like you're overdue for a haircut."

Tai twitches his ear at me. The rude gesture is the only acknowledgment that he heard me.

"I'll take three of your shifts," Locke offers.

"Very tempting… Any three?" I clarify.

"Any three." Locke leans back in his chair and props his feet up on the desk. He lifts an eyebrow, the one with a scar right through the center, as he scans the room, daring anyone to outbid him for the post. He's mastered the art of intimidation, never giving us an answer for how he got the scar through his brow, along with the half-moon-shaped scar on his cheek below it. Everyone around him avoids eye contact. Bennet looks especially defeated.

Locke's offer appeals to me the most, but I really can't pass up the opportunity to mess with Bennet. We all win if he lets me give him a cut. Well, everyone except Bennet.

"Tough choice, but I've got to go with the shears. Bennet, congratulations—First Watch Sergeant."

"Okay, enough of that," Commander Rialto says and relieves me of the podium. "The humans assigned to MuraDome IV will be arriving in the next EM. It's our job to make sure everyone is safe, follows the rules, and it's out of our pay grade to determine what happens next."

"One last thing," Deputy Petrok says. "In an act of solidarity, the Council has asked us to adjust our dietary options to match the humans."

"What does that mean?" Tai asks.

"It means we're eating noodles, boys." No one dares to complain about this in front of the commanders, but I know I'm going to hear about it later.

Everyone thumps the desk with their palms in unison, acknowledging his instructions. The announcement of our new visitors makes my mind wander back to the treaty reception on Earth. Throughout the entire night my eyes kept wandering back to a woman. I watched the way she would duck her head every time someone would congratulate her. She held onto her champagne glass like it was a lifeline. Some unknown part of me needed to go stand next to her, to shield her. Clearly the man following her around like a lost quinstak wasn't providing her any support. Before I could go introduce myself to her, she disappeared.

"There will be no fraternizing with the humans. You will not discuss your personal beliefs on matters of interplanetary policy. You will not bring in outside contraband. The humans will be restricted to MuraDome IV. That all being said, they are not our prisoners. Be accommodating and make sure they feel welcomed. And most importantly of all, don't fuck this up."

The room erupts the moment Rialto steps out from behind the podium. "Aro, with me," he orders.

I follow him into his office and he sits down at his desk, leaving me standing while he settles into his chair.

"You obviously knew about this prior to today."

"I did, sir."

"You know how important this treaty is for us. I expect you to keep everyone in line," Rialto says.

"Will do, sir."

"Our top priority is making sure we uphold our end of the treaty. If we lose Earth as allies, we're vulnerable. Make sure the humans get what they need. The sooner they finish their research, the sooner they can get back to Earth."

"Understood."

"Now go make Bennet earn his post."

"Yes, sir."

As soon as I'm done with Bennet's hair, I'll get a trim as well. I want to look good when the humans arrive.

05

Elowen

Coming out of stasis is a lot like waking up from surgery. Sounds happen first. A soft rhythmic beeping wakes me up. I slowly open my eyes. They are dry and scratchy. After a few tries I get both eyes open and can focus on the darkened ceiling. I clear my throat. My mouth feels like it's full of sand. I'm shivering from the cold room.

Once I've regained all my senses, I notice movement across the room. Medbots quietly putter around me and one other person in the shuttle's recovery room. A small tray extends out with a steel bottle of water and a nutritional gel pack. I push up to a sitting position, squeeze the tasteless gel into my mouth and take a small sip of water to wash it down. I am absolutely starving, but I force myself to go slowly. I want to eat as soon as possible, and that means being patient. I've learned from past experiences to not rush this process. As a kid I would toss back the gel as quickly as possible and wash it down with gulps of water and end up puking for hours.

It's been six years since my last stasis trip. Thankfully they've made some improvements on the gel. It used to be flavored in a poor attempt to imitate actual food. Whoever makes this stuff finally gave up on the pretense. Now it's tasteless and much easier to get down.

The worst part of stasis travel is the dreams. A weird twilight sleep of random images, memories, and hallucinations. Growing up, my stasis dreams were mostly about not being able to find my parents. As I grew, they became more about showing up to class unprepared for finals. I suppose those feelings of constant striving for approval and success haven't been resolved. This is my mind humbly reminding me of my unresolved issues. When I return to Earth, I'm demanding a refund from my therapist.

A more pressing matter pushes those thoughts away: noodles. It takes me a long time to get down the short hallway. My legs are stiff and sore. The narrow halls of the transport support me as I slightly stumble along. The last door holds the reward I'm desperate to reach. I press my palm to the door's sensor. It slides away and the smell of warm noodles hits me.

I sit at the first table within staggering distance from the door and swipe my finger across the ordering dashboard that's flush with the table. Two buttons light up, a red one with three squiggly vertical lines for hot, the other blue—a small prism for cold. I tap the red option and moments later a mechanical arm extends up from under the table and drops the steaming bowl in front of me. I grab my chopsticks, scoop an impolite amount of noodles, swirl them around, and shove them into my mouth. Now that's what I'm talking about.

The door slides open and the other person from the medbay walks through. Her movements are stiff and disjointed. Broth splashes my face and shirt as she sits down across from me. She looks as disheveled as I do, her pink hair tied up in a messy bun. She rubs her green eyes, still trying to wake herself up.

"What's a girl gotta do to get some food around here?" She nearly growls. I like her already.

"Hot or cold?" I ask as I activate the dashboard on the table.

"Hot, please."

I tap the red button and dive back into my bowl. If I had better manners, I'd wait for her food to arrive, but I'm starving—and that is taking precedence at the moment.

"I'm the worst. I should properly introduce myself before demanding food. I've never been this hungry in my entire life. I'm Brisa, but everyone calls me Bri."

"No worries, I'm Elowen. Stasis messes me up every time. After two more of these, I'll feel human again," I say, nodding at my bowl. "Was this your first stasis?"

"Yep, first stasis, first time off Earth, first whatever the fuck that gel thing was." The robotic arm swings up and delivers Bri her noodles. She digs in with enthusiasm.

"Damn, this is good. Wait, are they actually this good, or am I just super hungry?" she asks, her mouth full.

"Probably just hungry. Soon you'll be going for a stale protein bar over these bad boys." I hate to be the bearer of bad news. Our dietary options are extremely bleak for the foreseeable future. Noodles are standard for space travel. They're the perfect nutritionally modified food. They don't expire, and they don't take up much room. But one does get sick of them pretty quickly.

After a few bites, Bri breaks the silence. "I can finally think straight. That was crazy. I guess that's what happens when you don't eat during a five-month fever dream. You seem like you know what you're doing. I take it you've been off planet before?"

"Yeah, I grew up all over. I was only really on Earth for the last rotation. And for the record, there is nothing in the universe like that first bowl of noodles after waking up."

I like Bri. She's one of those people who draws you in immediately. Her casual confidence puts me at ease. I'm barely awake and I already have a friend. This trip is off to a good start.

"What team are you on?" I ask, hoping we will be working together.

"Genetics."

"I'm on botany."

"That's great! Oh man—I'm not feeling so good." She clutches at her stomach and the smile fades. She lets out a shaky breath and turns a sickly pale. I know that face. She probably rushed the gel, and it's catching up with her.

"Let's get you back to the medbay," I say as I help her up to walk her back as swiftly as I can. I know what happens next, and I'd rather not be present for it.

06

Elowen

Bri and I spend the next few weeks going through training modules. The cumulative effect of seeing all the rules at once is starting to irritate Bri. She huffs as she swipes through the course on the financial responsibility of the "enrollee" to cover any equipment they damage. I'm not worried. I have a perfect record with lab supplies. I've never even broken a beaker.

She lets out a loud gasp when she realizes we won't be able to leave the muradome the entire time we are there. I'm not as bothered by the rules. I like rules. They let me know exactly what is expected. I chalk up the strict protocols to diplomatic overreach. A lot is riding on this alliance.

Bri pauses our module on planetary safety after it covers fire hazards.

"Seriously? No fire? At all?!" she pouts.

"There's a high risk of fire because of the extra hydrogen in the atmosphere. The smallest spark could be catastrophic." Maybe if she knows the reason the rule is there, she won't be so bummed. "Don't worry—we'll improvise some birthday candles for you." I rib her a little, hoping to cheer her up.

"Well, what am I supposed to do with my flamethrower?" She bites her bottom lip, holding back a smile. It seems the reality of being so far from home and on a different planet is starting to set in.

From what I can tell, Hycea 34, or j'Tilak, is not that different from Earth, minus the way we've devastated our natural resources and brought about our own doom. The customs and social norms aren't that different. I'm grateful. I've been to places with really strange gender roles and rigid economic status conventions, and places where the weather is so extreme that survival requires specialized equipment.

Hycean planets are my favorites to visit. Their environments are most like Earth's, sometimes even better. On j'Tilak, their environment, proximity to their two primary suns, and size encourage a thriving, biologically diverse, and vibrant ecosystem.

The drastic differences between regions make the species on Hycea 34 extremely diverse. I'll be stationed at MuraDome IV on the continent pt'Clanik, which is milder and more temperate than some of the others. All the images I've seen of pt'Clanik make it look like an ideal pastoral painting from centuries ago. Rolling hills, bright blue sky—none of the scars from an industrial revolution that went too far. Hycea 34 is the Goldilocks of worlds. Not too hot, not too cold. Not too big, not too small. Just right.

After we finish our modules each day, I spend the few remaining hours preparing with Dr. Kahn so we can start our research as soon as we get there. The clock is ticking on Earth's unstable food supply. For centuries, we've been trying to save our pollinators. For the first time we might actually have a solution. If we can figure out how to recreate the pollination process from Hycea 34 and make it work on Earth, we could save millions of lives.

When I'm not working, I torment Bri with everything I know about the flora on Hycea 34. I particularly like torturing her with plant facts during dinner.

"Vegetation has hypermobility there," I tell her. "Plants and trees can uproot themselves, seek out sunlight, nutrients, hydration, pollinators—whatever they need to ensure survival. Each plant emits a signature electrical pulse that's received by any compatible plant in the surrounding area." I look up from my noodles at her deadpan face and continue with a smile. "Over the centuries, crops have evolved to rely more heavily on cross-pollination. Wheat used to be able to self-pollinate, but now we use pollinator bots to get them to germinate."

"Please don't make me regret being your friend," she says. I've quickly learned Bri prefers not to discuss work outside of business hours.

"Well, I'm your only friend at this point, so you don't have much choice."

"I don't hold you hostage and talk about genome sequencing." Bri levels me with an accusatory stare.

"That's because we both know that genetics is boring."

"Hilarious." She glowers at me.

"Thank you!" I place my hand on my chest, dramatically accepting her insincere compliment.

"Do you see me laughing?" she asks.

"I think you're laughing on the inside." I give her a squinty smile and she rolls her eyes.

"Okay, I think we're done here," she says standing up. I rush to keep up with her as she walks down the narrow hallway towards her room.

"You know what's not boring?" I ask.

"Wait—is this the setup for a joke?" Bri asks, eyeing me skeptically.

"Nope! Did you know that oak trees use mycorrhizal networks of fungi to share resources and information about the environment? On Hycea 34, plant life's ability to uproot and move is what makes this place so unique." I continue my monologue, just to annoy her a little bit more.

"What do you think the locals are like on j'Tilak?" She changes the subject the moment I stop for a breath.

"Big, blue, and extremely suspicious of humans," I say. We just finished our sensitivity training on the complicated political situation between Earth and Hycea 34. The ink on the Apollo Treaty is hardly dry and our research team will be the first to arrive. It's up to us to assimilate and reassure everyone we can peacefully coexist. A lot is hanging on this arrangement.

"Oh, believe me—I know what they look like. The Tilak men are smoking hot. I'm just wondering how welcoming they will be," Bri says.

Bri's comment takes me back to the treaty signing. They stayed mostly to themselves. The Earth delegation ended up touring them around and hosting state dinners to build a strong relationship. When I saw them, the Tilak were all standoffish and quiet. The most cynical of the media tried to blame their distance on a general mistrust. One thing that drives me crazy about humans: they are always so quick to think the worst.

"Bri, ask me how long a day is on Hycea 34," I say. On a shuttle with not much to do, annoying Bri has quickly become my favorite hobby.

"No, I don't think I will."

07

Aro

"Barracks inspection, sir?" I did not expect this when I got called into Rialto's office this morning.

"You heard me, and I want it done by 1000," Rialto answers without looking up from his handheld transparent yuriOS. His attention is fixed to the device. His quick swiping creates a blur of glowing blue and green across the screen.

"And why are we doing this?" I ask.

"Aro, I don't have time for you to question every directive that comes through. I've been instructed that a barracks check needs to be completed before their arrival, and I'm ordering you to do it." I hesitate long enough for him to clear his throat and tighten his grip on his yuriOS.

"Yes, sir."

"The only things that can stay are on this list. If it's not on this list it's got to go."

He swipes it over to my yuriOS. The listed items are familiar.

"*If*, sir? This is a very short list."

"You just can't help yourself, can you?" Rialto says, finally looking up at me.

"If I knew why…" I scan down the list. I know the unit won't be shy in expressing their feelings about surrendering their belongings. I'd like to be able to give them a reason.

A voice interrupts us through the intercom. "The unit has been notified and will be ready for inspection at 0800."

Rialto looks up at me exasperated. "Report back once the inspection's complete. You're dismissed." He swats at the air, sending me away.

I look through the list a second time as I walk through the office towards the barracks. No one's going to be happy about this. The list is ridiculously short.

Maak meets me at the entrance to the barracks and I show him the list without a word.

"You've got to be kidding me," he says as he runs his eyes down the list.

"I wish."

"When was the last time you had your bunk tossed?" he asks.

"Week two of Intros, just like everyone else." I remember the inspection well. Barracks inspections are usually only done during Introductions to ingrain discipline. I got caught with an unmade bed, a mistake I never made again.

"You're going to catch heat for this."

"I'm well aware. I tried to reason with Rialto, but this came from above."

"Only you could get away with questioning the commander," Maak says.

The housing unit door slides open. Tilaks stand at attention down the long hallway. Maak and I stop in front of the first door, and he strides into the room with a predatory look on his face. I can tell he's going to have fun with this. He loves hazing the new guys.

"Toss that bed, recruit," Maak orders the nervous soldier.

"Sir?" He looks at me and sounds terrified.

"I said, toss the fucking bed! This is disgusting. When's the last time you cleaned these quarters?" Maak's voice booms down the corridor. I look around the pristine room. It's in better condition than mine.

"Maak, knock it off," I tell him. "Lugo, anything not listed here needs to go." I use my yuriOS to project the list onto the far wall. He scrambles to grab all the stuff.

"You never let me have any fun," Maak whines.

"Let's get this over with, preferably without getting elbow deep in anyone's dirty laundry."

"You're losing your edge," he mutters, trying to shame me for taking this one task seriously and not turning it into a game.

"I've got plenty of fucking edge."

"Prove it," he challenges.

I just roll my eyes and head down the hall. "You're a child."

Maak goes farther down and bellows at the next soldier waiting for his turn.

"Only things staying are on the list. I can take it, or you can send it home," I say as I approach the next waiting soldier.

"Yes, sir." He springs into action, no doubt grateful he got me rather than Maak.

I'm making good time. It's not long before I approach Tai standing at attention toward the end of the hall. His rigid posture shows his annoyance.

"The humans aren't even here yet, and they're already a pain in my ass," he grumbles.

"This list came from the Council, not Earth," I correct him.

"I didn't think I signed up to babysit a bunch of helpless humans," Tai continues. Even though he's perpetually in a bad mood, Tai's still my closest friend. He's honest and loyal. I'd trust him with my life.

For how much Tai is dreading their arrival, I'm getting more excited by the day. There is a lot of speculation about what will happen when they get here. I wonder most of all about her, that woman. She's supposed to be part of the team here at MuraDome IV. I've made it my mission to meet her.

"Get your shit so I can be done with this." I check the time. Rialto wants it done by 1000, and I'm cutting it close. I'm not willing to burn up some of my goodwill with the commander over something stupid like not finishing this barracks inspection on time.

"Yes, sir," he says sharply. He clangs his bionic hand against the metal door frame as he steps into his room. The thump is supposed to be an acknowledgment of orders. Maybe it's his tone or posture, but I don't get the feeling that was his intention just now.

08

Elowen

An update flashes across my yuriOS, briefly turning my room red from the bright light. My alarm woke me up a while ago and I'm still trying to muster up the motivation to get out of bed. Any other day, I would have just slept in, but not today. Today is special. We get to refuel and get off this shuttle for a few hours. I can't wait to feel solid ground under my feet and breathe fresh air.

"Travel itinerary: Update" scrolls past the screen on repeat. I swipe through the voyage log on my yuriOS. We have been rerouted from our scheduled stop on planet Nebulon to a nearby fueling station instead.

The pit stop on Nebulon is all we have been talking about for days. We were so excited to get off this shuttle. Instead of a day with our feet on solid ground and fresh air in our lungs, we get a few miserable hours of subjecting ourselves to the worst sort of degenerates on a space station.

Fueling stations are bottom-of-the-barrel pit stops—categorically dirty, neglected, and hardly functioning. Most people avoid them at all costs. The really nice ones have a bar or diner with a wide range of food from across the galaxy, delicacies that the obscenely wealthy travel light-years for. The station we are going to today will likely only serve something that expired before I was born and will result in intestinal distress for at least forty-eight hours.

Dr. Kahn is heading down the narrow hallway when I step out of my room. She's got her arms out to steady herself, doing everything to keep her balance. After all these weeks she still hasn't gotten her sea legs.

"Did you see the update?" I ask.

"I did. I really could have used a few hours off this shuttle," she says. "I might regret this, but I'm still going to walk around. I need a change of scenery."

"On the bright side, at least we'll get to j'Tilak a day ahead of schedule."

"I'm sure Bri is excited to see her first fueling station," Dr. Kahn says.

"Dr. Kahn, she's going to be very disappointed."

"We are millions of miles away from Earth—call me Andi. It feels weird to be so formal while we are hurtling through space," she says.

"Okay then, Andi, I suggest you hold onto your valuables while exploring the station. You're about to get a lesson in the underbelly of space travel."

Our shuttle circles around the wagon-wheel-shaped station looking for an empty dock. All but one are already occupied. Fantastic—it's going to be busy and overcrowded in the hub. As we slow down and approach the last available spot, my stomach lurches from the sudden change in speed.

We hover here for almost an hour trying to dock. The delay doesn't bother me at all. It means less time Bri is going to drag me around on the station. My tiny window has a perfect view of the countless failed attempts at connecting. I can tell from the aging tech that this is a particularly old fueling station. In a universe of gross fueling stops, we might have found the worst one.

I'm going to be a good friend and go with her. I'll brave the grimy station, but I draw the line at eating station meat. It might be my last chance to eat something other than noodles, but I'd rather be safe than sorry. I don't want to spend the rest of the trip hunched over a toilet.

Green lights flash overhead, giving us the go-ahead to exit the shuttle. That's my signal—let's get this over with. I'm hoping Bri will take one look around and come running back to our shuttle. She is about to realize there are worse things than cabin fever.

"Finally! Let's go. I'm so excited." She's bouncing when she finds me in the hall.

I can smell the station before we even step onboard. It's a combination of malfunctioning air filters, something fermenting, and decades of grime, deposited by the thousands of different species who pass through.

"Wow! Okay. You weren't lying," Bri says and covers her nose.

"Let's just take a quick walk-through—then we come back." I'm well aware of my shitty attitude, and I have no plans to act any differently. Right now, I could be walking under a clear sky, fresh air, and solid ground. Instead, I'm holding my breath as we step over the threshold. I wonder if Bri realizes that the deteriorating tunnel we've entered is the only thing standing between us and being vacced out into space.

"Is this place going to have any redeeming qualities?" she asks, dodging a pile of garbage propped against the wall. Half-empty noodle containers teeter on top of each other, waiting for someone to tip the whole disgusting tower over. The wall it's relying on doesn't look good either. The metal has started to rust at the seams, and empty holes dot the length where screws should be to hold it in place. At one point in the distant past, the wall was probably smooth and shiny. Now it's rusted, dented, and looks like it could fail at any moment.

"Probably not. This place is disgusting. I'm going to need a round of antibiotics after this," I say and step over a heap of metal that appears to have been a mechanic bot.

"Someone's in a bad mood today," Bri points out.

"I really needed fresh air."

A long line of aliens is at the fueling window in the center of the hub, each waiting for their turn to purchase fuel. They all seem as eager as I do to get off this heap of metal floating in space. Many are hunched over so their heads don't hit the low roof. This station was not built to accommodate its current clientele of giant aliens.

Across the hub, a neon sign flickers over a doorway. Its bright lights attempt to spell out "dive bar" with an R that ran out of neon decades ago.

Bri looks at me. "After you." I motion for her to go in first. She can confront whatever terrifying scene we are walking into.

Bri walks through the door without hesitation and I reluctantly follow her in. I'm not able to see much as my eyes adjust to the darkness.

A wall of colored glass bottles comes into focus along with a tentacled Pyrrion pouring drinks and wiping down the bar top. All nine of their long arms work independently to serve the crowded bar. The fermenting smell is absolutely coming from here and there is no way I am eating or drinking anything from this place.

"Elowen? Elowen Carson, is that you?" I hear my name come from a dark alcove at the other end of the bar. Whoever said it sounds like they've already been in the bar for a while. Frantically, I try to decide between bolting from this place and figuring out who could possibly know me here. As if she can read my mind, Bri steps closer to my side and hugs my arm to her body, locking me in place. Or maybe she's finally starting to appreciate the reality of where we are and doesn't want to get left behind.

A short figure with a hairless head, large wide-set black eyes, and a small mouth bracketed by two small tusks comes into view. In this dark room it's hard to see exactly who is coming my way, but I can tell it's a Na'Lorskan female. Her clothes are a little worse for wear, and she's missing the traditional headscarf worn on her planet. Who is that?

I cling to Bri just as tightly. Whatever is happening, we are in this together. In fact, I partially blame her. I hear my name again and still don't recognize the voice it's coming from. Our soon-to-be attacker roughly knocks over a chair in her rush to get to us. I turn towards the door to flee when I'm wrapped into a tight hug from two boney arms.

"Get back here, Elowen—it's me! It's Priya!" she says.

"Priya? No way!" I'm shocked to see her. It takes a second, but I finally recognize her familiar face. She hasn't changed much at all since I last saw her more than a decade ago. But in this awful place far from her home planet and in these clothes, I could have walked by and never realized I had missed my closest childhood friend.

"Bri, this is Priya. She is one of my oldest friends."

They exchange introductions and Priya wraps me in another tight hug, the top of her head only coming up to my chest. I step back and look at her, still in complete shock.

"What are you doing here?" she asks.

"We're on our way to j'Tilak. What are *you* doing here? Shouldn't you be on some gilded throne writing decrees?" Priya is the Na'Lorskan chancellor's daughter. When we were young I loved to tease her about her royal lineage.

"You know we don't have any thrones." A dozen heads turn towards us at her booming laugh. She's always been loud for such a small thing. "I'm an ambassador now. Our system is formalizing some trade procedures, and the duty fell to me," she says.

Even though so much has changed, it feels like no time has passed since we last saw each other.

"Why aren't you at one of those luxury fueling stations? The ones with, you know… stuff?" I ask.

"Don't insult me. I am a woman of the people. Come have a drink. It's going to be a while before any of us get any fuel."

The three of us squeeze between tightly packed tables, earning a few grunts from the other patrons when we bump our way through. At Priya's table, I take the seat facing the room. There is no way I am turning my back on this place. The seat cushion is cracked and the broken chair pitches me forward awkwardly.

It seems like I'm the only one bothered by the dilapidated state of the bar. Bri and Priya look like they are having the time of their lives. Priya swipes in an order of drinks for us on the menu screen. Seconds later, a long Pyrrion tentacle extends and drops the drinks off on our table. I'm surprised by how quickly we get served. Priya must have already generously tipped the bartender. I skeptically watch mine, not sure I want to chance fate by drinking it.

"Priya, please tell me you're not going to drink that," I say.

"It's not so bad. There are worse places in the universe—trust me," she says. This is not the Priya I remember. She grew up in the height of luxury, with no shortage of bots ready to meet her every demand.

"Wow. A lot has changed in the last ten years. I never thought I'd see the chancellor's daughter defending a place like this."

"To old friends!" Priya raises her glass of murky alcohol. Our glasses clink together and after everyone else has taken a long gulp, I grudgingly take a sip. The fizzy, slightly bitter drink goes down easily, and a warm rush hits my bloodstream.

Bri takes another long drink before setting her half-empty glass down. She turns to Priya. "Start at the beginning. I want to hear every single embarrassing thing Elowen has ever done."

Priya looks between us with a smirk. I steel myself, preparing to be the entertainment for the evening. I give her a look, begging her to go easy on me.

"The first time I saw Elowen, she walked into class midway through the term with her clothes inside out and backwards." She gets halfway through the sentence before she's gasping for breath laughing. More heads turn in our direction.

"Oh no!" Bri covers her mouth to hide her smile.

"I had never seen those clothes before, and my mom was very confident when she helped me get dressed that morning."

"Don't worry. I didn't let her walk around like that all day. I got her straightened out and from that moment forward, we were inseparable." Priya is right—she helped me adjust to life on Na'Lorska and quickly became my closest friend.

Our families joked that we were twins, even though our appearances were opposite in almost every way. Even as a kid I was tall, and Priya's people never grow past four feet. I kept my long dark hair pulled back in a single braid, and Priya's smooth hairless head was always wrapped up in a colorful headscarf.

"Elowen was awkward, but that didn't stop my brother from falling deeply in love with her," Priya says. She drains her drink and orders another round.

"How is your brother these days?" I ask.

"He's great! He has a baby on the way." Priya beams with pride.

"Looks like we're gonna be here for a while. Next round is on me," Bri says with a raised glass.

"I'll drink to that!" Priya cheers. The three of us clink our drinks together, and I tip my glass high, swallowing down the rest. My aversion to the station slips away while we reminisce and catch up. I almost manage to forget how grimy and terrifying it is here.

09

Aro

"The humans' flight path was redirected and they'll be here a day early," Rialto announces to the briefing room. "They will be landing at the pt'Clanik base at 0600. Upon arrival they will officially be under our supervision."

Deputy Commander Petrok continues the briefing. "The cargo bay will be used as a staging area for their arrival. There we will connect each visitor with their precleared personal effects and escort them to their assigned room. Transpo will report to the cargo bay at 0500. Everyone else reports here at 0600 to prepare."

Rialto adds, "Check your yuriOS for job assignments. Final inspection reports are due by 1500. Dismissed."

I've been assigned the northeast quadrant to prep for the arrival of the humans tomorrow. The four sections spread out from the central hub which contains the mess hall and security ops. Each of the zones have a similar layout with a lab, a recreational space, and sleeping units. The gym, medbay, pool, and storage areas are scattered throughout the sectors.

"Don't we have bots to do this sort of thing?" Tai mutters as we look over our tasks for the day.

I'm just glad to have something to do instead of sitting around and waiting for the humans to arrive.

A red alert pops up on my yuriOS. "I'm showing a malfunctioning cleaning bot. Come with me to check it out."

"I really don't want to go to the human quarters. Find me when you're done," Tai says.

"Don't tell me you've fallen for that Anti-Human movement." There's a small vocal group of Tilaks that don't want humans here. No one takes them seriously. I'm not really sure they take themselves seriously.

"No, I honestly don't care about the humans," Tai says.

"Good. I better not catch you chanting 'Stay True to the Blue,'" I say, mocking their ridiculous rally cry.

Tai chuckles. "The 'Beat Feet, Pink Meat' morons are an even bigger pain in my ass than the humans." I can't help but laugh.

"Those fuckers are so dumb. I swear I heard one of them say, 'All Blue No Hue…mans.'"

We cut off our laughter before Rialto hears us. His office is just around the corner. He can't catch us having too much fun or he'll find more work for us.

"Are you doing Transpo tomorrow?" I ask.

"Yeah, don't remind me. Where will you be?"

"I'll be here at the cargo bay making sure it all goes smoothly. Don't be a grumpy asshole when you pick them up tomorrow. It's not their fault you don't like to work," I tell him. "If you show up with a porter full of terrified humans, I'm pulling rank and demoting you."

We walk together to find the cleaning bot in question. I locate it by sound. The cleaning bot has jammed itself between the bed and desk of one of the sleeping units. I crouch down and gently pull it out. These little guys break easily, and it's worth being careful with them so I don't find myself on mopping duty in the future.

"I'm fine with them being here. I don't see why we need to go to all this trouble. It's annoying."

"Let me get this straight. You're throwing a fit because it's an inconvenience for you?"

"When you put it that way…" Tai fades off. He watches over my shoulder while I test out the omni-wheel on the bot. It's not moving as smoothly as I'd like. The bot chirps and beeps happily while I slide open the shell to look inside.

"Just toss that one. I can go grab another from storage," Tai says and moves towards the door. I pull out the carpet fibers that had jammed the brush roll and close it back up. I pat the bot's lid and send it on its way.

"No need. It's still good."

10

Elowen

It starts out as a small vibration under my feet. The air gradually thickens as the shaking builds. By the time we are deep into the atmosphere, everything is rattling. I keep my eyes glued shut and let the heavy pressure of the descent push me against my seat.

I hate landing. I have trust issues when it comes to being in a situation where I can easily be engulfed in a giant ball of flame. There are too many things that can go wrong. It would be a shame to blow up into a million pieces right before we reach our destination.

I focus on my breathing and chance a look at Bri once the vibrating stops. She's retching into an emesis bag. I should have warned her against eating breakfast this morning. Andi passed out from the descent, her head hanging awkwardly to the side. The rest of the crew seems to be handling it pretty well.

We hover for a few minutes while the landing gear extends and I know the worst is over. There is a collective sigh of relief when we gently touch down on solid ground for the first time in six Earth months. Bri already looks better—now that we are on solid ground.

My entire body's shivering from the adrenaline. I wish my hands would stop shaking so I can get out of this harness. j'Tilak is just beyond the hatch and I cannot wait to see it. My legs feel like jelly when I stand up. I grab onto the overhead rail while I find my balance. After months of very little physical activity, they aren't used to supporting my full weight. My feet tingle with pins and needles with my first few unstable steps.

The hatch to the lander opens up and I'm blinded by the bright light of two suns. Someone casts a tall shadow in front of me and I can finally see.

It's a giant blue alien with a yuriOS and a stern look.

"Your transport's this way," he grumbles, waving a shining silver prosthetic arm across the base.

"Nice to meet you too," Bri mutters under her breath as she brushes past me down the ramp. She's holding onto her used puke bag as she slowly exits. I'm following close behind and bump into her back when she comes to an abrupt stop to take in our new surroundings.

The sudden shift from the quiet of space to the chaotic military base is disorienting. I gasp when two porters zip around us and narrowly miss each other at top speed. Grumpy Pants rolls his eyes at my sharp intake of breath. He's subject to the names I make up for him until he introduces himself.

We have to jog to catch up to our guide. His long strides coupled with our atrophied leg muscles lengthen the distance between us. Eventually he turns back and realizes we have fallen behind. He impatiently swipes his yuriOS while waiting for us to catch up.

"A souvenir?" he asks, nodding at the bag Bri filled up during the landing.

"Very funny. Where can I dump this?" She holds out the bag, but he's already walked away. She looks at me. "No, seriously—where can I put this?"

"No clue."

The same type of spherical porters as we use on Earth glide to a stop in front of our small group. The doors slide open and I eagerly climb into the closest one, ready to sit down after the short but strenuous walk. I should have done the recommended exercises on the shuttle over. I'm regretting my decision not to.

Pouty McPoutface climbs in and starts up the porter without a word. Still holding the used bag in her lap, Bri mutters, "Great."

"Maybe he's just shy?" I whisper.

"Maybe he's just a dick," she says in a loud whisper.

He clears his throat. I dig my elbow into her side. She just needs to keep it together a little longer. Soon we'll be at the muradome and she can lose her shit in the privacy of her own room.

"Identify yourselves." He barks an order at us without looking back.

"Elowen Carson and Brisa Mitchell," I answer for both of us, not giving Bri a chance to make some snarky comment.

A jolt forward throws us back in our seats. Captain Cranky jerks the porter around anything in our way, not caring to make it a smooth ride for us. We leave the base and I get a full view of the landscape for the first time. It's so beautiful I could cry. If I weren't seeing it in real life, I would think it was genAI. It's so pristine it can't possibly be real. The colors— everything looks bright and vibrant.

We head in the direction of the rolling hills in the distance. I turn and watch the huge metal gate close behind us. I settle back into my seat.

No more anticipation. We finally made it.

Bri laughs, "Where are we? Is this real?" She knows exactly where we are, but I know what she means. It's hard to believe we're here, and it's beyond my wildest dreams.

"You're on j'Tilak," our driver says.

"That was a rhetorical question," Bri says and rolls her eyes.

A wide field surrounds the base. I watch the terrain with my face pressed against the plexi, trying to see everything. All too quickly the porter rises up to ascend a hill and I feel like I'm a roller coaster. My stomach drops to my feet. From up here the view extends. In the distance giant trees rise up, their branches fanning out, forming a dark green canopy. A wide glittering river winds through the valley below. Golden grass covers the ground like suede with the occasional patch of brown.

We take a sharp turn to the left and speed our way down toward the outcrop of trees. Bri slides across her seat and holds the bag as far away from her as possible as it sloshes from the erratic turns and bumps.

"Careful with that," Mr. Sourpuss instructs, his eyes briefly landing on her from the rearview mirror.

"I'm trying!" She rechecks the seal on the bag, her frustration simmering near the surface.

"Be nice," I tell her through a clenched smile. "We're guests here." A lifetime of diplomatic training kicks in. These first few hours are crucial. My mom's voice rings in my head. *You can only make a first impression once*. It's not unheard of for a newcomer to break some cardinal rule and wake up on a prison planet. It can usually be ironed out after a few weeks, but I get the feeling Bri wouldn't take kindly to being locked up for any period of time.

She returns the fake smile. "I am."

The sky turns dark when we get to the tree line. We are now under the shade of the canopy. Wood creaks over the porter's gyroscopes.

I can hardly believe my eyes when a massive tree pulls a thick root out of the ground and heaves it forward. I smack Bri's shoulder and point to the massive tree that leaves behind a deep trench in its wake.

"Holy shit!" she says and leans over to see. We're moving too fast to see the tree make any progress. Broad trunks block our view as we continue on our way. Our driver could have at least slowed down so we could witness this for the first time.

We ride in silence for a while, completely overwhelmed with everything around us. I'm desperately watching the forest around us, hoping to see more movement, when I notice a very large shadow shift. A second later a two-legged reptilian creature the size of a small house lets out a roaring bark and jerks its head in our direction.

Three green eyes focus on us, pupils contracting into terrifying slits, tracking our movement. Its elongated snout is slightly open, displaying rows and rows of razor-sharp teeth. Its muscles are bunched up under green camouflaged skin, ready to pounce. Before it can make a move, our porter picks up speed and continues on uninterrupted through the trees.

"What was that?" A shiver creeps down my spine.

"That is a very angry female Allometradon. Did you notice her hatchling?" The driver doesn't sound very concerned. "We were safe. There is no way she could have gotten to us. These porters are mostly impenetrable."

Bri and I share a look when it hits us both that he said "mostly."

"All I saw were teeth. I've never seen anything like that before." Bri's voice is a little shaky. Unease settles into the air as Bri and I silently wonder what else we could encounter on our drive to the muradome.

The large white dome comes into view—home sweet home. It's bigger than any other research facility I've ever seen. It's the size of a small town, rising three or four stories tall. The porter circles the dome and slows as we turn into the cargo bay.

Bri and I step out, her small bag still in hand. Again, she looks around for a place to throw it away. A Tilak with the worst haircut I have ever seen approaches us. He looks self-conscious about his appearance and tries to smooth down the clumps of hair sticking out in every direction.

"I'm sorry, ma'am. You can't bring that in here. All personal items are required to be checked in ahead of time." Bri rolls her eyes at his comment and holds the bag out away from her body, threatening him with it.

"I don't want to keep this. I've been trying to find a place to dump it since we landed," she unleashes on the unsuspecting Tilak, her frustration finally boiling over. She desperately looks around for somewhere to put the container.

"Here, I can help you with that," a deep voice says from behind me. I spin and smack my face directly into a white shirt covering a hard chest. I look up and a friendly blue face smiles down at me.

"There's a receptacle right here. Just swipe and select this icon," he says patiently and points to a diamond-shaped outline with a hieroglyph in the center of a machine that's next to where we're standing. A small door slides up and Bri drops her bag in and promptly wipes her hands on her pants.

"Thank you," Bri says with relief.

He's handsome, like the rest of them, and his helpfulness makes me like him immediately. It was a matter of time before the contents of that bag ended up on the ground, or worse—on me. I'm about to thank him when the Tilak with the terrible haircut steps between us.

"Welcome to MuraDome IV. I'm Bennet. I'll show you to your rooms." Bennet, a.k.a. Choppy Haircut Guy, herds Bri and I toward the door leading to the rest of the facility. He catches Bri gawking at him and pats down his hair again.

"I've got this one, Bennet," the Tilak behind us says, the helpful one with the nice smile.

"But... Aro—sir. They're on my list. Did I do something wrong?" Bennet sounds confused and panicked at the thought.

"I can take it from here," he says, stepping forward.

"But sir, the list. I don't—"

"We're on your list? Lead the way," Bri says and follows Bennet, cutting off the discussion between him and the one he called Aro. "Can those giant three-eyed Allometr-whatevers get in here?"

"Oh, you met Millie! She won't bother us here," Bennet says.

"Good. I have a strict 'no dragon' policy," she says.

I hear a few chuckles behind us as we leave the cargo bay and head towards our rooms.

11

Aro

Fucking Bennet. He should have let me step in and walk them to their rooms.

I recognized her the moment she stepped out of the porter. Gone was the timid, nervous-looking female I saw at the reception months ago. This time she looked confident and happy. She looked like she was in her element.

If Bennet had just been cool about it, I would know what her name is and what room she was assigned to.

What I do know for sure, is that Tai didn't follow my order about having a better attitude. He looked more irritated than ever when he arrived with the two women. I didn't have a chance to follow through on my threat to pull rank. A dozen porters had filed into the cargo bay all at once. I barely managed to control the chaos, but we got everyone settled into their rooms without causing an interplanetary crisis.

I do a walk-through of the entire muradome after everyone is checked in.

Unfortunately, I don't find her. Instead, I end up fetching towels and extra pillows for a few of the new residents. I've retreated back to the Central Hub when Bennet walks in. He's all smiles. He whistles while he straightens up his workstation. I do my best to ignore him.

"Aro, sir."

I glare at him, hoping it's enough to get him to shut up. "For tomorrow should I—" Bennet cuts himself off. "Uh, never mind," he says and steps towards the exit.

"Did you have a question?" I ask. That came out more tense than I had intended.

"Not when you're in this mood." He leaves as quickly as he arrived, probably for the best.

He's not wrong about my mood.

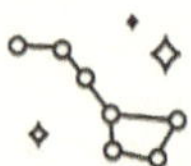

The next morning, I wake up ready to put a new plan into place. I head straight to Rialto's office to get his sign-off.

"Sir. I'd like to do another inspection in the labs now that the humans are here. I think we should double-check they didn't move anything around or whatever." I do my best to sound like a concerned authority figure.

Rialto looks up and seems to see right through me. "No, I think it's fine. I can't imagine they have even been to their labs yet."

Okay—that one didn't work. I've got a back-up.

"I'd like to volunteer to do one final survey, to make sure every-thing is working. I found a broken cleaning bot in my quadrant before they arrived. I'd like to double check to make sure everything's in good order."

"That's a good idea. Put Lugo on it. I need you to brief the Council on the humans' arrival. They want assurances that everything went smoothly." Rialto goes back to his yuriOS.

"I'm happy to do the inspection myself."

"As captain, you were overseeing the arrival, and I want you to brief the Council." Rialto rubs his temples like he's warding off a headache.

I suspect I might be the headache.

"Yes, sir." I turn to leave before he thinks of another assignment.

"I want a full report from yesterday on my desk by 0900," Rialto calls after me. I stop to acknowledge that I heard. I close my eyes, let out a silent sigh, and continue on my way.

Being cooped up in the security hub is going to make it a lot harder to happen to run into each other.

But I'm still determined to find her.

12

Elowen

I yawn and push back from the desk. The room is much brighter now than when I first hunched over my microscope late last night.

Oh shit—it's morning.

The only natural light in MuraDome IV comes from high narrow windows I'm too short to see out of. Exhaustion has kicked in. I can't decide if I'm more hungry or tired. Both, equally. My stomach rumbles loudly. I'm still getting used to the twenty-eight-hour days here on j'Tilak. I typically finish up in the lab and go straight to my bunk to pass out, but last night I totally lost track of time and ended up working much later than usual.

The airlock engages and blasts me with steam before I'm released to the locker room. My steri-suit hangs unzipped from my waist while I splash some cold water on my face. I jump when the door crashes open with a loud bang.

Bri bursts in. "Where were you last night?"

"I am so sorry. Right when I was finishing up for the night, a new specimen was delivered marked 'Urgent,' and I totally forgot. Can I buy you a bowl of noodles to make up for it?" I muster my most apologetic tone.

"I already ate breakfast, but I'll have a coffee while you eat. And you can't 'buy' free noodles. It's going to take a lot more to get you out of this. You owe me."

I haven't stopped working around the clock, even though the newness of the research has worn off and most people have settled into a routine which includes off time. Not me. I worry it's only a matter of time before Bri takes it personally and realizes I'm a terrible friend.

"Girl, you need a shower." Bri takes a giant step away from me.

"I'll just throw on a fresh shirt," I tell her. I'm hungry and want to eat before I pass out.

"I think you're overestimating the power of clean laundry." She laughs and waves her hand over her face, wafting air towards herself.

I pull on a white T-shirt and drop my steri-suit in the laundry chute. A shower will have to wait.

"Come on, I'm starving. I will explain the anatomical features of the flower I'm working on."

"Please, no." Bri fake cries.

We push our way through the crowd of people leaving the mess. Cleaning bots swarm most of the tables, wiping them down and sweeping underneath. I grab the last bowl of noodles. It's cold and slightly congealed. I make my way towards an open spot, Bri at my heels with a freshly refilled cup of steaming coffee.

There is a raucous group of Tilaks at the other end of the room. The gorgeous aliens are impossible to miss. They appear nearly human, outside of their color and size. Similar facial features, only their brows, cheekbones, and chiseled jaws are more prominent. Hard interior plates and sinew protect their vital organs, making them look even more fierce and imposing. This morning they all match in their white short-sleeved shirts tucked into khaki cargo pants. Bri and I sit down opposite each other, and I tear my gaze away.

"Like what you see?" Bri asks.

"Just observing," I answer innocently. "So, what did I miss last night?"

"If I'm being honest? Not much. Dr. Lee and I tried to teach a few of the security guys Cubes. They weren't into it." She slouches back into her chair with a huff. I'm surprised Bri got her program director to play Cubes. He's old and stuffy and, unlike Dr. Kahn, has never given us permission to call him by his first name.

"I'm really sorry. I would have made it worse though. I'm terrible at that game."

I look up to give Bri an apologetic smile and something catches my eye behind her. I accidentally make eye contact with a Tilak over her shoulder. I avert my gaze so it doesn't get awkward, but my eyes wander over again and he is watching me with a smile spread across his flawless face. It takes a second for me to recognize him. He's the Tilak that helped Bri with her puke bag when we first got here. I smile back and give a halfhearted wave in his direction.

"I think kicking your ass at Cubes is exactly what I need to cheer me up," Bri says. "I don't think I was made for this life. Being stuck in a muradome is way worse than I thought it would be. They keep denying my requests to leave! They say I don't have sufficient reason to leave the dome, and 'muradome security must be prioritized over individual requests.'" She mimics the deep Tilak accent speaking the universal language.

"Bri, I…" My eyes drift from Bri's face to the Tilak again, and my train of thought evaporates. He is still staring at me and smiling. "I, uh—"

She notices I'm looking past her and turns to see what—who—I'm looking at. She bites the corner of her mouth trying to suppress a smile and looks back at me with one eyebrow raised.

Before I can remember what I was about to say, he stands up and approaches our table. I try not to stare as he walks toward us. Definitely not looking at the low-slung pants on his waist. Or the white T-shirt stretched across his broad chest. I look everywhere except his half-cocked smile and refuse to acknowledge when he pushes his dark hair away from his face. His hair waves casually back, looking effortlessly handsome. His dark eyes narrow on me as he approaches.

I feel like I'm in one of those vintage vids, the ones where the camera zooms in and pulls back at the same time. The movement messes with my head. The focal point looks like it's getting closer and farther all at the same time. I'm almost dizzy by the time he gets to us.

Panicking, I look around the room searching for an escape route. I have been working around the clock and can't remember the last time I showered or ran a brush through my hair. Bri's comment about needing a shower was accurate—I'm disgusting right now. This is not my idea of a good first impression. And to top it off, Bri is loving every second of my torture.

He stops at the edge of our table. "Good morning, ladies," he says without looking away from me.

I clear my throat and swallow my food. "Good morning." I try to make my voice sound casual. I'm not fooling anyone. Bri sits there lapping up my awkwardness. Her eyes darting between me and the alien.

"Good morning," Bri says in an overly chipper voice. "Elowen and I were just talking about how our applications to leave the dome keep getting denied. You don't happen to know how to get those approved?" she asks sweetly.

"You're Elowen? I'm Aro." He doesn't look toward Bri once.

"And I'm Bri. You can call me 'Elowen's friend,' since that's all you're going to remember from this riveting conversation." There's an edge to her voice. She's only partially joking.

"Enjoying your noodles this morning?" he asks with playful interest, completely ignoring Bri's snarky comment.

"Come to think of it, these are better than yesterday's," I quip back.

"Aro! You're going to be in deep shit if you're late again." Aro looks over his shoulder to see his friends leaving.

"You go ahead. I'll catch up," Aro tells them. He sits down on the bench and slides up next to me.

"Make yourself at home," Bri says.

"'I've seen you before, at the reception after the signing ceremony," Aro says to me.

"You were there?" I ask. A bite of cold noodles lodges in my throat. I set my chopsticks down so I don't choke to death in front of this gorgeous being.

"I was. I haven't seen you since you landed. I wondered if you were hiding."

"I've been around. Maybe you just haven't been paying attention," I reply. This guy's arrogance is making me feel feisty.

"Not possible, I would remember," he says confidently.

"Elowen's what we call a workaholic," Bri interjects.

"Workaholic?" he asks, testing the word out.

"Someone who only cares about work," she explains.

"I don't *just* care about work. I like other things too," I say.

"Like what?" he asks.

"I don't know! You can't put someone on the spot like that. It's like asking a comedian to say something funny," I say.

"I've heard your jokes. I'm not sure that's the analogy you want to go with," Bri says with a grin.

"Oh yeah? Well, what do you call a flower and her best friend? Buddies!" I'm the only one laughing at my joke.

"Oh, wow…" Aro says with a slightly frightened look in his eyes.

"I told you she's a workaholic," Bri says to Aro under her breath.

"That's a bad example. Regardless, I'm not a workaholic," I say to both of them.

"I'd love to stay and let you redeem yourself from that awful joke, but I do need to get to work." Aro shoots me that crooked smile for a few additional seconds before he turns and walks out the door.

"Thanks for help with the barf bag!" I call after him, but it's too late—he's gone. That's fine. I don't like how desperate I sounded.

"That was interesting," Bri says, sipping from her cup.

"Did I just make a complete fool out of myself?" I ask.

"A little bit," she says.

I groan and rest my forehead on my palm. "I panicked."

"It's criminal to look that good," Bri says.

"They certainly don't make them like that on Earth… That's the last we will be seeing of him. I think I sufficiently scared him off with that joke."

"That's too bad. That would have been a fun little distraction," Bri says.

"Probably for the best. I can't afford any distractions."

"You're just proving my point for me." She mutters a little more under her breath. I swear I hear the word "workaholic" in there somewhere.

"I am going to take me and my corny jokes to bed. I'm exhausted."

"Make sure you go straight to your bunk, and not to the security hub to your new boyfriend!" Bri calls after me. Trying not to smile, I shoot her a look as I drop off my half-eaten breakfast in the trash receptacle on my way out.

13

Aro

I walk around all day with the image of that little human stuck in my head.

14

Elowen

"Good work the other night," Andi says as she drops off another set of slides for me to work on. "I appreciate the quick turnaround. At this rate we should finish up cellular review and move onto the full specimen observation in the next few days."

"We're making good progress." I'm starting to feel like we're going to succeed in our mission here.

"Absolutely. We're ahead of schedule as far as I'm concerned. How are you holding up?" She settles against the counter.

"I'm good! Great! Things are really good," I say enthusiastically. Maybe a little too enthusiastically. That urge to be the teacher's pet is alive and well inside me. I swivel my stool to face her.

"Okay." She pauses, not sounding convinced. "That's good. I don't want you to get burnt out."

"No burnout yet."

"Good. Stay focused on what's right in front of you. All the other stuff is just a distraction," she says and steps into the airlock.

"No distractions here!"

I set the new samples aside. I chastise myself for not asking her about a job after the program. I've been waiting for this chance to bring it up, and this was the perfect moment.

My eyes are tired from squinting all day. I need to look at something larger than a micrometer for a while.

Down the hall I see Andi and Dr. Lee walking toward the mess for dinner. I've been given a second chance to talk about my future. This is even better—now I can talk to both program directors at the same time.

I turn on my heel and follow them rather than going straight to my room. I'll get their attention, charm them with my intellect, and drop some hints about a job at the University when we return to Earth. I can play it cool. I got that awkwardness out of my system earlier. I'm totally normal now.

By the time I get my noodles the dining room is mostly empty. It would look suspicious if I sat too close to them. I'm strategic about where I'm going to eat. Close enough to engage with them and far enough to not make it too obvious.

Andi is speaking quietly to Dr. Lee. I look down at my dinner. I'm trying to emit a casual confident aura when a tray of food slides right in front of me and a big blue shape blocks my view. Aro sits behind the tray and grabs his chopsticks.

"Hey," he says with that same infuriatingly adorable smile.

"Hey," I echo back at him, distracted by the people he's blocking from view. He takes an oversized mouthful of noodles.

"I've been trying to think of an answer to your friend's question," Aro says with a crooked grin.

I'm completely transfixed by the way his mouth moves. Why does that work for him? Why is that hot? Any other time, I would be grossed out by someone talking with their mouth full. I watch him take another bite. That's when I notice how he holds his chopsticks. I watch him swallow. He notices me staring and quirks his head slightly and smiles again.

Something is definitely wrong with me.

I clear my throat before trying to speak. "Huh?"

"Yeah, she wanted to know how to get approval to leave the dome." Aro lightly drags his teeth over his lower lip.

He knows this is doing something for me.

"Oh, yeah. Don't mind Bri. She's bitter about being stuck in the dome. She's never lived like this before. She'll get used to it."

I lean to the side to look over Aro's shoulder at Andi and Dr. Lee. They're still eating. They are one table over, but they might as well be in another galaxy with this giant blue alien between us.

"If you weren't human, which species would you want to be?" he asks.

"Hm, I like that question. Where did you get it—sensitivity training?" We must have taken the same module. I can't help but tease him about actually using the corny exercises they gave us so we could imagine being in each other's shoes.

He laughs. It's consuming and immediately addictive. "Got me."

"Those classes can be pretty boring. I'm impressed that you were paying attention," I tell him.

I had found myself dozing off during my cultural sensitivity module. It's an important message with an awful delivery. The scenarios in the training were not realistic at all. To make matters worse, it seemed like the genAI character had never spoken the universal language before. Bri and I spent the rest of that day entertaining ourselves by speaking like the old AI in the vid with stilted speech and awkward hand gestures.

"I wanted to make sure I didn't say the wrong thing the first time I talked to a human. You know, like… tell a bad joke or something." As if I need a reminder of my earlier awkwardness.

"Admittedly, that was a low point."

"It's not too late to bring it back around. I believe in you," he says with a smirk.

"Don't get your hopes up."

"Don't sell yourself short! You seem to have a pretty good grasp on the subtleties of comedy."

I swirl some noodles on my chopsticks and right before I take a bite, he asks a question that makes me drop them back into the bowl.

"Is your boyfriend disappointed to be left behind?" he asks.

"Did you just ask if I'm single? I ask, surprised he would be interested.

"Are you? Single?" he asks as he slurps a mouthful of noodles.

"I am. Bri's right though—I'm a workaholic," I say, trying to keep some distance between us. I try to get a bite without flinging broth everywhere. I'm mostly successful.

That should set him straight. Literally minutes ago, I was telling Andi that I am free of all distractions. This alien is trying to make me a liar.

"I still don't think you're a workaholic, and I'm going to give you the opportunity to prove it," Aro says.

"That should be easy enough. I'll prove it right now. I'm heading back to work," I say with a smile and set my chopsticks back down.

"So easy to walk away? I was hoping you'd be fascinated with me by now."

I wish I could say his arrogance was misplaced.

"I find all local organisms fascinating. Especially Lumbricidae…" I can't resist the urge to tease him and insinuate he as at the same level as an Earthworm.

"Did you just compare me to a worm? I think I'm a *little* more interesting than a worm." His defensive words are undercut by the broad smile across his face. He's probably never been compared to something so humble before, and I'm thrilled I get to be the one to do it. If I've offended him, he's not showing it. In fact, he looks like he's enjoying the challenge. He also gets bonus points for getting the reference right away.

"Worms are a very important part of the ecosystem."

"So, you're saying I'm important… I'll take it. Even though I think there are more accurate analogies you could make."

Andi and Dr. Lee clear away their empty bowls. Damn—I'm missing my chance. I shove one last bite of noodles into my mouth and stand up. I'm going to try and catch them in the hallway. I brush by Aro, quickly dispose of my used dishes and head toward the door.

"I'm sure you'll think of a more fitting metaphor," I throw over my shoulder toward him. Before leaving, I take one more look at Aro. He's sitting there laughing.

"I'm sure I will."

Leaving him there in the mess hall feels like a power move, one that is only going to raise the stakes with a guy like Aro.

I'm sure a little harmless flirting here and there over a bowl of noodles is fine. He is sorely mistaken if he thinks I'd jeopardize my place in this program by taking it any further. My rational brain is listing all the reasons why I should avoid him completely.

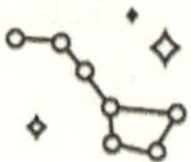

1303 Incoming message from Aro pt'Burosa

Aro: I need some advice.

Elowen: Unless you want to talk about botany, you're coming to the wrong person.

Aro: Not botany. I'm still racking my brain to find something fun for us to do.

Elowen: Don't you have more important things to do with your time?

Aro: Absolutely not. This is my top priority.

Elowen: That's concerning. You may need to reevaluate.

Aro: I'd like to give you an opportunity to act on all of those dirty things you were thinking about during our date.

Elowen: Our date?! In the mess hall? What makes you think I was thinking dirty thoughts?

Aro: So you do remember it.

Elowen: I think we have very different interpretations of what happened.

Aro: We should probably meet up and get our stories straight.

Elowen: Creative way to ask me out.

Aro: I am a creative thinker.

Elowen: Has anyone ever told you that you're arrogant?

Aro: Never. Actually, not true. My sister tells me every chance she gets. I don't want to start our relationship off with a lie.

Elowen: Relationship?

Aro: Yes. And quit trying to change the subject. What are you interested in for fun?

Elowen: Right now, I am interested in the gamete of a lumen'entem.

Aro: Oh really?

Elowen: It's the specimen I'm detailing right now.

Aro: Well, you might be interested in what the plant is used for.

Elowen: Alright, you have my attention.

Aro: In the past Tilaks used it for ceremonial purposes to achieve enlightenment. Now it's just used for the psychedelic effects.

Elowen: My concern is purely scientific.

Aro: In that case, don't get any of the pollen directly on you. You might enjoy the effects, but I doubt your boss would like you tripping out while you're supposed to be working.

Elowen: Have you done it before?

Aro: Once. It's something that should be done with a guide. It's a powerful experience that can go in many different directions…

Elowen: Good to know.

Aro: I have to cancel our dinner plans tonight. I'm covering a shift.

Elowen: We didn't have dinner plans for tonight.

Aro: Yeah, I know, but you were hoping we would. Now quit bothering me, I'm very busy and important.

Elowen: Again, with the arrogance!

Aro: I think you misspelled charming.

Elowen: I know how to spell a lot of words, for instance: insufferable.

Aro: How about irresistible? That one in your lexicon?

Elowen: I am familiar with the word presumptuous.

Aro: You got me there. When can I see you next?

Elowen: I'll be around.

Aro: I like that you're making me work for this.

Elowen: Incorrigible.

Aro: I also like that you know a lot of big words.

Elowen: …

15

Elowen

"You made it!" I don't blame Bri for sounding surprised.

I still feel guilty about standing her up last week even though she seems to have let it go. I'm flipping through an old copy of National Geographic in the rec room while she settles onto the couch across from me.

"Check out this magazine. This artifact is worth more credits than I'll see in my entire life." I'm gingerly turning the pages to avoid getting fingerprints on the glossy pictures. "This issue covers the first human expedition out of the Milky Way. How did they even get this?"

"Let me take a look at that." Bri reaches out for the magazine. I carefully close it and hand it over to her. She promptly drops it on the coffee table between us without any consideration for its fragility. "What a nice piece of non-biodegradable history. Did you ask Andi about getting out into the field?"

I scowl at her for being so rough with the magazine. "We are swamped in the lab. She's not going to request a field trip for me just because we're bored."

"Elowen, we have to be assertive. We've got to make them tell us no. If there is any chance we can get out of here for a single minute, we have to try."

Bri is relentless. I feel bad for Dr. Lee. Bri claims she earned her position on this trip by sheer force of will. When her program director announced they would be picking someone to assist him, she assumed the spot was hers. She approached him and started preparing for departure without ever being formally invited to come. After seeing how brilliant she was—according to her—Dr. Lee decided she should go. I wonder what it's like to go through life with that sense of unwavering self-confidence.

"If it comes up organically, I'll say something."

Bri and her team of geneticists are also working around the clock to identify ways hypermobile plants could survive on Earth. Something about tossing it all into the CRISPR. I have no idea how that works. I wasn't kidding when I said genetics is boring.

We're all under a ton of pressure, and we deal with it in our own ways. I have a hard time turning it off at the end of the day. I'll be able to relax once we've figured this all out. Bri needs something to focus on other than work in order to keep herself motivated.

"Bri, it's going—"

Bri interrupts with, "Oh hi, boys!"

Aro and another Tilak appear out of nowhere. I'm caught off guard, but Bri is suspiciously unsurprised. Aro plops down on the couch next to me, and the other sits down next to Bri. Her bright smile fades when she recognizes the metal bionic arm from the day we landed.

"You," she says with disdain. She stops herself. Sitting next to her is our less-than-friendly chauffeur, and apparently Bri's mortal enemy. I don't think she will ever forgive him for making her carry her puke the whole way here.

"It's good to see you again," he says when it's clear she isn't going to finish that sentence. "I'm Tai."

"You've got a lot of nerve," she says with daggers in her eyes. He looks over at Aro confused, looking for support.

"I think she's talking about the vomit," Aro says, accurately guessing why Bri is holding a grudge.

"I thought you were keeping that for some weird human custom. I didn't know you were trying to throw it away," he says defensively.

"Why would I want to keep a bag of puke? You were just trying to torture me."

"You seemed really attached to it," Tai says, stifling a laugh.

Bri throws her hands up in the air, frustrated by his lack of apology. She gives up with Tai and turns her attention to Aro.

"Not the best pick for wingman," she says.

"Wingman?" Tai asks.

"A wingman is like a backup, a buddy to help you get the girl. Guys on Earth sometimes need some help feeling confident enough to approach a… a…" I offer a rambling explanation but stop myself from saying "love interest." I don't want to presume that is what's happening here.

It dawns on me that Bri has orchestrated this situation.

Tai laughs. "Glad I can help you out, 'buddy.' It's good to see you acknowledging your lack of confidence."

Aro glowers at him.

"So, what's the plan for tonight?" Aro says as he stretches his arm out on the back of the couch behind me.

I level Bri with an accusatory stare, she brushes it off. She is up to something.

"No plans, just taking the night off," she says convincingly with her doe-eyed innocent act. Tai has already checked out of the conversation, his attention focused on the group of Tilaks at the other end of the room.

"Aro, you tell us the plan. I hear you've been trying to figure out what Elowen is 'into.'" Bri is straight to the point. I realize my mistake too late. I should never have told her about the flirty messages.

"Brisa," I warn.

"Well, actually Elowen gave me a good idea a few days ago." Aro turns to Bri. "Wait, I thought your name was Bri."

"I'm surprised you remember," she says, sounding genuinely impressed.

"It's a human custom that we shorten each other's names or give a less formal name to friends. It's a way of showing affection." It feels like I'm rambling. I am rambling. I need to stop talking. Why am I still talking? "Like, shortening the name Robert to Bob, or Elizabeth to Lizzy. You guys don't do that here?" Someone really needs to step in and stop me.

"I didn't know that. I like it. I'm glad you consider us friends already, Bri." Aro lets me off the hook. I would have just kept rambling until I ran out of air and passed out.

"I wouldn't go that far. Everyone calls me Bri. Unless someone were to, say, break my best friend's heart, then it would be Brisa," she directs at Aro. Tai, who's been silent, snorts out a laugh and watches with an amused smile.

"Point taken." Aro stares back at her, not backing down.

"Tai, do you know how to play Cubes?" Bri changes her tone, sounding more friendly now that she's gotten that point across to Aro.

Tai's amused smile from watching Bri and Aro fades. "I don't," he says slowly. I surmise he is trying to find a way out of being roped into the game by his hesitant response.

"Come on, let's play a few rounds." Bri nods toward an empty table a few feet away. Tai looks at Aro. I know that look. It's the same look Bri gives me when she means, "You owe me one."

"Wish me some first-person luck," Tai says while hoisting himself up from his comfortable spot on the couch.

"It's 'beginner's luck,' and you're going to need it," I tell him.

I've underestimated Bri's boredom. She's now spending her free time playing matchmaker. I haven't seen her smile this much the entire time I've known her. She's clearly enjoying every second of this, and it's absolutely terrifying. Bri cocks an eyebrow and her eyes dart back and forth between Aro and I. Bri is a lot of things, but subtle is not one of them.

Aro shifts his weight a little closer. His hand resting on the back of the couch nearly touches me. A tiny bolt of electricity radiates from the sensitive spot between my neck and shoulder. It wouldn't take much for me to lean back and brush against him…

No, this is just harmless flirting. No touching. Absolutely not.

"Do you miss Earth?" Aro asks.

"Not at all. I mean, I miss my parents. Earth, not so much."

"Really? I always thought Earth was this amazing place that nothing could ever compare to."

"Don't get me wrong, Earth is great. I never really thought of it as home, so I don't have that same attachment to it. There's this weird 'Earth exceptionalism' thing that I've never quite understood."

"Where did you grow up?" he asks.

"I've lived in nine different systems. My parents took me all over," I say.

"And you're how old?" he asks.

"27".

"A new place every three years. That's a lot."

"Look at you—doing math in your head," I tease. The trash talk keeps the rambling at bay.

"I didn't even need to use my fingers this time," he jokes back. "That's a lot of moving around. How does j'Tilak compare to the others?"

"I don't know. I haven't seen anything outside the muradome since we arrived."

"Well, how much of the dome have you seen?" Aro asks.

"Not much. Actually, I haven't even left this section." I wince.

"Well now is a perfect opportunity to fix that. Let's go for a walk, and I can show you around a little," Aro offers.

Before I can give him an answer, he's up with his hand out to help me off the couch. When our hands touch, that same electric pulse passes between us. My "no touching" rule is already out the window.

"Was this Bri's plan or yours?" I ask.

"It was all Bri. She gave me strict instructions to show up on time and bring a friend," he says with a laugh, then clears his throat. "It did take a little convincing to get Tai to come along." He confirms what I already suspected. Tai was an unwilling participant in their little plan.

"He doesn't look very enthusiastic about it." I hope he's sullen and bored the whole time and makes Bri miserable with his bad attitude. She deserves a little bit of karma for trying to mastermind the situation between me and Aro.

"He'll be just fine. Bri will have him wrapped around her finger in no time." Aro already seems to have a pretty accurate insight into her.

He leads me to a section of the dome I've never seen before. I'm anxious about where he could be taking me. I quickly brush away the possibility that he could be leading me to his room—that is not going to happen. As I continue following him, I promise myself that if we end up at his room, I will not step through that door. I'll turn right around and find my way back to the rec room.

"This way leads to the south side," Aro points out as we walk down the hallway. A dozen knee-high cleaning bots whir past, pushing us up against each other as they sweep the floor. My pulse picks up and my hands get clammy at his proximity. I jump away when they are gone. This is exactly why I shouldn't have taken his hand to get up. Touching just leads to more touching.

Aro activates the next door we come to. He presses his palm against the square touchscreen next to it. The screen lights up green when it scans his hand and the door slides open.

I follow him into a cavernous room that is easily four or five times larger than my lab. In tidy rows, stacks of uniform black storage containers rise nearly to the ceiling.

"You brought me to the warehouse?" I choose to ignore the twinge of disappointment I feel at our destination.

"As you know, there isn't much to do around here."

Aro saunters down the aisle. I follow him from a safe distance. The tension between us feels manageable with some space. We reach the back corner and Aro picks up his pace a little.

"Follow me. There's something I want to show you." Aro ducks into a smaller room that's separated from the rest of the warehouse by a clear plexi wall. The safe distance away from him is erased when I step into the confined area.

It's darker in here, the only light coming from a dim control panel that runs the length of the room. Aro lights it up with a swipe of his finger. He taps through the glowing hieroglyphs without any explanation.

"Here we go." The panel emits a soft hum at his touch. Aro slides his finger forward and a lit-up cube on the panel follows his movement. Simultaneously, metal and gears grind together in the warehouse. At the other end of the room a magnet activates and lifts a crate into the air. It raises up and lowers down, synchronizing with Aro's finger on the panel. He taps twice and the box drops to the ground with a clang. Aro picks up another crate, swings it through the air and stacks it on top of the first one he moved. He arranges the stacks effortlessly.

"Want to take a turn?" he asks me once the containers are all lined up. "Just select a unit here and slide it up."

I gently rest my finger on the control pad over the lit-up cube. A container at the far end of the warehouse rises. The panel vibrates as I move it up, down, and side to side. "This is fun. You come in here to play blocks when you're bored?"

My quick glance at Aro takes my attention away from where I should be looking. The crate crashes into the next row, knocking a few boxes to the ground. I jerk my hand back like it's about to be bitten.

"Shit, I'm sorry. I got distracted." I step back wanting him to take over the panel. With a few swipes he has everything back where it should be.

"You should've seen the first time Bennet worked the panel. He destroyed the entire place." Aro laughs. "Now let's get out of here before you break something." He playfully nudges his shoulder against mine as he leads me out of the room.

"Let's see if I can find somewhere that's Elowen-proof. I'd hate to see you having to explain to your director that you destroyed millions of credits' worth of equipment," Aro says nonchalantly.

"What's in the boxes?" My stomach drops to my feet.

"Not exactly sure, but it must be something important to be stored in a secured room," he casually tosses over his shoulder.

My legs stop and I feel like every ounce of blood has drained out of my body. "Oh no."

Aro turns around to look at me and laughs. "The crates are empty. You didn't break anything. I wish you could see your face right now."

"You scared the shit out of me." I playfully punch his chest for emphasis. Before I make contact he flicks my fist aside like he's shooing away a fly.

"Be careful, little human. You keep touching me like that, I might think you're flirting with me."

"I should kick your ass," I say, narrowing my eyes at him.

"That gives me an excellent idea!" Aro beckons me to follow.

He scans open each door as we walk through twisting hallways. I've completely lost any sense of direction and have no idea where we are now.

Aro's pace slows and he activates a door for us. "After you."

I'm surrounded by workout equipment and monitors. The gym is mostly empty, with a few Tilaks working out. They briefly acknowledge Aro as we walk through, but no one takes notice of me. We come to an open area with soft purple mats covering the ground.

"Alright, take your best shot," he says and sinks down into a defensive fighting stance.

"What?" I laugh at his ludicrous posture.

"Try not to hurt yourself."

I bounce on my toes back and forth, imitating a combative posture. "You ready for this?" I push out my lower lip in mock seriousness.

"Let's see it then." He motions me forward.

I take a jab at him. He ducks out of the way and steps away from my strike in one swift motion. We circle around each other, both of us smiling and waiting for the other to make their move.

I look down when my foot finds the edge of the mat. That's all the opening he needs. He swats at my ass and jumps back a safe distance away before I can even flinch. My face heats red from the smack on my backside.

"You humans turn the cutest shade of pink when you've been beat," he says.

"Beat? Not even close." My bravado sounded real even to my own ears.

I turn and take another swing. This time he grabs my wrist and turns my body so my back is up against his chest. I squirm to get away, but his arm across my upper body holds me in place. I can feel his solid chest against my back. I clutch his forearm and it loosens a fraction at my touch.

Luckily, he can't see my face. I'm smiling as I step to the side and sweep my foot across his ankles, bringing him down to the ground. He lands on top of me caging me in on the mats. I turn over to face him and he grabs both of my wrists, holding them to the sides of my head while his knees straddle my hips.

He smiles down at me. "Hm, I like the view from up here."

I'm not ready to give up without a fight. I push my hips up and yank my wrists out of his firm grasp all at once. I grab his shoulder and use his momentum to roll him to his back with my full body weight on top of him. Pressed together, our chests rise and fall against each other. Our position makes heat radiate from between my thighs. It all began with him helping me up and less than an hour later, against all better judgment, I'm now straddling him on the ground. He could easily lift me up and toss me aside and there is nothing I could do about it.

"What are you going to do now that you've got me here?" he asks quietly.

He wants to see who yields first, and now I'm feeling stubborn. I look around to see if anyone is watching. The others in the room are oblivious to us, focused on their own workouts. I arch my back and move upwards to meet his face. I sweep my hair behind my shoulder and bite my lower lip. His eyes settle on my mouth.

"I think I could do anything I want," I say, imitating his cool confidence.

The space between us feels heavy and I'm powerless to the gravity pulling me down. I wonder what his lips would feel like on mine. Maybe just a tiny, little...

Someone drops their weights with a loud clang. I pull away and collapse onto the mat next to him and try to catch my breath. He shoves a hand through his hair and his ear does a little twitch.

"Um. I'm gonna go," I mumble. I push up off the floor and suppress the urge to bolt from the room like a coward. I straighten my shirt and do my best imitation of a confident walk. I glance over my shoulder when I reach for the door, hoping he doesn't see through my act. He's lying on the ground staring up at the ceiling.

16

Aro

I still feel the imprint of Elowen's perfect round ass pressed up against me. She absolutely did that on purpose. There's no other way that little human could have brought me down. In that position she could have made me forget my own name. Now is not the time to think about her on top of me, with her coveralls unsnapped and gaping open. That spark in her eyes when she looked down at me is seared on my brain. I would conquer worlds to have her look at me like that again.

I was definitely getting the go-ahead until she jumped off of me. Is this what rejection feels like? Things are usually so much more straightforward. She's totally interested in me. I know what that feels like. I know it's there. So why did she stop? It doesn't make sense.

There's got to be a reason I've felt this pull towards her since the first moment I saw her across the crowded ballroom. She seemed uncomfortable that night. I noticed every fidget. I was completely distracted the entire time. I should have been paying attention to the important discussions of planetary policy around me, but I couldn't bring myself to care about anything except getting her attention. At one point we made eye contact, but her eyes darted away before I could do more than raise my glass. There was a hint of that same unease earlier last night, but it faded away pretty quickly.

Elowen is this little puzzle I'm determined to figure out—starting tomorrow.

"Captain!" Commander Rialto's stern voice snaps me back to reality.

"Yes, sir."

"We're waiting."

I step up behind the podium and clear my throat. "Good news, boys. Today is Tactical Ground Operations Training." I love T-GOT, especially today. It's a perfect time to get out of the dome and do something physical to keep my focus on work and not on the apprehensive feeling weighing on me from last night.

"T-GOT!" I hear from the back of the room.

"Check your yuriOS for team assignments, and whoever takes down the target will get an extra day of paid leave, courtesy of Deputy Commander Petrok." Almost in perfect unison the unit looks down at their devices and starts murmuring about their roles for the training.

"You said you needed that day for a private matter." Petrok crosses his arms and frowns at me.

"Oh yeah… I got it from here, boss," I tell him with an awkward smile.

"Hey, Aro—I'm going to need your sister's number so I can take her out on my day off!" Locke yells over the loud group.

"That's never going to happen." Someone in the back yells, "Dayum!" Locke can't handle Kiera, and he'd be too hard to replace after she kicks his ass for saying something asinine.

"I look forward to beating you all for the—what is it… sixth consecutive time?" I can't resist taunting them a little.

"Fifth," Tai mutters under his breath.

"Let's go, it smells like desperation in here," I say and grab my yuriOS. "You've got five minutes to report to your rally point. Training begins at 0700." I've barely finished my sentence when the room erupts, everyone rushing to their assigned posts.

"What team are you on?" Tai asks as we leave the briefing room.

"Alpha Recon."

"Just like old times. Who else is with us?" he asks.

"Maak and one of the new guys, Lugo."

"The one Maak messed with during barracks inspection?"

"One of many. I've paired them up for the day."

"Good. It serves him right for being a dick," Tai says.

Everything we need for the training is waiting for us at our rally point in the cargo bay. Tai shoves supplies into his pack while I inventory the weapons in our pile.

"You need to find someone else to entertain Bri next time," Tai says.

"What? You got off on such a great start!" It was fun to watch them bicker.

"She's a cheat," he says.

"That's a pretty serious accusation. I think you're just a sore loser." He flairs his nostrils at me. I'm sure the truth is somewhere in the middle. I wouldn't put it past Bri to cheat, and I know firsthand that Tai is a sore loser.

"What's going on with you and the female?" Tai asks as he straps blaster cartridges to his belt.

"I don't think they like being called that," I correct him.

"Whatever. What's going on between you two?" he asks again.

"I don't exactly know," I answer honestly.

"I'm not complaining. At least your mood has improved." He looks up at me with an accusatory stare.

"Oh, come on. I wasn't that bad."

"I know I don't need to remind you of the rules, and we both know you'll just do whatever you want anyway. Just be careful. A lot of shit could hit a very large fan," he says, using one of the human phrases we learned before they arrived.

"I'm aware. I'll be careful." I say what I think he wants to hear. Tai's not wrong, but I'm not about to admit that to him. The door behind us slides open and Maak walks in, catching Tai's comment.

"Careful about what?" Maak asks as he crouches down and carelessly shoves supplies into his bag.

Lugo's eyes go wide the moment he steps through the door and sees that he's on the same team as Maak.

"Don't worry about it, brother. I'm always careful," I tell Tai. He doesn't need to be worrying about me.

"Ha!" Maak lets out, interjecting himself into our conversation again.

"I say we go for a good old-fashioned rope-a-dope," I suggest to the team once everyone is packed and ready to head out.

"Rope-a-dope, sir?" Lugo asks.

"Come on, noobie," Maak grunts.

"Maak, knock it off. This is what training is for," Tai says and roughly hands Maak the loaded pack, hitting him square in the gut.

"You and Maak are Team Alpha, Tai and I are Bravo. Once we locate the enemy, Alpha will set up a defensive position and draw them out. Once Special Forces arrives, we will attack from the rear after they've used up all their ammo on you two," I explain.

"Yes, sir," Lugo says, sounding every bit the fresh recruit. Maak shakes his head and steps out of the cargo bay. I like the new kid. He reminds me of myself. Even though he's young, he hasn't complained about Maak's hazing. He's tougher than anyone gives him credit for.

I drag in a deep breath of fresh air. My head feels clearer and more focused right away. Using the trees for cover, our team moves in opposite directions out of the dome. The weight of the weapon feels good in my hands. This is where I like to be. Something about T-GOT just feels right. It's like time slows down and every movement matters. It switches on that ancient part of my brain that's trained for survival, the one that still lurks after all these millennia.

The muradome is in a secluded part of pt'Clanik. There is nothing between here and the military base, and it's about half a day by porter to get there. We're smack in the middle of a forest, a perfect place to train the unit on how to move around without being detected.

We get to the expansive grassland beyond the trees. Elowen would like it here. No—focus. I'm not thinking about her right now. I've got a record to defend.

I extend my arm and pat the air down, ordering the unit to get low to the ground. The tall grass gives us some cover as we keep moving forward. I direct them to follow me as I take a sharp turn, heading north instead of east like we had planned. Going north will give us the high ground. Maak audibly huffs from the back. I snap my head back and glare at him. If he gives our location away now, we might as well pack it in.

We continue north until we reach the destination I set us toward. A singular tree at the top of a rolling hill. Down below a sea of flowers and grass swirl around. This is where I would bring Elowen if I could. I shake my head and bring my thoughts back to the present. We spread out along the ridge to scope out the valley below. I tap my visor at my temples and rest the plexi on the bridge of my nose. I focus my eyes on the tree line in the distance and the visor automatically zooms in, giving me a better look. We scan the landscape for a while, looking for any signs of where to go next.

"Target located," I hear in my earpiece. Shit—we should have just gone east. Maak rips his visor off and throws it into the ground.

"Alright, let's go." I drag myself up off the ground.

"What were you thinking dragging us up here?" Maak asks, visibly upset.

"I thought this was a good vantage point." My excuse sounds lame even to my ears. The truth is: I wasn't focused.

"I could have used an extra day off." Great—now even Lugo has turned on me.

We head back to the dome in silence, the tension thick between us. I feel guilty for letting them down. And there goes my winning streak.

"What's that?" Lugo asks, sniffing the air when we are about halfway back to the dome.

I take in a deep breath. The smell burns my nose as we get closer. Maak stops in his tracks and crouches down. I look past him and see black ooze spreading over a tree. Tai's ears twitch and his head turns as he tries to tune his hearing to anything around us. The four of us freeze in place, watching and listening.

I order the other teams to fan out and search the area to find whatever made this mark.

All other teams report back—nothing.

I scoop up some of the sticky black sludge into my empty canteen and seal it shut, hoping it might help us figure out where this came from.

17

Elowen

Even though the lab is at full capacity this morning it's quiet enough to hear a pin drop. We are a sea of identical steri-suits hunched over microscopes, all focused on our work. Andi's making her way through the aisles, checking in with staff and dropping off samples as she goes along.

I grab a new slide to analyze. I secure it on the stage and adjust the focus of the eyepiece. There are more technologically advanced methods of magnifying things, but nothing beats the sensation of using these old microscopes. Looking through them is so aesthetically pleasing. The cool metal pieces. The simplicity of the knobs. Using a physical object to maneuver the mechanisms that click into place. Metal sliding against glass. It's nostalgic, and I love it.

I switch the slide from the microscope over to the ion-selective electrodes to measure the concentration of potassium. I jot down the measurement and move the sample over to the "finished" pile. The plant I've been studying has a lower potassium concentration than that of its closest equivalent specimen on Earth. I mark my notes with a question mark as a reminder to follow up.

"Elowen, I need you to take these samples down to the genetics lab," Andi says and leaves a box on the table next to me.

"Have you noticed anything odd about the potassium concentration in your data?"

"Yes. We've already marked it as a non-significant finding." She glances over my notes briefly before going on her way.

I should have known it was already noted. I berate myself all the way to the genetics lab.

Intellectually I know it's not normal to know the status of every single finding—but those are the kinds of unrealistic expectations I have for myself.

Bri is waiting for me. She takes the slides and loads them into the reactor. She puts her hands into the machine's attached polygloves and manipulates the components.

"I feel like I'm seeing a whole new side of you lately," she says without looking away from her work.

"What do you mean?"

"Anytime you're around Aro this sassy trash-talking side comes out. I haven't even heard you explain some oddly specific fact to him yet. I'm not complaining—I like that Elowen."

"He brings out that side of me. I feel like he needs someone to keep him humble."

"It's your subconscious telling you that you're going to bang," she says.

"It's just a little harmless flirting."

"For now. Who knows where it could lead? I could use a little something-something to go somewhere, if you know what I mean." Bri's a master at multitasking. She can effortlessly do her job and pry into my personal life at the same time.

"There's always Tai," I say. My comment makes her stop moving and she looks over at me.

"Absolutely not. He is the worst. He threw an absolute fit when I beat him at Cubes. We ended up fighting about the rules for an hour."

"There is a fine line between fighting and fucking," I tell her.

Her loud cackle echoes through the quiet lab. She tries to stifle her laughter when everyone looks up from their work to glare at her.

"There's that Elowen. I was just talking about her and there she is," Bri says.

"You need to focus on your work. We can talk about your obsession with my personal life later."

"Wait! Don't go. I can do both at once," she pleads. "I want to hear more about the gorgeous Tilak who is obviously in love with you."

"We'll talk later, and he's not in love with me. That would be absurd."

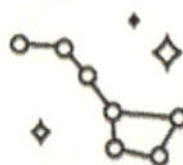

1130 Incoming message from Aro pt'Burosa

Aro: I'm going to need to smooth things over with Tai. He's still not over it.

Elowen: It couldn't have been that bad.

Aro: Bri beat him three times in a row. There have been accusations of cheating. It got a little out of hand.

Elowen: She's ruthless when it comes to Cubes.

Aro: Tell her to take it easy on him next time. He may not recover from the beating she handed out.

Elowen: He'll just have to get better at the game. You have to know by now that there's no reasoning with Bri.

Aro: I'm going to need a new wingman.

Elowen: Finally admitting that you need a wingman. This is progress.

Aro: Hungry? I'm starving.

Elowen: Nice change of subject. I can't eat right now. I'm stuck in the lab for a bit longer.

Aro: I need to eat.

Elowen: Then go!

Aro: I don't like eating alone.

Elowen: There are about fifty other Tilaks you can drag to lunch.
Aro: I want to eat with you.
Elowen: Okay, give me an hour, but it will have to be quick.
Aro: See, that wasn't so hard.

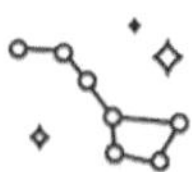

Aro is waiting with two bowls of noodles when I get to the mess hall. He motions to the noodles across from him. I'm nervous about seeing him again after our walk through the dome. Butterflies don't even begin to describe it.

This is the closest thing to a date I've had in a while. What if he doesn't think this is a date? Do his people even date?

The noodles in front of me look different. What is usually clear broth now has a reddish tint with some texture. "What do we have here?" I ask.

"I got you some noodles." He watches me intently, waiting for me to take a bite.

I twirl some noodles on my chopsticks and take a small bite to test it out. "That's good." It's spicy and salty, so I slurp in another big bite. "What did you put in it?"

"It's my secret recipe, and I'm not going to let the cat out of my sack."

I bite my cheeks to stop a laugh from coming out. "You mean, 'let the cat out of the bag.'" Maturity means not laughing at his incorrect usage of the word "sack." I'm proud of myself.

"That doesn't make any sense," he says.

"I know." It's cute he messed up the saying.

I go back to my delicious lunch. This is a huge upgrade from the food I've been eating for months. Noodle fatigue is hitting us all. I'm very tired of eating the same thing three meals a day.

"Thank you. You've made my day exponentially better. I thought I had something with my research, but it turned out to be nothing."

"Glad I can help," he says. "Exponentially." He tests the word out and looks over at me.

I look around the mess to see if anyone is watching us, still feeling self-conscious about eating a meal alone with Aro.

"I realized last night that I know all about you, and you don't know anything about me," Aro says.

"What do you know about me?" I ask with a nervous laugh.

"For starters, I know you're funny as hell even though you tell terrible jokes, that you're a good friend. Sometimes you ramble when you're nervous. You're an only child who has seen more of the universe than anyone else I know. You're brilliant at your work, and that you like a challenge," he says confidently, ticking each attribute off on his fingers.

"How could you possibly know all that about me?"

"Your comedic timing is impeccable, and you can't fake that. I've seen you with Bri, you make an effort when you're tired or don't want to be around people. You do it for her so she doesn't feel so alone here. You talked about moving around with your parents and never mentioned siblings. You're here, so you must be brilliant. And the challenge—well, that's just a guess."

I look at him with new eyes. I would never have guessed that he paid that close attention.

"Impressed, right? Ask me anything," he says with that cocky assurance I usually find irritating on men, but lately it's having the opposite effect on me.

I bite my cheek to hold back a smile. "Are we going to get in trouble for this?"

"Eating noodles? Well, technically speaking I'm not supp—"

"Not the noodles, *this,*" I motion back and forth between us.

"I'm more of an 'ask for forgiveness not permission' type," he says.

"Well, I'm more of a 'follow the rules and not get kicked off the planet' type."

"I think there is a way we both get what we want," Aro says with confidence. "We'll have to wait and see how that goes. Next question."

"How old are you?" I ask.

"30 Earth years," he answers.

"What's your job here?"

"I'm a captain. I tell these knuckleheads what to do and when to do it."

"If you weren't here right now, where would you want to be?"

"Honestly? I wouldn't want to be anywhere else right now," he says and nudges my knee with his under the table.

"How many times have you used that line?" I ask. There is something about him that brings out this side in me. Maybe he's right about me liking a challenge.

"Once—just now," he answers without hesitation.

"Tell me about your family," I say.

"That's not in the form of a question. You're going to have to rephrase."

"You mentioned a sister before. What's she like?"

"Kiera. She's a few years younger than me. We are really close."

"What do you want to be when you grow up?" I ask.

"I don't have much choice in the matter. My father is Bajimr for the pt'Burosa House."

"What's that?"

"He's the head of one of our ancient noble houses. And at some point, I'll take over."

"I didn't know I was speaking with royalty. I would have been more deferential," I say with a tiny bit of sarcasm. I'm impressed it's taken him this long to tell me about his identity. In my experience, people with proximity to power want to make sure everyone around them knows it right away.

"Sometimes people get weird when they realize who I am," Aro says.

"Well, I'll probably say something weird. At least it won't be about that."

"I wouldn't expect anything less."

"That explains why you were at the treaty signing."

"Can I be honest? I noticed you that night and waited for you to come over and introduce yourself," he says.

"I felt a little out of my element with all the politicians and dignitaries and university presidents."

"They all seemed pretty impressed with you," he says.

"Then I guess I have them fooled."

The way he smiles at me is a problem. Actually, the way my body reacts when he smiles at me is the problem.

18

Aro

My head snaps to the door every time it slides open. I'm disappointed when someone other than Elowen walks in. I've had her bowl of spicy noodles ready for a while. I came in early in case she decided to get lunch before the rush.

The broth is starting to thicken in a very unappealing way. There is no way I can give Elowen these noodles now. I dump the bowl into the sani-unit and grab a fresh one. After returning to my spot, I remake her lunch, taking care to add enough seasoning without making it too spicy. I slide the bowl across the table and turn it a few times. I want it to look just right for when she gets here.

I watch the door impatiently and swirl my own food without taking a bite. I want to wait until she gets here so we can eat together.

I check the time again. She's late—later than usual. The tables around me start to clear. Lunch break is about over, and she still hasn't shown up.

I look ridiculous sitting here with two bowls of noodles, clearly waiting for someone who isn't coming. I grab both bowls, dump them, and go back to the security hub.

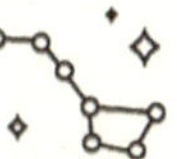

Dinner finally comes after an agonizingly slow day. I do the same thing I did for lunch. I replace her cold noodles three times before I give up and call it a night.

She's avoiding me.

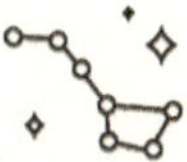

It's been days since I saw her. I've managed to grow more irritable. Today I have a pounding headache from my perpetually clenched jaw. I told myself I would be patient and wait her out. That resolution has proved to be more difficult than I was prepared for. Every day I go through my routine hoping she will appear. I lurk in the mess hall and rec room, hoping she'll walk through the doors and put me out of my misery.

19

Elowen

Bri and I are opposites in most ways, but we share a disdain for early mornings. The synth-coffee only makes matters worse. I've given up on it, but Bri drinks the stuff hoping one day it will taste like the real thing.

I should be mad at Andi for scheduling the All Staff this early, but the good news she announces makes up for the ungodly hour. She happily tells us all teams are making great progress and sends us off with news that our initial findings will be sent off by the end of the week.

"So, where's the boyfriend today?" Bri asks me while she zips up her steri-suit.

"Not my boyfriend." I plonk down on the bench and pull up the thick suit I'll be stuck in all day.

"I've been seeing Aro at the mess hall with two bowls of noodles, growling at anyone who tries to sit down with him. It's pathetic," Bri says while we step through the airlock and enter the lab. She says it the way you would talk about a sick puppy. The ones with the oversized watery eyes.

"How much longer are you going to torture this poor guy? Hasn't he passed the test yet?" Bri asks.

"I don't know what you're talking about. I'm not testing anybody."

"Please. Don't play innocent. You're avoiding him to see if he will track you down. I get it—make sure he's truly interested before going any farther. I think that he's proven himself by now," Bri says.

"I have been avoiding him, but not to test his interest in me. I've been avoiding him because I want to keep my job, and that means not getting distracted by the first hot alien that smiles at me."

"You're not going to lose your job. That's a convenient excuse," she says. "I'm just saying, he's clearly interested, and I think you could use a little diversion."

"When we have a pollination solution, then I can think about a potential relationship. Until then, I've got to stay focused on work."

"You know that you're allowed to have a personal life," Bri says.

"I can have a life once we fix the giant mess that's waiting for us on Earth."

"Can you hear yourself right now? It's preposterous that you feel like you have to put your life on hold, and single-handedly save humanity. It's a pretty narrow view of success—you don't have to achieve everything to earn happiness."

Bri's eyes don't let go of mine. She is dead serious. She wants me to truly hear what she's saying. Intellectually I know she's right.

"You aren't ready to hear any of that yet. The last thing I'll say—I just hope you realize that I'm right before it's too late."

"I hear you, and I'll think about it. I promise."

If I didn't love Bri so much, she would irritate the shit out of me. Not only does she command the main character energy I've lacked my whole life, now she has the gall to go and be insightful and emotionally intelligent.

"I'll be eating dinner in the mess hall tonight, like a normal person. When you're ready to stop hiding, you can find me there," she says with a teasing glint in her eye and heads to her workstation.

Is it ego that has convinced me I have to be the one to figure this all out? Every day, people balance a personal life with their professional one. I've put this limitation on myself that I can't do both. The idea of letting go of a tiny bit of control to see where things could go with Aro sends anxiety through my entire body.

20

Aro

There she is, sitting there casually slurping noodles as if she hasn't been in hiding for an agonizing nine days.

I put my tray down in front of her and stand for a moment with my chest thrusted out proudly. I feel like I won some unspoken game we've been playing. She finally looks up, her gaze sweeping over me until her eyes meet mine.

"Good morning," I say, like she hasn't been evading me for over a week, and that I haven't been desperate to track her down.

"Good morning," she says and goes back to her yuriOS.

"Look who came out of hiding."

"I don't know that it's possible to truly hide in a muradome," she says sweetly. I see right through her innocent act. She's been avoiding me.

"That's true..." I say and fill my mouth with noodles.

"Yet here I am, hiding in plain sight." A blush creeps up her chest and neck when we make fleeting eye contact.

"Well, I'm glad you're back," I say, smiling broadly.

"Let's just say it was observed that I haven't been as... available. Accusations were made, and I'm proving the point that I'm not hiding from anyone."

"Translation: Bri pointed out that you're avoiding me, and you don't want to seem scared. Are you going to eat all your meals here now?"

She smiles at me, and I could die from happiness.

"Can I fix those noodles for you?" I ask, letting it slide. I won't make her answer the question.

"I thought you'd never ask."

"I was worried you wouldn't approve of my little act of rebellion," I say mixing in the seasonings. I move slowly, a little retribution for avoiding me all this time. I can feel the impatience radiating off her. I go even slower.

"What rebellion?" she asks, curiosity piqued.

"The spices. I was supposed to get rid of them before you all got here."

"What? Why? That doesn't make any sense," she says.

"For some reason, it ended up on the list of stuff we weren't able to have. I have a theory though." I slide the bowl over to her. She takes it with greedy hands and digs right in.

Fuck—a part of me that feeds off of taking care of someone else just roared to life.

"What's your theory?" she asks, wiping away some splatter on her cheek.

"I think that our meddling governments wanted us all to bond over how shitty the food is. They told us that it was an 'act of solidarity.' I hate feeling manipulated, so I socked away some spices. Welcome to the resistance."

"You're telling me I'm complicit with your rule breaking? I'll allow it, just this once. The real crime here is how bad the noodles are."

"So, I'll see you at lunch?"

She swallows heavily. "Baby steps..."

I understand the meaning of her human saying. This small opening is enough for now.

"The dome is all yours for the next few days. I've been summoned to Bihar," I tell her, gauging her response.

"That should be a nice break," she says neutrally.

"You can *really* prove Bri wrong, and even eat during regular mealtimes."

"I thought we already established that I'm not hiding. Just going about my work, staying focused on my job."

"Sure. Of course. Staying focused. Me too."

"Good. I'm glad we are on the same page," she says.

"Maybe you'll miss me enough to let me take you on another tour of the dome," I suggest.

"I think I've seen enough, but thanks."

"I'm sure I can find something better than a storage unit this time."

"I don't know if there's any topping that," she jokes.

Good. She's teasing me again. This is progress.

"I bet you that I can find something better than the storage unit. And if I can't, I'll leave you alone. No more cornering you at the mess hall… or conspiring with Bri to find you in the rec room."

She hesitates, watching me through squinted eyes.

"You have a deal." She reaches out to shake my hand, sealing the agreement the way humans do. I reach out, and the moment our fingers make contact, I feel her touch throughout my body. I can tell she feels it too. She looks up at me with big bright eyes. Reluctantly, I let her go when she pulls back. I drag my fingers along her hand until she finally breaks contact.

21

Elowen

"I thought about what you said," I tell Bri. I caught up with her in the gym. From the way she's sweating and breathing heavily, she's been at it for a while. Unlike me, who chooses sleep over exercise every single time.

"Is it time for me to say, 'I told you so'?" she says, coming to a stop on the tread.

"I'm not one-hundred-percent sure about Aro, but you did raise some really good points. I appreciate you being the kind of friend to call me out on my shit," I tell her.

"I sort of want to hear you say the words…" Bri trails off, waiting for me to be crystal clear. She faces me and taps her toe, waiting.

"You were right."

"Oh, damn. That feels good. Being right is a hell of a drug." She closes her eyes and throws her head back, relishing the moment.

"I shouldn't put off having a life because of my career… and I don't need to earn the right to find happiness… and it's possible that I've been hiding because the idea of trying to juggle both is absolutely terrifying," I say, putting it all out there.

"I'm proud of you. My baby bird is ready to leave the nest."

"To be clear, as far as Aro goes, we are just friends," I remind her.

Right when I say the words, a message from Aro pops up on my yuriOS. I try to hide my excitement at seeing his name in my notifications.

1625 Incoming message from Aro pt'Burosa

Aro: Hey.
Elowen: Hey.
Aro: Meet me for lunch tomorrow?
Elowen: Sure. I need to spice up my noodles. Can you bring back a jar for me?
Aro: Nope, that's not part of the plan. If you can fix up your own noodles, what would you need me for?
Elowen: This is true.

Bri snaps her fingers in front of my face, getting my attention. "That smile on your face right now." She points. "That's not the face of someone messaging their 'friend.'"

"You're reading too much into this," I tell her and turn back to my message screen.

Elowen: When do you get back?
Aro: Hopefully tonight.
Elowen: I'll see you tomorrow, better have those noodles ready when I get there.
Aro: I will. And I miss you too.
Elowen: Presumptuous.
Aro: You know what it does to me when you use big words.
Elowen: Intransigent.
Aro: Now you're just torturing me.

Bri wipes a towel over her face. "I love this for you, by the way," she says, waving in my general direction.

"When did you get so perceptive?" I follow her to the next machine she's going to use. For a brief moment I'm inspired to also work out but quickly change my mind.

"I always have been. It's a gift and a curse."

"Ever point any of this insight at yourself?" I ask.

"That is a completely different set of skills. I like to save my wisdom for others. I prefer to glide through life joyfully ignorant."

22

Aro

I hate politics. Six hours ago, my father and I walked into this room, sat down and we haven't moved since.

He shoots me a death stare and I stop my knee from bouncing. I even got an "ahem" when he caught me messaging Elowen during a particularly boring monologue from one of his advisors.

Maybe I'm not that good at faking my interest in this meeting.

My father selected these nine Tilaks over the last twenty years. I'm sure he picked each one based on their individual strengths, but at this moment, they are all a giant waste of my time. I prefer more direct communication, specifically where I don't have to sit in the same room for hours waiting for someone to get to the point.

Over the course of the day, I figure out they have split into two factions. One group is blindly supportive of my father and will follow whatever he says. He has been talking about opening our planet to other species for a while now, and it's no secret that he hopes the Apollo Treaty with Earth is the first step in that direction.

The other group is very comfortable with the status quo on j'Tilak. Their mumbling and body language give away what they would never have the audacity to say outright: they don't think humans or any other species belong here. I wouldn't be surprised if they were working with the protesters who definitely need better slogans if they are going to be taken seriously.

Besnik's voice breaks through my thoughts. "Commander Rialto, thank you for joining us here today. We have analyzed the sample your team collected outside MuraDome IV. We have determined that it is mire from an Atorum."

Finally, we get to the reason I'm here today.

Rialto's eyes widen for a fraction of a second in surprise. I don't know what an Atorum is, but it doesn't sound good. He brings the room up to speed on what happened the day we discovered the black ooze.

"What is an Atorum?" my father asks.

"It's a GMEO, a genetically modified eradication organism. They're used to eradicate harmful viruses, bacteria, or invasive species. Simply program what you want removed from the environment, and they take care of it while leaving everything else largely untouched," Besnik explains.

"What is it doing here?" my father asks.

"No way to know with only the mire. If we are able to intercept the Atorum, we could possibly trace it back to where it came from," Besnik says. She's a newer advisor. I've been unable to get a read on her in our limited interactions.

Great. A programmable killing machine is loose. Fan-fucking-tastic.

"Where is it now?" a soft-spoken voice says from the back of the room. I haven't bothered to learn that one's name. However, they might be my favorite because they have spoken the least out of everyone today.

"We don't have any leads at this point," Besnik says reluctantly.

"That's enough for today," my father says, bringing the meeting to a close. The council members file out quietly, their feet shuffling on the stone floor. I slip into the back of the line to follow them out.

My father intercepts me before I can leave. "I hope you're not trying to run off before you say hi to your mom," he says with an affectionate slap on the back.

"Wouldn't dream of it," I say, even though that is exactly what I had planned to do.

"You didn't seem to be enjoying the meeting today. It won't be too long before you can appoint your own council," he says.

"It was fine. A little too long in my opinion. I just wish everyone would be more straightforward and say what they were thinking. It's pretty obvious that a few disagree with your decision about the treaty," I say.

"I'm aware. I wanted to have advisors with different backgrounds, different ways of thinking. It's dangerous to be surrounded by people who will only tell you 'yes.'"

"Differences of opinion are one thing. Giving consideration to those with dangerous ideas is another," I say.

"You were paying attention!" he says.

I guess I did pick up more than I thought.

"Go see your mother. She's waiting for you at home, and she made me promise that I'd send you there the moment the meeting ended. I have a few more things to wrap up. I'll see you at dinner." That last part sounded like an order.

I'll be here in Bihar longer than I had hoped. I guess can stay here for the night and still be back to the dome by lunch tomorrow.

I don't want to avoid my mom. We're close. I usually go out of my way to see her when I'm here. I don't know if I'm ready to go into detail about my personal life at the moment. My mom's powers of perception are high. She has a knack for getting information out of me. I don't know how she'll react to me being interested in a human. She's supportive of my father's goals to open up our planet to others. I'm not sure how far that support extends.

I take a shortcut through empty rooms and corridors over to the residency where my mom is waiting. It's been years since I've lived here, but I still know all the shortcuts. It makes me happy to be back. It would be even better if Elowen was with me. I think she'd like hearing about all the trouble Kiera and I got into when we were young.

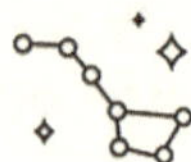

Sounds of clinking direct me towards the kitchen. Anytime I need to find my mom, I know where to look first. She passed down her love of cooking to me. This is where we've always bonded.

"You kept me waiting," she says with mock seriousness.

"Not my fault. I was ready to leave hours ago." I drop a quick kiss on her cheek.

"You're here now. Grab a knife and start chopping." She motions over to a pile of veg on the counter. "How have you been? Things at the muradome must be busy. I haven't heard from you in weeks." She pauses her movements around the kitchen to watch me. She's always had the uncanny ability to see right through me.

"It's not too busy. I mean, I've been busy, but the dome is boring… but busy." I trip over my words and laugh a little. This must be Elowen's influence rubbing off on me.

"So which is it—busy or not busy?" Her dark eyes stare into me.

"Busy. I've been busy."

"If it's not the work keeping you busy, then what is?" she asks. My mom has a unique way of asking questions. If it were anyone else, it would be an interrogation. She manages to get away with it. I'm not going to bother resisting. I might as well just tell her what's going on.

"I've been spending time with one of the scientists."

She silently urges me to continue.

"She's funny, and smart, and completely unimpressed with me," I tell her.

"She sounds perfect," Mom says and pops a bite of veg in her mouth.

"There's one tiny insignificant detail," I say sarcastically. "She's human and will be returning to Earth once her research is done." I brace myself for her reaction, but none comes. She continues to cook.

I haven't stopped to think about how this could all play out, and I don't want to now. There is just something about Elowen that feels right, and I'm going to follow that instinct. We can figure everything else out later.

"Who's to say what is significant or not? Things are always changing. Who knows what our world will look like in a few rotations?" She shrugs like this is all no big deal.

"I'm starving!" My dad declares when he walks into the kitchen. He greets my mom with a kiss on her cheek and steals a bite of veg.

"Aro was telling me about his new friend at the dome, a human." My mom brings him up to speed.

"Rameera," he warns. My dad is much better at giving me space when it comes to my private life.

"Roman." She mimics his tone.

I'm hardly listening while the two of them recount their day. I keep replaying what my mom said. It didn't bother her at all that I'm interested in a human. My family's support would make it a lot easier on both of us. If only I can somehow convince Elowen to stay after the program is done.

23

Elowen

"Ready to lose that bet?" Aro asks, appearing out of nowhere. He could've very loudly approached me, and I still would have missed. I was so fixated on my work, I could have missed a herd of stampeding elephants.

I brought my work to the rec room today. I wanted a change of scenery from the lab, and it's usually empty in here while everyone works.

"I'm not easily impressed, but that storage room was *pretty* spectacular," I tell him with a note of sarcasm.

"Let's go. It's now or never."

"Right now?"

I worry we look too much like a couple. I'd be lying if I said I wasn't attracted to him, but this is still a no-go.

The fact that I let my eyes wander all over him when no one's paying attention is my own little secret.

I follow him through the hall, and I watch him walk. That's really not the right word—it's a goddamn swagger.

"If we hurry we can get there during shift change in the greenhouse, and it will be empty for a little bit. Now's your chance to check it out," he explains, and I match his stride.

"Then what are we waiting for?" I say as I pass him, turning back briefly to smile. It's safer up here. I'm not tempted to let my eyes linger on him from here.

Aro pulls to a stop outside a door like all the rest. He scans his palm to open it, and I'm immediately hit with warm fresh air. It's enough to knock me over. There is no comparing it to the recycled air we've all been breathing. The entire ceiling is clear plexi, and I look at the blue sky for the first time in months. It feels like heaven—the warm suns on my skin. The smell of soil draws my attention down. There are dozens of rows of large raised gardening beds.

"The seedlings sprouted a few days ago. They'll be ready to start their migration soon," Aro tells me as he walks toward the short soft tufts of greenery.

I lean down and watch a sprout slowly unfurl and sway. I'm too afraid to touch the small leaves. They look so fragile at this stage. I'm transfixed, watching the tiny movements of the green barely peeking out of the soil. Little fingers wave back and forth, reminding me of a tiny sea anemone's tentacles moving with the ocean current.

I had no idea we were cultivating in the dome. This definitely beats the storage room.

I walk up and down the aisles between the raised garden beds, completely spellbound. Their little roots are secure in the soil for now, but in a short amount of time, these little sprouts will be fully mature and ready to seek out resources and pollinators.

"In a few weeks, my team is going to disassemble the boxes so the flowers can rove," Aro explains. "I was just in here going over the plan with the greenhouse staff and I thought you would like it in here."

"They have you guys doing yard work now?"

"Gotta put these muscles to good use," Aro says. I detect a tiny flex in his chest and avert my gaze back to the plants.

"I bet it's amazing to see them move around."

"It is. They remind me of you. These beautiful little things exploring, searching for what they need," he says.

"You make my drifting sound so poetic."

"I think it is," he says and walks farther into the greenhouse.

His observation stabs me in the chest. I'm surprised by the sweetness behind his words. I thought I had him figured out. But he's not just a perpetually joking arrogant alien—he's so much more.

"Can I take one of these? I want to analyze the apical meristem," I ask Aro, even though it's not his approval I would need.

"The what?" he asks.

"They make the plant grow. I want to see if they're similar to the ones on Earth," I explain.

"I have an idea, and go with me on this. Why don't we just sit and watch? The microscope can come later. Let's be in the moment," he suggests.

My mind races with the discoveries this could uncover. "This could be the key that unlocks a breakthrough. I haven't looked at this stage yet."

"You can do that later, right? Come sit with me."

Aro sits between two raised beds cross-legged and leans back, using his arms as support. I make a mental note to come back and collect a sample before the sprouts grow too quickly.

I settle in next to him, using the frame as a backrest. I try to make myself relax, but I'm eager to take a closer look in the lab. This might be the critical stage I'm missing.

"You really can't turn it off, can you?" Aro asks, sensing I am still in my head, and not in the moment with him. He picks up a small rock and turns it in his hand.

"I don't know how you *can* turn it off," I say, confirming his suspicion. "How do you stop your mind from racing? Worrying about every possible outcome?"

"I dunno. Right here right now feels pretty nice."

I take a deep breath to give myself a chance to think of what to say next. The air smells so good. I close my eyes and savor the feeling of the suns on me once again.

I slowly open my eyes and Aro is watching me. "See? That wasn't too hard."

"And you live like this every day?" The idea that someone can do that blows my mind.

"Not all the time."

"I'm not very good at being in the moment."

"I'm sure my father wishes I was more like you," he admits.

"Don't change. Overthinking is a rough existence."

"Really? It doesn't bother you that I don't have a ten-point plan for the future?"

"Not at all. I like you just like this." I'm surprised at my own words. It's the most spontaneous, in-the-moment comment I've ever made to someone. There were no equivocations, no disclaimers. Simply a statement of fact about my feelings.

I keep my eyes on the ground, nervous to meet his gaze at my heartfelt confession. His finger gently lifts my chin and our eyes meet. His face is close to mine, so close that all I can see are his eyes. He leans closer and softly kisses me. His lips linger for a moment before he pulls away. I open my eyes to find him smiling. He leans in and kisses me again. I kiss him back—this time harder. His hand combs through the hair at the base of my neck, holding me to him. It's intoxicating. I can't believe I've been avoiding this.

The door to the nursery slides open and a group of scientists file in.

"Time's up." Aro pulls away slowly, like he's being dragged away against his will. I wish I could stay here for hours. Getting back to the lab is now the last thing on my mind.

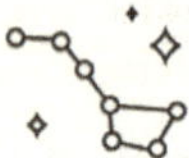

I toss and turn, trying to fall asleep, wondering what Aro is doing at this very moment. I picture him lying in his bunk with his shirt off. Conjuring that image immediately turns me on. I close my eyes and let my hand slip under the sheets along my belly. I picture Aro's hand sliding between my thighs. It's not the first time I've imagined us together. Some nights I think about him taking his time and torturing me with his touch. Other nights it's more urgent and demanding. I think about the dirty words Aro would whisper in my ear as he pleases me.

Memories of the sounds he made when we kissed today make me moan and I move my hand lower. I bring my wet fingers back and rub the pads of my fingers across my most sensitive place. I think of how hard he would be, pushing himself into my hip while he works his fingers in and out of me. I ride myself as I climb closer to the peak of my desire. I think of Aro pushing deep into me, and my muscles clench around nothing. My fingers aren't enough. I need more.

I clear my head of everything except him. It takes a long time to get there, and in my frustration, I almost give up. I keep picturing him, imagining what he would look like stroking himself while I got off. I tense and grasp a handful of my bedding when I cross over the edge and shake through my orgasm. My body pulses while I catch my breath and slowly pull my hand away. This takes the edge off, but I know there is only one thing that will fully satisfy this obsession I've developed for him.

24

Aro

I've dragged the whole unit outside for today's workout. They've been getting soft sitting around in the climate-controlled dome. I could also use the fresh air.

I need to get my thoughts straight. All I can think about is the next time I'm going to see Elowen. Now that I know what her lips feel like on mine, I'm obsessed. Something clicked into place in my chest when she said, "I like you just like this." No one has ever said anything like that to me before.

I separate the group into pairs, getting a twisted satisfaction when I put Maak and Lugo together. I'm still trying to even the score between the two of them. Today should be enough to tip the scale in the new recruit's favor.

"Listen up. It's been a while since we trained outside the dome, so I'm going to take it easy on you." I pause for dramatic effect. "Well, *some* of you." Maak isn't the only one that gets gratification from torturing the unit. Except I use my power for good. He's just a dick to the new guys.

"We're going to do some high-interval training today. I want a full-speed run to the sentinel bots and a recovery walk back. Oh yeah—I forgot to mention, for that run out you're going to be carrying your partner." I look over at Maak and grin. "The higher-ranking officer will do the carrying. Six intervals. Now, go!"

Tai stands at attention next to me, his eyes locked forward. His rank gives him the luxury to skip drills. Occasionally he and I will opt in for the workout, but not today.

"Sitting this one out, sir?" he asks.

"I've got to give someone else the chance to finish first. It's bad for morale if the captain always wins."

"You think Maak will learn his lesson after this?" he asks, knowing me well enough to know I strategically set this up for Maak's benefit.

"After I'm done with him, he'll be leaving the recruits alone."

We watch the officers running in the distance, some struggling under the weight of their heavy partners, silence stretching between us.

"You've been spending a lot of time with Elowen," Tai says. I wondered how long it would take for him to bring it up again.

"Don't worry. I haven't forgotten about what you said last time. No need to repeat yourself," I say.

"But... fuck the rules. You're going to do it anyway," he says.

"The rules apply to me, just like everyone else. I'm just more inclined to follow rules that make sense."

"This one makes perfect sense. The political situation between j'Tilak and Earth is brand new. Can you imagine the consequences of some little half-human-half-Tilak baby running around? The treaty doesn't address any of that," he says.

"I know what the treaty says," I say defensively. "Plus, you know we were all given the contraceptive shot."

"Then what are you doing? This relationship could jeopardize your future." He sighs heavily, looks around, leans in and continues. "Rules are a good thing. They keep us in line. Breaking rules leads to very real consequences." Tai absentmindedly rubs his bionic triceps.

He's never told me what happened to his arm, and I've never asked. I figured if he wanted me to know he'd tell me. He's had it since we met—day one of Intros. It's so much a part of him, it would seem odd at this point if he had two blue arms.

Maak and Lugo come to a stop in front of me, both out of breath from the run.

"Sir. Do you want me to take my turn carrying Maak now?" Lugo asks as he takes a gulp of water.

"Not necessary. We're moving on."

"Sir, I can do the heavy lifting," Lugo nervously looks between Maak and me. "I mean, obviously, I know you have a great reason for doing it this way… I don't mean to question your call, sir. So, what I guess, I'm saying is—"

"I agree, except for the blatant ass-kissing." Maak cuts him off, still struggling to catch his breath, glaring at me.

"You want to run, recruit, go ahead. Six more intervals. Maak, you stay here and give me a hundred pushups." Lugo looks over at Maak with an apology.

"Don't look at him, look at me. Go!" I yell.

"Message received, sir. No more hazing the new guys," Maak says as he drops to the ground.

25

Elowen

"I got a message from the Earth Galactic Alliance," Andi says not looking up. Her tone makes me nervous as it suggests she isn't happy to hear from the world organization funding our research.

"That doesn't sound good."

"They're concerned that we aren't making progress fast enough," she says, finally looking up from her microscope. She pushes back from the desk and pulls her goggles off to rub her eyes. She looks so tired.

"We have been making a ton of progress!" I say.

"Not enough, according to the fucking EGA."

"More resources would help. They could send more staff so we could go twice as fast," I suggest.

"It would take too long for another team to arrive. I have an idea…" She drifts off, deep in thought.

"What are you going to do?"

"I'm going to ask for an exception to allow me to leave the mura-dome for some field observation. Maybe there is something out there that we aren't seeing in here," she says.

"Can I come?" I would love to get out in the field. The dome has been feeling claustrophobic for a while now.

"I want you to stay here and keep chipping away. This could be a total bust, and I don't want to fall behind in the lab."

I swallow down the rising disappointment that bubbles up. She's right. Now's not the time to slow down because I want to take a field trip.

"Why the sudden rush? Did something happen?" I ask.

"They didn't say. I got the impression it had more to do with politics than anything else. It might be enough to get me an escort out for a few hours," Andi says. "Elowen, we're going to figure this out."

"I know." I give her a weak smile.

We go back to our microscopes and work in silence next to each other. The thought of how many people will suffer while they wait for us to figure this out hangs in the room. I try not to think about what happened the last time a major crop failed. I need to stay focused. We *can* do this. I repeat the mantra in my head the rest of the afternoon. *We can do this.*

26

Aro

"Did you see this?" Tai points his yuriOS at me.

Elowen found me this morning and warned me that her boss would be reaching out. My initial reaction was to deny the request, but Elowen explained the situation back on Earth. I found it impossible to tell her no.

"Apparently, she needs to do some field observations. I already approved it," I say and go back to my work.

"And you're sure about this?" he asks. I bristle a little at his tone. Now I know how Rialto feels when I second-guess him.

"It'll be fine. A quick trip out of the dome never hurt anyone."

"What's the security arrangement? What team will be escorting her?" he asks.

"It's just going to be Lugo. I can't spare any other staff right now. He's the only one who's available."

"He doesn't have the experience. I'll do it," he offers.

"No, you have a shift tonight, and there's no one to cover for you," I say.

"You could do it." It almost sounds like an accusation. I square up to face him directly. He needs to hear what I say next because I'm done having this conversation.

"I have another commitment." I don't go into detail. It's none of his business what I'll be doing instead, and he knows better than to ask.

"You have to be fucking kidding me." He turns away and goes back to the security feeds across the wall of the hub.

"No, I'm not kidding. Lugo will babysit the human, as you like to say, and they will be back before breakfast."

"I don't like this," he says, turning his head back to me but avoiding eye contact.

"You don't have to like it. The decision has been made."

I stomp out of the hub. Being around Tai is ruining my good mood. I've got a special night planned for Elowen. I did some research on courting customs on Earth. I am taking her on a human date. There are a few popular options, none of which are easy to pull off in a research facility. I've managed to patch something together and I'm pretty sure she'll like it.

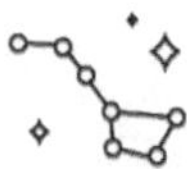

I've got a small office blocked off. It's out of the way. We won't be interrupted. I'm going to grab us dinner from the mess, set it up, and surprise her with dinner—just the two of us. Ordinarily it would be a nice restaurant or eating outside on a blanket, which sounds really uncomfortable to me.

We get… an empty office with the same noodles we've been eating for months. Now that I think about it, I'm less confident she'll be impressed.

I balance the tray of food as I make my way through the halls. I take the long way through the dome, making extra effort to avoid running into anyone. I don't want to answer any questions.

It doesn't take long to set up. The noodles are ready. I keep a steel cover over the bowls to keep them warm. I spread some nano lights out over the table and look over the room over once more. It doesn't look too bad.

I change into black trousers and a stiff black shirt. I fiddle with the neck clasp. I check the mirror and close the clasp, then open it again.

I'm overthinking this. She'll probably be wearing the same thing I've seen her in each day. I don't think she has anything other than the coveralls that the humans wear. But I'm not complaining. I'm often distracted by the thought of what is under them.

She makes the bulky uniform look good. Every once in a while, she'll tie the sleeves around her waist. I've spent far too many hours imagining myself untying that knot and pulling them off her.

27

Elowen

The door to my room slides open, revealing an Aro I haven't seen before. He isn't in his usual khaki pants and white T-shirt. He's in all black and I practically beg my eyes to stay on his face, even though his crooked grin might actually kill me.

"What's the special occasion?" I ask.

"We are going on a human date," he says, sounding proud of himself.

"You missed one crucial step."

"What? I did a ton of research. You don't even know what it is yet!" he says.

"You're supposed to ask the other person if they want to go on a date first," I tell him.

"Is there such a thing as a surprise date?" he asks. He looks a little defeated. Bri's accusations that I'm torturing him come to mind and I decide to go along with his plan.

I nervously look down the hall to make sure no one's in sight. I point my finger at his chest. "You better not get me in trouble," I say. "Wait right here." I close the door on his gorgeous face.

I look down at my clothes, the same outfit I've been wearing every day since we left Earth. They are wrinkled and not at all what I would choose to wear on a first date. I desperately spin around in my room looking for something else— anything else—to wear. I fling open my closet doors. More coveralls hang inside.

I roughly dig through my drawers and pull out a tank top. Why didn't I think to pack something other than the basics? I grab a pair of black leggings. It's just barely better than what I was wearing before, but it's all I've got.

I glance in the mirror on my way out the door. I fiddle with my hair and pinch my cheeks a little. The door slides open and I'm second-guessing my wardrobe change. Now I look like I'm trying too hard. When I'm finally brave enough to look up at Aro, his gaze is traveling up my body. Our eyes finally meet and he hits me with that incredibly sexy half-smile I've been trying to stay immune to.

"You look great."

"Better than dirty coveralls, I suppose," I say, trying to hide how self-conscious I feel.

"You won't hear any complaints from me."

He takes my hand and pulls me through the hallways. Every time we cross someone's path I release his hand. The moment we're out of sight, he grabs my hand again. He's making a point. It's clear he is not concerned about hiding from anyone. I, however, don't want to get caught.

I'm just now getting comfortable with the idea of having a fling with Aro while I'm here. My concerns about the "no fraternizing" rule haven't gone away completely. Maybe I'm getting more comfortable with the risk, or maybe it's just getting harder to deny myself when it comes to him.

We get to a darkened office and Aro slides the door open with flourish. Inside the softly lit room I see two bowls of noodles on a desk that's been adjusted to sit lower to the floor and nano lights scattered over it, casting a romantic glow.

"You did all this?" I ask.

"I wanted to take you on a human date," he says and pushes a strand of his wavy black hair back out of his eyes.

"You can just call it a date. And I love it. Thank you," I say.

I shorten the distance between us and look up at him. "Do you know what usually happens at the end of a date if it goes well?" I ask.

"I didn't get that far in my research."

I reach up and grab his shoulders and pull him down to me. I push up on my tiptoes and surprise him with a kiss. My heart pounds in my chest when he steps even closer, bringing his body against mine. A rumble comes from his chest while his grip tightens on my waist. I break the kiss and watch his eyes slowly open.

"I like human dates," he says and lowers his mouth to mine again. I push on his chest, stopping him. I want to enjoy all the effort he went through before this goes any further.

"The noodles are getting cold," I tell him and turn to our little setup for the evening.

We eat and talk for hours. He tells me about all the places he's been on j'Tilak throughout his time in the military and what it was like growing up. He tells me some funny stories about his sister, who I'm convinced is already my new best friend.

I tell him what it was like as a kid bouncing back and forth between galaxies. Some of my favorite places we stayed and other not-so-favorites. I deliberately avoid talking about Earth. I don't want to ruin our good time by talking about the renewed pressure we are under.

I tell him how I've always wanted to come here, and what it could mean for my future. I'm surprised when I admit to him that my goals aren't completely altruistic. Yes, I want to contribute to fixing the pollination crisis, but I also want to make a name for myself. I want to accomplish something and prove to myself that I'm successful. I like this version of me with Aro. I feel like I could tell him anything and he wouldn't judge me.

The nano lights flicker on and off, signifying they are running low on battery. We've been holed up in the office most of the night, completely unaware of the time.

Reluctantly, we drag ourselves up from the floor and stretch. I'm stiff from sitting for so long. Aro is the perfect gentleman and walks me back to my bunk. I don't trust myself enough to invite him in. With a door safely between us, I lean back and imagine his lips on mine again.

28

Aro

My mind replays the look on Elowen's face when we stepped into the office. Nothing can ruin my happiness today. I've even forgiven Tai for irritating me. I clap him on the back when I get to the security hub. He lurches forward at the contact and presses his lips together. Maybe he hasn't moved on from our last interaction.

"Lugo and Andi didn't return last night," Tai says. And just like that, my smile fades. Tai steps aside from the floor-length touchscreen that's displaying all the interior security feeds. I tap through each one, magnifying each stream to check for them. Sure enough, there is an empty charging space in the porter bay.

"Anything on comms?" I ask.

"We haven't been able to reach him since his initial check-in at shortly after they left," he says.

I hurry over to the other side of the room that has the exterior sentinel bot feeds. I scan through each feed quickly, not seeing them there either. I go back to the view right outside the porter bay and reverse the feed until I get to when Lugo's porter left last night.

His porter leaves the cargo hold and turns south. His porter slowly moves through the densely packed trees. Little furry forest dwellers with bulging eyes freeze in the beam of light from the porter then skitter out of the way when it passes. It all seems completely ordinary.

"They go out of view here." Tai stops the feed when the porter passes by the last sentinel bot.

"Lugo probably got lost. I'll go get them."

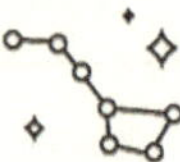

I get into a porter and leave the cargo hold, heading the direction Lugo went last night. Poor guy is never going to live this down. He'll be back at square one with the rest of the unit.

Between the trees, the light of the two suns glares off something in the distance. The shine draws my attention to the left. The missing porter comes into view. I can tell right away something isn't right. Rather than hovering over the ground, it's half buried in the dirt. I use my yuriOS to activate my body shield. The fuzzy feeling of the energy field spreading amplifies the dread weighing me down. I tap my coordinates into the yuriOS and send them to Tai. I get out of the porter and quietly move through the narrow space between trees.

I can now see that the plexi has been smashed. I peer over the edge into the porter. Everything is covered in black mire. Past the porter, thick black sludge covers Lugo from the neck down, holding him in place against a tree. His eyes are glazed over and unfocused. "Lugo! Can you hear me?"

He shakes his head, rousing himself. "I'm okay. Get to Dr. Kahn. She's over there." He nods his head pointing me in her direction.

She's on the ground leaning up against the next tree over. Her body is limp. Eyes closed. She's splattered with black mire. Blood seeps from a wound on her side. I drop down on my knees next to her and check her pulse. It's faint.

"Dr. Kahn—Andi—can you hear me?!" I don't get a response. I peel back Dr. Kahn's soaked coveralls. Bright red blood is still coming out of a wide gash along the dark skin on her rib cage. I pick her up and carefully take her to my porter. Help is on its way, but she needs medical attention now. I'm not waiting until backup gets here.

Tai was right—I should have been the one out here last night. I should have never sent Lugo out on his own.

I set the porter's course to the dome and work on getting the bleeding to stop. My field med kit has the basics, just enough to get someone to the bay in case of an emergency. I rip open the packaging, spilling a fine white powder over her wound. This will temporarily stop the bleeding. I roughly swipe away the sweat pouring down my face.

I clean away some of the blood on Andi's side. The adhesive will stick better on clean skin. She whimpers and shifts a little when I get too close to the opening.

"It's okay. You're going to be okay," I tell her. I have no idea if she can hear me or not. I squeeze the adhesive out of the tube in a thick line tracking along the wound. It thickens immediately and draws her skin together.

I sit back against the wall of the porter for the rest of the trip back. There isn't anything else useful in the med kit. I have a chance to think about all the ways I fucked up. I shouldn't have sent Lugo last night. I should have gone. He's too new and inexperienced, and I was overconfident in his ability. The weight of this responsibility is heavy on my chest as it all sinks in.

Med staff is waiting for us when I pull into the dock. Andi is laid down on a gurney and rushed into the medbay. I wipe the drying blood off my hands and onto my pants as I head towards Elowen's lab. She deserves to hear what happened from me.

Elowen is sitting cross-legged on a bench facing Bri in the locker room. I hear a muffled comment from Bri. Then, Elowen's laughter. She looks so happy in this moment. I'm about to destroy all of that. She looks over and sees me. Her bright smile feels like a stab in my chest.

"Hey!" she says as I sit down on the bench next to her.

"Something happened." My voice cracks. "Andi and Lugo were attacked by an Atorum last night. She's in the medbay—getting help." Shock falls over her face like a mask.

"She's okay?" She says the words so quietly I can hardly hear them.

"I don't know."

Bri gasps, tears already streaking down her face. Elowen hardly moves, completely numb from the news. She falls towards me. I catch her and wrap my arms around her shoulders. She clings to my shirt while silent tears collect on my chest.

29

Elowen

Another Tilak in a med-coat hurries by without a glance in our direction. We have no idea how long it will be until we can see Andi, but I'm
going to sit here as long as it takes. I'm not leaving until I know she is
okay. She needs to know she isn't alone.

"Here I am having one of the greatest nights of my life while Andi
and Lugo were..." I can't bring myself to say the words.

"You're a smart woman. Don't turn off that brilliant mind whenever emotions run high. Logically, the two things have nothing to do
with each other," Bri tells me, her gentle tone softening the blow of her
brutal honesty.

"Thank you? I think I heard a compliment in there somewhere."

"It's absolutely a compliment. You're smart and focused and
determined. Now's the time to tap into that, not forget it when you
need it the most. Don't dissolve into one of those sniveling women who
collapses when shit gets rough." She's right, and strangely enough, her
straightforward approach does make me feel better.

"Now, I am dying to hear the details of your 'human date,'" she
says imitating Aro's deep voice.

"It was the most romantic thing anyone has ever done for me."

"Noodles in an office?" she asks skeptically.

"No—I mean yeah. It wasn't just noodles in an office. He put a lot of thought into it. He researched human courting and planned it out. It was incredibly sweet."

"I think you're blinded by the sex haze," Bri says.

"Sex haze?"

"You know, when everything feels magical and wonderful. It's the best sex ever because it's new. Then the haze lifts and you realize you're eating the same boring noodles in a dusty office," she explains.

"I don't think it's like that." I'm not exactly sure what it is, but it's not something that's fading the more I get to know him.

"So, is it the best sex ever? I'm curious about the heat these guys are packing," she asks.

"I wouldn't know. We haven't slept together. And if you're so curious, then why don't you get out there and check for yourself?"

"Don't get me wrong, they're all super hot, but for some reason they aren't doing it for me." As the words leave her mouth, a Tilak in scrubs steps out of the medbay just in time to hear her.

"Oops!" Laughter bursts out of her.

"You're going to get us kicked out of here!" I smack her arm and crack up with her. It feels good to laugh. I can feel the tension from the last few hours lift a little.

A few minutes later someone comes out of the medbay and scans the room. I jump up hoping they are here for us.

"You can come in now. She's out of surgery."

Bri and I rush into the medbay. Andi lies motionless on a gurney with tubes and monitors stuck to her body. Lugo is in the chair next to her. Medbots wipe away the stubborn black sludge from his face and body. She smiles weakly when we step to her side. I grab her hand and do my best to show a brave face.

"How are you feeling?" I ask, not knowing what else to say.

"Better than ever," she says with a raspy voice.

"She's going to be okay?" Bri asks the room full of med staff.

"She's expected to make a full recovery. Once she is stabilized, she'll be transferred to the hospital in Bihar for further treatment and tests," her nurse answers nearby.

"Is that really necessary?" I ask, all of a sudden worried again that she'll be separated from us.

"Don't worry, Elowen. They're just being extra cautious," Andi answers for them. She seems to approve of their plan, which eases some of my worry.

"You going to be okay too?" I ask Lugo.

"Yeah. I wasn't hurt. The Atorum slimed me to the tree so it could get to Andi." He swats the medbot's arm away from his face and wipes away the black splatters himself.

I look back to Andi and she's struggling to keep her eyes open. I gently pull my hand back and step away. I can relax now. She's going to be okay.

30

Elowen

Andi is too stubborn for her own good. We've all taken turns trying to talk some sense into her, but she is firm about "walking on her own two goddamn feet." Out of all of us, Lugo came the closest to nearly convincing her to be assisted. He has hardly left her side the last two days. Every time I've gone to the medbay to check on her, he's already there. Once I caught him doting on her, fluffing her pillow and gently forcing her to drink water. What surprised me the most is she didn't seem to hate it.

Bri and I surround her through the halls to the dock, at the ready if she gets dizzy or needs to stop and rest. She laughs and swats our hands away anytime we get too close.

Lugo has packed all her belongings into the waiting porter and holds out his hand to help her into her seat. I hardly believe my eyes when she takes his hand and steps up with a grateful smile.

"Elowen! I almost forgot. Make sure this gets to the lab." She hands me a large bag. I peer inside and see a lumen'entem flower. I delicately hold the bag to my chest, not wanting to damage the fragile petals.

Lugo's eager to leave. He slides the porter door closed while everyone is still saying their goodbyes.

"That was weird," Bri says and turns to leave.

"It's sweet. He wants to make sure she's okay. He's probably just protective from the attack," I tell her. I think it's cute. Maybe a little bit strange, but cute.

My feet are heavy while I walk to my lab. It doesn't feel the same here without Andi. I look into the bag again, and without thinking too hard about it, I turn down the hallway that leads to my room instead of going to the lab.

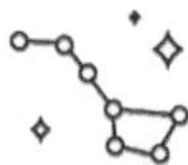

I turn the flower over in my hands for the hundredth time. I've looked at it from every possible angle. It's beautiful. The colorful layers are stunning. I graze my finger over the velvety petals careful to avoid the pollen Aro warned me about.

I had intended to take the flower to the lab hours ago, but a thought has lodged itself into my brain, and I can't seem to let it go. Aro told me what the flower is used for, and now that I have one in my hand—one that could easily "go missing"—I toss around the idea of experiencing the effects of the flower. I don't even know how to do it. I'd need Aro's help if this is something I really want to do. I'm nervous about feeling out of control and fully letting go.

I set the flower down and pace back and forth for a while. Weighing the pros and cons in my mind. I have no idea how long I've waffled back and forth when a light knock on my door snaps me out of it.

I slide the door open and Aro steps in. Seeing him infuses me with the last bit of confidence I need to make my decision.

"Andi gave me a lumen'entem flower before she left," I tell him. "She asked me to take it to the lab, but I kept it."

He raises both eyebrows in surprise. He waits for me to continue.

"I want to do it," I say definitively.

"Who are you and what have you done with my Elowen?" he asks with a broad grin.

"Don't be so surprised! I'm more of a risk-taker than you realize." He looks back at me skeptically.

"I knew you had it in you. When do you want to do it?" he asks. I sense how close we are in my cramped room, which feels even smaller with him in here.

"Tomorrow? What do you think?" I ask.

He takes the flower and turns it over a few times in his hand before setting it back down.

"Tomorrow's perfect."

"Well, well, well. To what do I owe the pleasure?" Bri says and welcomes me into her room. It's identical to mine, except her room has holograms of her family on the shelves and an abstract painting of what could be a DNA strand.

"That's cool," I say pointing to the artwork.

"My brothers gave it to me as a going-away present." She looks a tiny bit sad when her eyes linger on the image. I've never pried when she has hinted at feeling homesick. If she wanted to talk about it, she would.

"I'm going to tell you something. But you can't freak out," I warn her.

Her eyes widen and a maniacal smile crosses her face. "Yes. Tell me everything."

"I'm going to try the lumen'entem."

"The flower that unleashes your full unfettered desires and life's purpose?" she asks, knowing exactly the flower I'm referring to.

"Yes, that one."

"The flower that removes all your inhibitions and reveals life's true meaning?" She's messing with me, quoting a time I bombarded her with my findings on this flower.

"Yep," I say flatly.

"The flower that'll finally let you get over yourself so you can…"

"Don't be an ass. You know I overthink everything."

"Sorry. I am honestly impressed that you're considering it," she says and gives me a little clap.

"You'd tell me if I'm making a giant mistake, right?"

"Of course."

"Can you remind me that it's harmless fun, and I won't get in trouble?" I ask.

"You're overthinking this. It's a little harmless fun, and you won't get in trouble."

"And if my life ends up in shambles?" I ask.

"I'll take all the blame," she says with an excited little shoulder shake.

31

Elowen

I'm swallowing the last of my protein bar when Aro strides into my room. He's wearing that black button-down shirt with sleeves rolled up to his elbows, tucked into perfectly tailored black slacks. It's the same thing he wore on our date, and it still takes my breath away. The contrast of his rich blue skin and the black clothes—it does something for me.

"Are you sure you want to do this?" he asks.

"Yep, I'm sure," I say, trying to sound confident. A small part of me still wants to bolt from the room and hide.

"Okay, here's the plan. We're gonna go to the Northeast Rec room. That corner of the muradome is usually empty this time of night. Once we get there, I'll make the tea and it will take effect pretty quickly. That will get you high for about four hours or so. We'll hang out there until you're back to reality and I'll walk you back to your bunk. I'll run interference if anyone comes around. No one will suspect a thing." He walks me through the plan with military precision.

"Sounds good to me." I carefully pick up the flower and hand it to Aro. He tucks it away and grabs my hand.

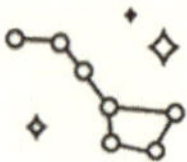

He is right about this side being empty. Light sensors flicker on, evidence that no one has been here in a while.

"Here we are." Placing his hand on my lower back he ushers me into the quiet rec room.

From the couch I watch Aro tap a few pollen granules into a mug filled with steaming hot water. "Remind me what's going to happen once I drink that." I stop biting my lip when he turns to face me, not wanting him to see that I'm nervous.

"It's different for everyone. Some people feel really peaceful and relaxed, others have hallucinations. When I did it all my thoughts and emotions were amplified. Time would stop and stand still then rush forward. I still don't fully understand some of what I saw," Aro explains while making the tea.

"Apparently, thousands of years ago our ancestors would drink this tea as a rite of passage. This is one part of an ancient ceremony that would mark a Tilak's ascension to full adulthood. The tea would help them tap into their subconscious and provide clarity or reveal their life's purpose. Occasionally, the experience will take a dark turn, but I won't let that happen to you. Only good vibes tonight."

I take a deep breath, and nod. "I'm ready."

Aro passed me the steaming mug and I cup it in both hands. I use it to ground myself through my nerves. I take a small sip and try to relax as it goes down my throat. Its vaguely sweet, a hint of flowers and citrus. I take a few more sips. "How much should I drink?" I ask.

"That's probably good for now. You'll know in a few minutes."

I sink deeper into the couch and fold my legs up to my chest. My face feels numb and fuzzy right away. I'm vaguely aware of a smile plastered on my face. My hearing is muted, like I was plunged underwater. Aro's back is to me while operating the coffee machine across the room. I unabashedly stare at his muscular back and thick legs. I imagine what it would feel like to run my hands up his arms and over his shoulders.

Aro turns back to me with a knowing smile. "How's it going over there?" He caught me staring again. Those black slacks are going to kill me.

"Good!" My voice comes out an octave higher than I intended. "I mean, I feel good, just a little numb." I go to extra lengths to lower the pitch of my voice and sound relaxed.

Aro sits down next to me on the couch. "Good. Ride the wave wherever it takes you."

I lean back and relax my body a little. Aro is taking up most of the couch with his legs spread out and his arms across the back rest. He softly blows into his steaming cup of synthetic coffee and takes a sip. An untold amount of time passes while I watch his mouth. I realize I'm biting my lower lip again, and not from nerves this time. My fingers ache to reach out to him as my body gets warmer and warmer.

I fan my chest. "It's so hot in here."

Aro chuckles. "Yeah, I think it's kicking in." He tosses me a stainless-steel water bottle that appeared out of nowhere.

The cool water touches my lips. It coats my mouth then my throat and everything on the way down to my stomach. It tastes amazing. I look down at my hands and they're leaving trails of colorful light as I move them across my field of vision. I stretch out my legs and drop my feet onto Aro's lap. Our touch reverberates up my legs into the pit of my stomach. I am suddenly aware of my clothes rubbing between my thighs. I clench my legs together to ease the sensation. My body feels feverish and I shudder. Aro rubs the soles of my feet, sending shots of colorful light up my legs.

"I'm glad you decided to do this. It's a completely unique experience. You might even be the first non-Tilak to do it." Aro's voice sounds gravelly and incredibly sexy.

"Hm," I say as I lean in toward him.

The movement shifts my perspective and all of a sudden, I'm weightlessly drifting through space, watching Elowen and Aro from above with a calm disconnect. Levitating above, I see Elowen nuzzle up to Aro's ear and whisper.

"And you're the lucky bastard who gets to supervise, but don't get too attached. I'll be sent back to Earth soon." And then she taps the end of his nose with her index finger.

"I like you, Aro," she says and leans back against the couch.

"I like you too," he says, eyeing her suspiciously. He is trying to gauge how much of this conversation is her true feelings and how much of it is the tea.

"Oh, now you decide to play it cool?" she playfully asks.

"I believe I have made my feelings toward you pretty clear from day one," he tells Elowen.

"Yes, you have. What's that all about anyways?" she asks him.

"When you know, you know."

"And what is it that you think you know?" She pushes him a little further.

"What I know with one-hundred-percent certainty is that I am at your mercy. Whatever it is you decide to do with me, I am powerless to resist, and I wouldn't even want to. I know that the moment I laid eyes on you, everything else just faded into the background." Elowen smiles at his confession.

Now she is the one sizing him up about his sincerity. He matches her eye contact, refusing to look away, daring her to say something. She is finally the one to break eye contact.

She says, "I have the best idea. Follow me." He's surprised at her quick change of subject.

I float above as she moves through the rec room with Aro following close behind. Elowen grabs Aro and drags him down the hallway. She makes an abrupt turn and goes into the pool room.

Elowen strips off her clothes. She pulls her shirt over her head and drops her pants down to the floor before kicking them away. She slides her underwear down her hips and lets them fall while unhooking her bra behind her back.

"Get naked. We're going for a swim." She walks to the edge of the pool and gracefully dives in.

Aro holds himself still, like he doesn't trust himself to move. "Nope. I'm staying right here. You have no idea how dangerous you are to me right now," he says and sits down on a bench facing the water.

My perspective shifts, and I'm seeing things through my eyes again as I come to the surface. The water is swirling around me like a whirlpool. Soft feather-like touches tickle my entire body. The water transforms into the tiny green sprouts from the greenhouse and they brush against me. The ceiling pulses up and down with my breathing. I float for a long time, letting my hair spread out along the surface. The greens make way for yellows and then pinks. I am in the center of a giant tie-dye pool, colors spreading out from underneath me.

The ceiling contorts into something menacing, so I dive back under the water to feel the peaceful weightlessness that welcomed me. It feels like I can hold my breath forever. Eventually the familiar burn in my lungs brings me back up to the surface. I take a moment to catch my breath and look over at Aro. The sight of him pushes all my fear away.

My vision fades and comes back into focus as I'm walking through the muradome. I hear a low din of activity around me and occasionally a friendly voice greets me just outside of my eyeline. I walk through the familiar hallways, smiling to myself as I wander through. There is an odd itch on my left hand, and I look down. I see a jagged cut on the flesh below my thumb. I bring it up to my face and when I can finally see it clearly, it looks like I had a long-jagged cut along my palm, but it's healed and replaced by a tidy white line, a scar with a slightly raised edge.

I open a door expecting to enter the mess hall. When I step through, I'm back on Earth. I walk along a valley framed with golden rolling hills.

I crest a hill and come to a rushing river. Water swirls around rocks in colorful waves. When I step into the water, chills run up my legs. I step farther into the river and eventually find myself floating along the moving current. The water speeds up and slows down, rushing me past rocks and around bends. Stars permeate the dark night sky. A brilliant red flower pulses open and closed against the dimly lit background.

The flower is barely out of reach. It slips past my fingertips every time I reach for it. The petals vibrate with each beat from the center of the flower. I give up trying to touch it and just watch it, consumed by the beautiful rhythmic motion.

I'm back in the pool and slip back down under the water, savoring the transcendent sensation of shifting through visions. I run my fingertips over the rough bottom of the pool. I watch the ripples of water shift colors as I poke my finger at the colors, like a kid popping bubbles. When I come back up for oxygen, I catch a glimpse of Aro smiling at me from the bench. He raises his eyebrows at me, silently checking in. Warmth radiates from my chest as I smile back at him. He's so beautiful. In a flash I'm watching Elowen again from above.

"Come on! It feels good. It's so bubbly!" Elowen's naked body is mostly obscured by the rippling water. I notice Aro is affected by her. He adjusts his pants and clenches his jaw.

"I'm staying right here. I'd never forgive myself for taking advantage of you right now." He stays resolute in his decision.

"If you won't come to me, then I'll come to you," she says and lifts herself out of the pool. Biting her lower lip and swaying her hips, Elowen slowly walks toward Aro. She looks like a predator stalking her prey. I watch as she drops down on his lap. She grabs his hands and places them on her hips. Her hands slide up his arms and rest on his shoulders.

She shifts her hips forward to get more friction between their bodies. "Hm, I knew you would feel good." She runs her fingertips from his jawline down his neck and shoulders to his wrists. "I really like this part right here," she says and slowly touches his jaw, coming to a stop on his chin.

He hisses through his teeth and his hands move up to her waist and stop under her arms. He gently lifts her from his lap and stands her up against him. Her pebbled nipples drag up his shirt and Elowen looks up at him.

"You look good tonight, and these pants are begging to come off." Elowen's voice sounds thick. She grabs his belt and works the buckle. Aro steps back to grab the folded towel next to him and wraps her up and rubs her shoulders up and down briskly.

Aro gives Elowen the water canteen. "Drink this," he instructs.

"Yes, more tea!" She giggles and reaches to grab the canteen.

"Just water from here on out," he replies.

"That's no fun," she huffs.

"Let's get you to bed." Elowen closes her eyes and drifts off while Aro carries her out into the hallway.

Seconds, minutes, maybe hours pass and the feeling of soft sheets brings me back to my body. My mouth is parched as I take in my surroundings. I'm in a bedroom, but it isn't my room. The bed shifts next to me. I am tucked into Aro's side with my head on his shoulder. One of my legs is splayed over his body and my arm is across his waist. I'm hyperaware of each place our bodies touch. My vision shifts when I try to clear my head. My stomach rolls from the change in altitude and I'm watching Elowen and Aro from above again.

He's lying on his back with an arm around her body. Elowen reaches out and grazes her fingertips down Aro's chest and abs. She keeps moving lower and wraps her hand around his cock and moves up and down slowly. He makes a pleased murmur, giving her permission to continue. She keeps moving up and down and sees a small drop of cum on the tip. Elowen leans down and spreads her tongue flat and licks off the wetness.

Elowen sits up and moves her body over his. Straddling his hips. They're both completely naked. He roughly grabs both breasts. Pulling until her hard nipples are between his fingers.

Elowen holds his dick and pushes him against her clit. She rubs up and down his shaft, pleasuring herself and spreading her soaked pussy around him. She looks down and watches his thick blue cock rub against her soft pink skin. Elowen's breathing speeds up and seconds later her orgasm crashes over him. Her entire body shakes and her hips jerk out of rhythm, using him until the last wave of pleasure leaves her. She leans down and softly kisses his mouth. He holds her down to him, their chests pushed together, his fingers indenting the skin on her rounded hips.

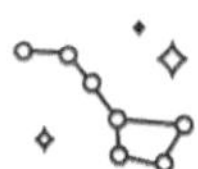

Eons of time are contained in an instant, and I'm looking through my own eyes as awareness comes back to me, memories muddled together. Shit. Shit. Shit. Shit. I'm mortified. Shit. I am such an idiot. It should have been some transcendent spiritual awakening, not a bunch of random visions and pent-up sexual frustrations.

The line between dream and reality is hazy as I try to recollect exactly what happened last night.

I'm pinned between Aro and the wall in his bunk. I try to slip out from next to him. When I move, Aro turns on his side and pulls me back tightly. Holding me close to his warm chest.

"Nope, you're staying right here," Aro mumbles. Something hard pushes into my lower back. "Ignore that and go back to sleep." He nestles his face deeper into my hair and his breathing evens out as he falls back asleep.

There is no ignoring what is pressing against me right now. The memory of his hard cock rubbing on my clit makes my entire body tense up. My traitorous body still feels the intensity of his touch. There is no possibility of sleep now. I inch my way to the bottom of Aro's bed and slide to the ground. I look down and realize I'm fully dressed in what I wore last night and Aro is shirtless, wearing gray sweatpants. His erection tents his pants. I don't take a second look as I slip out of his room.

32

Aro

I barely crack my eyes open to watch Elowen try to move silently around my room and out the door. It's laughable how she thinks she can slink away without waking me up. I nearly stopped her from leaving. I can't imagine anything better than waking up with her in my bed, listening to her breathe with her warm body pressed up against mine.

We both need to process what happened last night. I wasn't lying when I said everything faded into the background the moment I met her. I don't see that changing. She tried to remind me she'd be going back to Earth soon. I've decided that doesn't work for me. I can't make her stay, but I can be pretty persuasive.

It was clear what she wanted when she climbed out of the pool and pounced on me. I liked how assertive she was. It took every ounce of strength to resist giving her what she wanted. My self-control hung by a thread. Every time she arched her body against mine, that thread was pulled tighter and tighter, ready to snap. She wasn't in her right mind, and I'd be the worst piece of shit to take advantage of that. She slept like a rock the moment I laid her down on my bed. I briefly considered giving her the bed and finding somewhere else to sleep, but I ultimately wanted to be here if she woke up and needed something.

I remember what it was like when I took the lumen'entem years ago. My visions were a series of brief moments. Some were violent, like I possessed a terrifying power. Other times the visions were peaceful. Scenes so beautiful they drew tears from my eyes. Eons of time flashed before my eyes in an instant. I watched history pass before me. I saw my world change over millennia. It was more than my mind could comprehend at the time. I still struggle to understand most of it.

I know Elowen must have gone on an incredible trip. She floated in the water for a long time quietly humming and mumbling here and there. I wonder what the lumen'entem showed her. Maybe I'm a selfish bastard, but all I can hope is that it showed her a future here, with me.

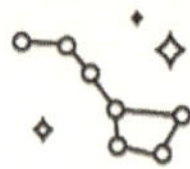

A bang on my door interrupts my self-reflection. There is only one person I'd be happy about knocking on my door this early, and she just snuck out moments ago.

"You're lucky. If you had pounded on my door like that ten minutes ago, I would have knocked you out," I say as Tai walks in and sizes up the room. "She's not here." I have a pretty good guess about who he's looking for.

"I distinctly remember having a conversation about you being careful with that one. I'm worried you have a misunderstanding about what 'careful' means." He sits on the only chair in the room. He kicks his feet out and casually picks at his nails. He's making a lot of effort to appear relaxed, but I'm not buying it.

"And I distinctly remember telling you not to worry about it."

"This isn't a joke, Aro. There have already been consequences from your little crush."

"I know," I say tersely. I don't need to be reminded of what happened with Andi. "Why are you being such a narc about this? Not to be a dick, but this really doesn't involve you."

"You know what? You're right. It doesn't involve me. But I know first-hand that one bad decision follows the next and you're already pretty far down that path. How many rules have you bent or broken for her?"

I stare back at him, unwilling to answer that question.

"They will never accept her," Tai says.

"Who the fuck is 'they'?" I snarl at him. My eyes narrow on him, trying to discern if he includes himself in the category of those who won't accept her.

"'They,' 'them,' everyone out there." He motions all around us.

"Then it's a good thing it doesn't matter because *I* accept her. She belongs with me."

"You have a briefing to lead in twenty minutes. I suggest you get your shit together and focus on your job because it's rapidly coming to an end. When it's over, you'll be expected to act like a leader, and not sulk around like a cub who didn't get his way."

"I don't sulk."

"And that is because you have always gotten what you wanted. But that isn't going to happen with Elowen. She is going to leave and there needs to be something left of you when she does."

33

Elowen

I keep waiting for the embarrassment to fade. I've tried to talk myself down from the horrifying memory of me literally climbing Aro like a tree, straddling him, and using him like my own personal sex toy. I'll be haunted for the rest of my life. I'll never be able to look him in the eye again. I'll never be able to look *myself* in the eye again. It wouldn't be that hard to avoid mirrors the rest of my life.

"I thought I might find you here," Aro says as he walks in the greenhouse like I conjured him out of thin air. I don't look up, not ready to deal with the consequences of my actions last night.

"I love it in here." I've been working here all day, hoping that being around the cute plants would help me clear my head. What were tiny green sprouts a few weeks ago have grown into beautiful purple and yellow blossoms. Their wispy petals swirl around like a choreographed ballet. Soon they will be tucking up their roots into the bottom of the petals and moving towards their ideal growing location. The structured flower beds have already been removed and the dirt has slid down into mounds covered with the beautiful blossoms.

One flower has already begun uprooting itself, well before the others. I lay my hand down on the dirt next to it. The petals slowly shift and roll onto my outstretched palm. I take a deep breath and say what needs to be said.

"I am so sorry I took advantage of you last night. I honestly don't know what came over me. I took things too far," I tell him.

"Wait, what? I'm confused."

"My awkward attempt at seduction… I am a complete idiot."

"Hold on, let me make something abundantly clear. Last night was the hottest thing I have ever seen in my life. I only refused you because you weren't in your right mind. And I would have never forgiven myself if that was the first time we were together. Trust me, it took every ounce of self control I had." He lifts my face up so I can't avoid his gaze.

"I would be more than happy to revisit it another time, when you aren't high off your ass. If that's what you want," he says, searching my face for an answer.

"This is going to blow up in our faces. The closer we get, the harder it's going to be to say goodbye."

"We can worry about all of that later. I will take anything you'll give me. So…" he says with a broad smile, "what do you think we did last night? And did I live up to expectations?" The glint in his eyes is back.

"What makes you think there were expectations?"

"Elowen, you've been eye-fucking me since the first day we met. I know you've been wondering what it'll be like."

"I cannot believe you just said that." My cheeks heat with embarrassment.

"We're getting it all out in the open now."

"Full transparency? What happened last night is between me and the lumen'entem. But just to be clear, we didn't have sex last night?" I ask and look back down to the blossom rolling over my palm and fingers. Holding my breath for his answer.

"We slept fully clothed. You drooled a little on me. That's it," he says and puts his hand next to mine, the flower moving over to his palm. "Look—this little guy's confused. Doesn't know if it's day or night," Aro says sweetly, watching the flower continue to roll around.

"What did you say?" I ask. Suddenly every synapse in my brain starts firing off.

"I said this little guy doesn't know if it's day or night," he repeats.

34

Elowen

I've been staring at the ceiling over my bunk for who knows how long. What Aro said struck me. It took me right back to the vision I had last night of the red flower. The answer is just out of reach. I squeeze my eyes shut, trying to block out anything that could take away from following this train of thought.

A light tap on my door jerks me out of my head.

I open the door as Aro raises his hand to knock again. He's dressed in all black, a pack slung over his shoulders. He closes the door behind him and looks me up and down.

"Put your boots on. We need to hurry." He frantically looks around the room for my shoes.

"Where are we going?" His rushing around my room is making me nervous.

"We are going outside," he says quietly.

"Woah, wait. Do I have time to think about it?" Panic shoots through me.

"Yes."

"How long?"

"The next twenty seconds," he says and hands me my boots.

"Aro, no. This is a bad idea. I can't leave the dome. I'd love to, but I can't." Aro reaches out, buttons the closures on my coveralls and pulls me along gently down the empty hallway.

"Yes, you can, I'll get you in and out. No one will ever know, and you'll get to see j'Tilak for yourself." His tone is all confidence.

I plant my feet on the ground. He makes it halfway down the hall before he realizes I'm not right behind him. He comes back for me, carefully, like he's approaching a spooked animal. I stand my ground. I've wanted to see more of this world, but not at the expense of my presence here. All of that, in addition to the killing machines lurking around! It's not a good idea.

"Elowen, you've dreamed of being here your whole life. This is your chance." I look up into his pleading eyes trying to decide what to do.

"It's not safe out there," I say.

"We'll be fine. I promise I won't let anything bad happen to you."

With a deep breath I nod. "Good girl. Now I'm going to need you to wait here for a minute," Aro says and softly pushes me into a cleaning bot closet I didn't realize was right behind me. He closes me in before I have a chance to protest.

The small dark closet is just big enough for me to squeeze into. My body pushes against all four walls. The cleaning bot rests in its charging dock between my feet. My nose twitches from the floating particles of dust. It's such a tight fit I can't even reach up to rub my nose, so I twitch my face to fight the sneeze that's building.

I can barely hear anything outside of my little spot, but I pick up on a muffled conversation between Aro and another Tilak. I have more time to think of all the reasons I shouldn't do this. It's too big of a risk. This is breaking the number one rule, the thing that could get me deported immediately. It would also get Aro into a shitload of trouble. I resolve to talk some sense into him as the door slides open. I squint from being in the dark closet to now the brightly lit hall.

Aro puts a finger to my lips before I can say anything. He knows right away I'm still trying to talk my way out of this.

"Too late to back out now."

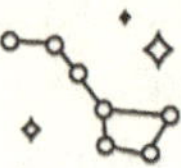

I find myself in the big empty warehouse where we first arrived at the dome, staring at the open cargo bay door. The closer we get to the outside the faster my mind spins, all the reasons why I do want to sneak out compile in my head. The cargo bay is lined with porters charging in their concave platform ports along the edge. Aro drags me behind him and we skirt the edge of the room, weaving in and out of the silver spheres charging for the night. I drag my feet as we get closer to the massive door. Aro continues pulling me forward, single-mindedly focused on getting outside.

At the end of the row, he crouches down and points straight above his head. A security bot hovers a few feet above him. I barely shift forward and the noise from my pants rubbing together sounds deafening. Aro glares at me and silently mouths the word "quiet."

My legs start to ache from crouching down so long. Aro holds his position until the whir of the bot moves to the other side of the room. He moves with lightning speed to the other side of the final porter. I follow him less gracefully in a half crouch half run. He watches the cargo bay while I catch up to him. Confident we're in the clear, he makes one last dash for the open door directly in front of us. He beckons me to follow him. I can't believe what I'm about to do. Ignoring all rational thought, I follow him out into the darkness outside.

35

Elowen

While my eyes adjust to the dark I take a deep breath of crisp air. The wind blowing through the tall evergreens is fresh and cool. Aro silently directs me to keep my back against the outer walls of the dome. We sidestep a few yards and then he pulls me forward toward a stand of enormous trees.

"Welcome to j'Tilak," Aro says and spreads both arms, his palms facing the sky. A proud smile stretches across his face. We're surrounded by a grove of tall trees, the night sky hidden behind the connecting branches above us. They're so tall I can't see where the trees end and the sky begins. My boots sink down into the soft dirt with every step.

"Aro, I…" escapes my lips while I take it all in.

"Let's keep going. We have a ways to go." He walks slower this time, heading toward the hills in front of us.

The adrenaline pumping through my veins helps me keep up with him initially. It only takes a few minutes before my feet feel really heavy and my heart rate picks up. Tomorrow—tomorrow I'm going to start working out. It should take a lot more than this to get me out of breath.

Aro looks down and smiles. "We can stop and rest as much as you need." I would like to disagree, but I'm so out of breath I can't get a word out.

We rest at the top of the hill so I can catch my breath. I look back and see the brightly lit dome nestled into the valley. It's a soft white glow against a backdrop of dark sky.

Aro places his hands on my shoulders and turns me to face him. "You ran off so fast earlier. I just want to make sure that you are okay after last night."

"I'm okay. I'll need some time to process all of it. I think it actually helped me put a few things together for the research."

"You are incredible," he says and pulls me to his chest and crushes me against him in a tight hug. "Let's get moving. We only have a few hours and there is a lot I want to show you."

I let go of all my worries and follow. I'm getting better at being in the moment with him. Aro occasionally looks back and smiles at me as we walk. An open field greets us when we break through the trees.

Tall grass tickles my fingers as I follow closely behind Aro. Up ahead, a patch of small blooms sway in the breeze. Aro sits and pushes down the grass to make space for me. I sit down, close enough that our legs barely touch. It's enough to feel the warm electricity between us.

"Check this out," he says and looks up to the sky.

My eyes follow his, and for the first time I see the unobstructed night sky. Millions of stars shine down. The small amount of darkness between each light isn't just black—it's dark shades of blue and green. Three moons in different phases line up above us. Along the horizon a nebula spirals in greens and reds. I'm stunned by the beautiful sky.

"I knew you'd like it here," Aro says with a smile.

"You have no idea."

I feel his eyes on me for a brief moment before he turns back to the night sky.

A bright meteor streaks across the sky. "Oh look! On Earth they used to call that a shooting star." I nudge his arm to get his attention and he snags my hand and laces our fingers together.
Woah! The memory of my stasis dream hits me. How peculiar. The way that vision played out in real life, I'm not alone. Did I have a

premonition? I'm stunned into complete silence. I enjoy the synchronicity with a warm, tingly feeling in my heart. We watch the night sky for a long time. I quickly lose count of how many shooting stars streak past us.

Aro turns on his side and props his head up. "There's still more to see." He stands quickly and pulls me up next to him.

"Let me know when your soft little human body needs to be carried."

"Soft little human body? Please. I'll be the one carrying you."

We both know I'm full of shit.

Back on our feet we walk a while longer. Aro is a perfect guide. He names all the different plants and tells me about the creatures that live in the area.

"Okay, we're close. Walk softly and follow my footsteps exactly."

I follow his instructions, and we finally come to the top of a hill with a lone tree. Aro slides off his pack and leans it against the trunk. We sit with our backs against the tree and take in the view. Shifting around like water in an eddy, flowers and grass move as one. Small groups of similar blooms spread out then come back together. I've never seen anything like this before. I look over at Aro and am surprised to see he's watching me and not the view.

"This is probably just another ordinary day for you," I whisper.

"Elowen, there is absolutely nothing ordinary when I am with you." He bends down bringing his face close to mine. His index finger lifts my face up to meet his, and his eyes drop to my mouth. Aro hesitates a moment before his lips softly brush against mine and it feels like warm electricity. He grabs the back of my neck and brings me harder against him. We both part our lips and his tongue slides against mine. I feel so cherished, he kisses me like I am something precious and adored. He softly kisses the corner of my mouth one last time and pulls away.

Reeling, he turns my head back toward the view and whispers, "You don't want to miss this."

I peel my eyes away from him and a few feet in front of us I see something drifting across the ground. A round ball with hundreds of flat petals rolls across the grass. It looks like the wind is blowing it away, but there is no movement in the air. Variegated petals in reds, pinks, and oranges tipped with silver move slowly in front of us. Each layer flops over the other as the flower moves toward its target. It approaches another flower. The blossom finally reaches the other flower and they delicately touch. The petals slowly tangle and move over each other. The moving flower rolls completely over the stationary one and then after a brief hesitation keeps moving.

Once again, I'm spellbound. I had given up the hope of experiencing this. I blindly grab for Aro, unable to look away from the view. He has given me the most incredible gift. I can happily go back to Earth when this is all over, with no regrets about missing this incredible place. Before I came here, my goal was to document the planet and use this experience to solidify my career. Now all I can think of is the overwhelming gratitude I have for being right here. Every time someone asks me about j'Tilak, I will think of tonight.

A sobering thought crosses my mind: someday Aro will just be a memory.

We sit in complete silence for hours watching the sky and field in front of us. He anticipates all of my needs. When I'm hungry, he hands me a protein bar. When I shiver from the cold, he tucks me into a blanket he has in his pack. An unfamiliar sense of serenity takes over.

Memories from last night come back. I'd watched myself with neutral curiosity, completely detached from any emotions or judgment. The more I think about it, the visions take on a meaning that settles deep into me. A knowing outside of language works into my very DNA. I'm cracked open and put back together. I feel peaceful at the sense that a small, bruised part of me is finally restored. I felt healed when I looked down at the scar on my hand. The harder I would try for something, the farther it would get from me. How I felt aligned when I let go.

"You thinking about last night again?" Aro whispers, pulling me closer to lean against his chest.

I turn my head to look back at him. "How'd you know?"

"Lots of deep sighing and you're not squealing at the little flowers anymore."

"I don't squeal," I clarify with mock seriousness. "I was thinking about last night. I'm still trying to figure it out. I feel different today than yesterday. Something shifted." I struggle to find the right words to describe my state of mind.

"I loved watching you in the water. You were stunning, floating there all serene and peaceful. How was it for you?" he asks, his arms tightening around me. I feel safe and warm, like I'm in an alternate reality where nothing could ever go wrong.

"It felt like something inside of me that's been holding me back is finally starting to let go. Speaking these words out loud exposes a vulnerability I really struggle to show others.

"Let's stay here forever," I joke.

"Don't tempt me." He sounds completely serious. Aro leans in for another kiss. I want to give myself over to him completely. He holds onto my bottom lip, gently tugging before ending it much too soon. I stay still for as long as possible, rooting myself to this spot. Locking away this memory for safekeeping.

Out of the corner of my eye, I catch a glimpse of a lumen'entem flower unfurling its petals. That doesn't make sense. "What is that flower doing?" I think out loud.

"It's getting ready to move, just like all the others," Aro responds without realizing what makes the lumen'entem odd to me.

"It's opening its petals at night! Of course! Its roots are too fragile to be exposed to the suns." Aro doesn't seem to pick up on the significance. "I've got to get to the lab."

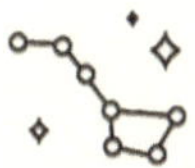

The primary sun peeks out on the horizon. Gray lights up the sky followed shortly by a bright red glow. He doesn't say anything. Instead he squeezes me a little tighter, acknowledging what I told him. I wish I had the courage to tell him how transformed I am. That for the first time in my life I don't feel like I am broken, or that something is wrong with me. I want to tell him that I still have work to do—that there are parts of me that I resented and that are now fully fused with who I am. That I can coexist with those feelings and memories—they're a part of the whole. I'm proud of myself that I am willing to even consider voicing this to him someday. I sit with these thoughts a while longer as the bright light spreads across the horizon.

We walk side by side back to the dome. The trip back goes quickly. Even though I'm excited about this breakthrough, I'm also not ready to leave this beautiful place. Aro breaks the silence. "I'm not sure if we'll have the chance to sneak out again." He says what I'm already thinking. Tonight was a once-in-a-lifetime opportunity, and I'll probably never experience this again.

The dome comes into view and Aro holds my hand again. "I don't think I could ever get enough of this place," I say as I look over at him trying to get my smile to reach up to my eyes. I am eternally grateful to him. Something I could only describe as grief takes over.

36

Aro

Elowen trails behind while I move strategically through the trees, carefully avoiding the sentinel bots. I pull her close a few times under the guise of avoiding detection, but it's just an excuse to feel her against me.

She looks radiant, the early morning light reflecting gold off her dark hair. Her eyes wide and bright, not missing a single detail around us. I don't like the feeling of going back to reality. Everything else ceased to exist for a few short hours. I'm greedy. I want more time with just us two. When we get back to the dome, I'll have to share her with the world again. For tonight, she's mine and it's been the best night of my life.

We circle around the outside of the dome, approaching through a blind spot in the security feed. When we get to the outer wall, we press our backs against it again and sidestep our way to the cargo bay. The hatch is still open from when we left hours ago. I'm surprised to see it's still open—I had programmed it to close behind us when we left.

I step into the cargo bay first and look around. Not seeing anyone I pull Elowen in behind me. We retrace our steps through the rows of porters. Right as I reach for the door sensor, I hear someone clear their throat behind us.

I spin around and pull Elowen behind my back, blocking her from view. Maak is leaning against a container watching us. I breathe a heavy sigh of relief at the sight of him.

"You go on ahead. I'll come find you later," I tell Elowen and usher her out of the bay.

"You scared me. I thought for a minute that we were caught," I tell Maak after Elowen slips through the door.

"You were," he says, his face deadly serious.

"I'm glad it's you. It would have been hard to explain to Rialto or Petrok," I say.

"You're not doing a very good job of explaining it to me. Because what it looks like from here is that you snuck a human out, against orders and against all fucking rational thought. Putting everyone in danger." I'm surprised by his reaction. He's seething. I wouldn't have expected him to care about this at all.

"Maak, it was a quick trip out. No one needs to know about this," I say approaching him.

"What do you think you are doing, Aro? This ridiculous obsession you have with this human is going to blow up in your face."

"It's not an obsession," I say.

"What is it then? It seems like you've picked this human over your own people when you do shit like this. First you blow off your responsibilities so you can fuck her, leaving Lugo out there alone to face the Atorum alone. Now you're sneaking her out of the dome, putting us all in danger."

"She's important," I tell him through clenched teeth. Maak has gone too far. I'm angry now.

"Well, go back to your human. That's all you seem to care about anyway. Just don't drag anyone else into your mess. Including me. I won't say anything for now, but if shit goes sideways, I'm not covering for you." Maak stomps out before I can try and reason with him.

37

Elowen

The answer is so obvious. It's been staring us in the face this entire time. I should have paid attention the day I noticed the difference in potassium concentration. It never sat right with me. When Aro took me out of the dome, another piece of the puzzle fell into place. I can't believe I didn't think of this right away.

The look on Andi's holographic face as I explain my hypothesis tells me everything I need to know. I can see her mind working one step ahead of me as I talk her through it. "Go find Dr. Lee," she says. The blue-tinted image of her dissolves before I have a chance to reply.

I'm breathless from the run over and get to the genetics lab just as Dr. Lee double taps the link request from Andi. Her image flickers to life on the huge screen that takes up most of the wall. She looks down at us with a smile, like a beautiful deity who's about to change the course of history.

"What do you know about turgor pressure?" she asks. It takes everything inside me to let him answer.

"It's the primary mechanism in the pulvinus cells that open and close a flower's petals according to the sun… or suns," he says, succinctly answering the question. My excitement bubbles over and I take the chance to interject.

"Right! On Earth, blossoms need to be open during daylight for photosynthesis and to attract pollinators. Here, flowers also open at night so they can move around without the suns burning their roots." I say, leading Dr. Lee to the same conclusion I came to.

"If we modify the pulvinus's DNA to keep their ion channels closed and retain the water, the blossom will stay open. We've been working on modifying the root-specific function DNA, and if we put that together with the turgor pressure, we have a viable solution. Elowen, you did it." Dr. Lee staggers back with a stunned look on his face.

Tears stream down my face as the realization sets in, and time stands still. We did it.

In a rush, everyone jumps into action. Dr. Lee directs the staff and everything speeds up. I'm numb as people I hardly recognize come up and shake my hand, offering their congratulations. We did it.

At the edge of my elation I have a nagging uneasy feeling. This means I'll be leaving sooner than I thought.

Dr. Lee climbs onto a table silencing everyone in the crowded rec room. He raises his glass. "Everybody, raise your glasses to Elowen. She followed her instincts and saw something everyone else overlooked. Her tenacious pursuit will alter the future of Earth. Her name will be etched in history books forever. To Elowen!" he says. Everyone's here to celebrate our breakthrough.

"To Elowen!" they cheer back.

The moment feels surreal. My face is warm from the champagne that seemed to appear out of nowhere. It was likely confiscated from a smuggler. Everyone is so happy from the accomplishment, and part of me is too. The other part of me is not ready to say goodbye.

"Speech!" Bri hollers from the back of the room. Something comes over me and I'm up on the table next to Dr. Lee. No hint of the stage fright that's plagued me in the past.

"This was a team effort. There's no 'I' in team—"

"BOO!" Bri heckles me, and the room erupts in laughter.

"Okay, okay," I laugh, holding up a hand. "Seriously though, we're all great scientists but we might be the worst diplomats in the entire universe. Don't tell the EGA, but had we just stepped out of our Earth-centric perspective and talked with our hosts, we might have buttoned this whole thing up months ago. But hey, we eventually got there!" I tip my glass back and take a drink, signaling the end of my speech. What I don't say is that I'm glad we didn't figure it out right away. I'm glad we overlooked the obvious more than once. It gave me time with Aro, and that probably makes me the most selfish person here.

"Now, let's get the party started!" Dr. Lee shouts. He climbs down from the table and animatedly talks to one of his team members. I laugh when he sloshes his drink all over himself.

The party kicked off as soon as the samples and findings were sent off to Earth so the scientists there can pick up where we left off. Everyone around me is elated and congratulating each other. I keep a smile plastered on my face, even though inside I'm devastated.

"You are absolutely incredible." I hear his familiar voice behind me. I turn and Aro is standing there, dressed in all black again, his tunic and perfectly tailored pants. He stands out with everyone else still in their uniform and coveralls.

The fact that he made the effort to get dressed up for the occasion is not lost on me.

"You deserve some of the credit, too," I tell him.

"No way. This was all you."

"You need a drink," I tell him, noticing he is empty-handed.

"Lead the way."

After endless rounds of toasts, the party slowly dies down. Aro and I have settled comfortably on a couch. I'm tipsy and my face hurts from smiling for so long.

"You're amazing," he says. "You've said that already," I say.

"I'll never stop saying it. I knew it the first time I laid eyes on you," he says.

"Yes, it is quite impressive that I didn't even know how to operate a garbage can," I say, reminding him of our first encounter when we first landed. My words blur together, making me sound more intoxicated than I am.

"That's not the first time I saw you," he says.

"It's not?"

"Nope. I saw you on Earth. I knew right then."

"That's right—you were creeping on me from across the room at the treaty reception." I playfully jab him in the ribs with my elbow.

He grabs my elbow to prevent me from pulling it away and tucks me into his side. Clearly not caring if anyone sees us like this. Maybe it's the lowered inhibitions or the realization that my time here is coming to an end, but I don't care if anyone sees us either.

"I couldn't take my eyes off you. You were so beautiful and nervous. I did not like that man who dared to stand so close to you," he says quietly next to my ear.

"Really?" I say with a yawn.

"You have no idea. Time for bed. Let's go," he says and helps me up.

I look around and note that we are the last ones awake in the rec room. It's the first time I've ever shut down a party. I'm usually the first to leave. Tonight, I wanted the party to go on all night. Because it marks the beginning of the end. Soon we'll be packing up our equipment and heading back to Earth to complete the final stages of our work.

In the quiet moment, I think of all the shoulds that have been plaguing me all day. I should say goodbye, but I can't bring myself to say the words to end whatever it is Aro and I have with each other. I look over at him, but the words refuse to come out. I can't do it.

"These idiots can't hold their alcohol," Aro says as we step over a passed out Tilak. I find a flattened pillow that hadn't been claimed and tuck it under their head. We pass by a couch where Bri is snuggled up with Tai.

"I did not see that coming." I point Aro's attention to our friends, the last two I would have expected to see in such an intimate position.

The floor is littered with knocked-over cups. Maak is lucky enough to have grabbed a cushion from the couch to get comfortable on the ground. Others are propped up to a sitting position against the wall, heads drooping at uncomfortable angles.

Seeing Maak reminds me of the awkward exchange we had the other night when he caught us sneaking back into the muradome. Maak kept his distance from us all night, choosing to celebrate on the opposite end of wherever we were. I'm sure Aro noticed, but he never said a word about it. Now that I think about it, Tai also kept his distance.

We walk hand in hand down the hallway. It doesn't seem that important to hide now that I'm leaving soon. Suddenly he stops and lays his palm on a door panel. I've probably walked past this door a hundred times and never noticed it. He pulls me inside and the dark supply closet lights up, sensing our movement.

The door slides shut behind me, and my back is against the closed door. Aro's forearms cage me in. He leans down and presses his lips against mine. I kiss him back, pulling him closer to me. I've been wanting to do this all night. His mouth trails down my jaw and throat. Small, punctuated kisses all over.

"I have one more adventure for us," he says between kisses.

"Aro, please. No more rule breaking. Let's get through this last part without any trouble."

"I'm going to take you to see Andi," he says and a sly smile spreads across his face. Damn, he really knows how to get through to me.

"One more adventure, but after this, it's by the book," I tell him firmly. There is something about him that makes me keep stepping out of my comfort zone. It's empowering and terrifying all at the same time.

"I love your cute little human sayings, even though they don't make any sense."

38

Aro

We need some help to get out of the muradome this time. Bri is really the only one for the job. I don't think she will mind conspiring with us. The thing about Bri though—she's a little unpredictable. I don't doubt her loyalty to Elowen, or her willingness to bend the rules here and there. What makes me nervous is what she could want in return. I'm sure about two things: she will definitely ask for something and whatever it is she asks for, I won't like it.

Bri and Elowen are in the rec room kicking back after a long day of packing up for the return trip to Earth, which I am still firmly in denial about. Elowen and I lock eyes as soon as I step into the room. My heart thumps loudly in my chest. She's nestled into the couch, her feet tucked under. Once again, I'm floored by her. She's in a soft sweater that's a few sizes too big, and she has the long sleeves tucked under her fingers, holding them to her palms.

Bri turns and watches me, her expression far less welcoming. I get the feeling I'm interrupting their time together. I don't feel guilty at all for monopolizing Elowen's time. I'm greedy when it comes to her.

"Look what the cat coughed up," Bri says when I sit down next to Elowen.

"I don't know what that means, but it sounds disgusting," I say.

"It is," Bri confirms.

"What's the matter? Not happy to see me?" I ask, unable to resist the urge to tease her a little.

"I'm ecstatic," she replies with that mildly intimidating monotone voice I can only imagine took her years to perfect.

"Hi," I say to Elowen.

"Hi," she says back.

"Bri, we have a favor to ask of you." Elowen initiates the conversation I've been mentally preparing myself for.

"You have my attention," Bri says, clearly trying to dampen her obvious excitement. Elowen has warned me that Bri has a flair for the dramatic.

"Elowen and I are going to go visit Andi," I say.

"And you need my help to sneak out." Bri understands what we need before I have a chance to ask.

"Could you cover for me for two days?" Elowen asks.

"Absolutely. Consider it done," Bri says.

"I think we need a plan for what you'll say when someone comes looking for me."

"Aro is the only one who ever looks for you, so I doubt anyone will be asking. I'll say you're in the lab."

"First of all, that's hurtful!" Elowen says, not sounding offended at all. "What will you say if someone in the lab asks where I am?" she asks Bri.

"I'll tell them you're in the mess hall," Bri says.

"What if they came from there?" Elowen asks, concerned that Bri isn't taking this plan seriously enough.

"I don't know. I'll make something up," Bri says, brushing aside Elowen's concerns.

"This isn't going to work. Maybe we should ask Tai," I suggest. That was apparently the wrong thing to say—or right thing to say depending on how you look at it—because Bri's posture changes immediately. She sits up straight and looks us both in the eye.

"Don't you dare. I've got it covered. Go have your lovers' getaway or whatever you're really gonna go do. I'll take care of things here. Plus, I like the idea of you owing me a favor." Somehow that last part feels like a threat, but that's Future Aro's problem.

"I appreciate it, Bri. I still think we should come up with a plan so that you don't get caught telling a lie and end up in trouble along with us if we get caught," Elowen says. She's clearly more concerned than I am, probably rightfully so. I like watching her negotiate with Bri over the details.

"I'll tell everyone you have diarrhea. There won't be any follow-up questions if I say that," Bri says with a laugh.

Elowen's eyes widen in horror. She turns to me for help. "Please don't do that."

"It's the perfect excuse. The moment someone mentions intestinal distress—boom—conversation over."

39

Aro

Elowen is radiating excitement as we enter the cargo bay. It's still dark outside. The suns will be breaking over the horizon soon.

Her door slid open the moment I stepped in front of it this morning. I didn't even have a chance to knock. She looked like she'd been dressed and ready to leave for a while. With her small bag strapped to her back, she followed me quietly throughout the dome.

We jump into the porter I have ready for us. Elowen smiles over at me while she buckles in. Every cell in my body lights up with that one look from her.

Elowen watches the view and I watch her. Her head is turned away from me taking in the scenery, but I can see the wonder on her face in the plexi's reflection. I'm excited to show Elowen my planet. I dutifully point out everything we come across on our way to Bihar. Birds, plants, animals, trees—anything I can think of. As long as we are talking, I'm not thinking about her leaving.

"Want to see something cool?" I ask, already knowing the answer.

"Absolutely," she says without hesitation or needing more information.

I pull the porter to a stop. "You stay here. I'm going to make sure it's safe." I jump out and run a perimeter check. There haven't been any Atorum sightings since that day weeks ago, but I'm not taking any chances.

I get back to the porter and open the door for her. She uses my hand to steady herself when she steps out.

"We need to be quiet or we'll scare them off," I tell her.

"*Them?*"

"You'll see."

We creep our way through the tall, high grass. It's almost up to Elowen's chest. She gently bats it away as we go. The suns behind us light her up in ethereal light. Everything she does is so beautiful it makes my chest hurt.

I hear the trickle of water. I crouch down and motion for her to do the same. I silently point to the far end of the stream. She follows my finger and sees what I wanted to show her. A pair of mid-sized, fuzzy, green, barrel-shaped animals are bent over with their blunted snouts in the water. They come up and wipe their long whiskers with their pudgy paws. Their antennae are at attention, listening for danger.

The creatures scamper back into the grass and bed down near a fallen log, circling around before settling into their nest of leaves and grass. They groom each other before tucking into a tight ball and closing their big round eyes.

I bring Elowen up next to me and whisper, "Those are quinstaks, a male and female pair."

"They're so cute! They look like a little family," she whispers.

"Quinstaks pair off to mate and then go back to their colony once they have a kit on the way. They're prolific breeders and mate for life. One mated pair can produce hundreds of offspring," I explain after we have backed away, giving them space to sleep.

"We interrupted their honeymoon!" she says tenderly.

"Some animals on Earth have lifelong mates as well. Penguins are my favorite. They're these little flightless birds that live in a really cold climate. The male penguin wins over the female by giving her little pebbles. They use the pebbles to build a nest where they lay an egg and take turns keeping it warm and raising their baby. They return to that nest every year and do it all again." She is so cute when she's explaining stuff. I could listen to her rattle off facts all day.

"That sounds like most things here. They all have their own mating rituals and pick one mate and stick together. All except those slutty little flowers that just hit it and quit it." I'm proud of my usage of the human saying, and I'm pretty sure I said it correctly this time.

"Aro, are you slut-shaming the flowers?" she says trying to hold in laughter.

"No shame whatsoever."

"My flowers are just doing their part to reproduce," she says.

"Tilaks used to have mating bonds like the quinstaks. It hasn't happened in centuries. Some believed couples were brought together by fate, or maybe it's biology. Regardless of why, it was much more than a romantic relationship. It's a connection that empowers each Tilak to reach their highest potential and makes it so together they could accomplish anything and be the best versions of themselves."

"What do you believe? Biology or fate?" she asks.

"There's no disputing the biological reasoning behind it. But when two individuals come together in a deeper way, they fulfill the universal truth that there is something beyond science. It's something that we don't fully understand, but we feel it in our bones." As the words pour out of me, I push down the unfamiliar feelings starting to bubble up. We're talking about these cute little animals, but I've never felt so vulnerable with someone before.

"How does free will fit into that?" she asks.

"There's always free will. We're always given a choice."

"Choices always come with consequences," she says.

"And there is the magic of j'Tilak. This world from the tiniest creature to this whole planet—our society and spiritual structures all hang in careful harmony. You see it right here." I wave my hand back to the quinstaks.

"I see it too. It's what makes this place so special. I've never seen a world that has so fully embraced the power of balance. It's so fascinating, because it's not symmetrical or totally predictable, but it's this constantly moving shifting thing holding everything together."

I sit back and watch the way her face moves while she thinks. I love the way her mind works.

"Think those little guys back there have these kinds of conversations?" I ask. Feeling the need to lighten the mood. I recognize a sliver of fear inside me, that if I push too hard, I could lose Elowen.

"I hope so. If they are lifelong mates, what could be more important?"

Elowen has a piece of grass poking out of her hair. I reach over and gently pull it out, trying not to tug on any strands. She catches my hand and inches closer to me. I look down at her. Before I can kiss her, she pulls my head down and her lips tug at mine. I savor the feeling of her on me. She kisses me sweetly, and it's over too soon.

"I like being out here," she says, sounding happy and content.

"I do too. Growing up we used to spend summers out away from the city." Memories start to pop up. Most are good, but one is harder to think about. My mouth starts talking about that one before my brain has a chance to tell it to shut the fuck up.

"Sometimes my sister and I would hide in the woods when it was time to go back to the city. One last adventure before we had to go back to real life. My parents were in on the game, but the last time we hid my dad was furious about it. He accused me of avoiding my responsibilities and then gave me the silent treatment all the way back to Bihar."

"Balance, right?" she says and slides her hand into mine. It feels like home. With two words she shined a light and dissolved all the ache from the memory.

I can feel Elowen sensing how I'm feeling. She pulls me into a hug and rests her cheek on my chest.

40

Elowen

Bihar is unlike any other city I've seen before. The space between buildings has been over taken by flowers and trees. Vines climb up the walls around us. Tilaks mill about between massive skyscrapers. High overhead, mazes of bridges connect tall buildings.

It's impossible to tell where the ground is. I would be sure we were on the base when the road would drop out from beneath us, exposing another even lower level. I kept my face plastered to the glass of the porter the entire time, in a constant state of awe.

Unlike the cities on Earth, there is serenity here. The most modern buildings and tech, surrounded by nature. Ever the devoted tour guide, Aro points out his favorite places to get a meal and all the local tourist traps. He keeps a hand on my knee the entire trip to the hospital.

We come to a stop with a group of porters, waiting for our turn through a busy intersection. We pull up to one with a Tilak child, who is staring at me through the plexi. They point towards me, trying to get their parents to look at what they see. I wave back and the child ducks down, embarrassed they were caught.

"You're making quite the impression," Aro says, laughing at my interactions with the little one.

"Gawking at a new species is one of those few things that every-one does, regardless of where they're from," I say. I remember doing the same thing as a kid, but I was usually the one everyone looked and pointed at.

"News is going to travel fast that there is a human on the loose," I tell him.

"The program is essentially over. What are they going to do—send you home a few days early? They need you to pack up all that research."

"There isn't much left to do," I whisper. I hate that this came up.

"Don't remind me. I'm over here pretending like you're going to stay and you have the nerve to ruin my fantasy," Aro says.

He's been not-so-subtly dropping comments about me staying here once the program is done. I've even allowed myself to live in that delusion for a little while with him. It's getting harder and harder to pretend I won't be leaving soon. Now that it's come up I have a pit in my stomach. The brightness of the day is dulled by the reality of our circumstances.

He looks over at me and I force a smile, but it doesn't quite reach my eyes.

"Let's just be here today. We can worry about the rest later," he says and grabs my hand. His ability to stay present is admirable. He is relentlessly present.

"You got it."

Aro goes back to pointing out his favorite spots in the city. The deeper we go into Bihar the older the buildings get, eventually leading to ancient ruins at the center. Crumbling stones form arched temples that are barely visible from the overgrowth of plant life slowly taking over. Narrow dirt paths wind between the old ruins.

"Eventually j'Tilak will overtake the remains of those buildings. After a while we might build new ones or just let it sit," he tells me. I hope they let Tilak reclaim what was once hers.

"We're here," Aro announces when we pull up to another build-ing that looks like it's being overtaken by nature. More creeping vines crawl up the walls and columns. Trees huddle around the walls, their branches making a canopy over the roof. Flowers and grass grow in fractal shapes along the bottom. It's the densest foliage I've ever seen.

"This is not what I expected. Hospitals don't look like this on Earth."

"The plants and trees come here to counteract the concentration of illnesses and injuries," he says.

Aro tells me how the patients with the most critical injuries are closest to the outside natural environment. They believe that the close proximity to nature can help heal. The scientist part of my brain immediately questions the validity of that, but I switch off that cynical voice and believe what I have seen with my own eyes here on j'Tilak.

"This place will never stop amazing me."

I admire the shifting grass as we walk to the hospital. I attentively step between patches to avoid smashing their delicate leaves. Aro confidently leads me through, and the plant life darts away from his strong and steady steps.

Andi's room is at the far end of the building on the ground level. Before we even get to her room, I can hear her voice. She sounds happy. I can't detect a trace of pain in her tone. Other voices murmur back and forth with hers. I quicken my steps, eager to finally see her.

I lightly tap my knuckles on the door frame before stepping into her room. She's sitting upright on the bed. It's impossible to tell that mere weeks ago she was injured so badly.

"Surprise!" I say and come to her bedside.

"Elowen! What are you doing here?" she asks.

"We're here for you. I had to see you with my own eyes."

"Aro! I can't believe you brought her!" she lightly scolds him.

He steps out from behind me. "Dr. Kahn, you are looking well." He sounds nervous. I take his hand in mine and give him a squeeze. I want him to know I'm here for him. I'm realizing now he has been carrying guilt from what happened.

"I feel great, and please call me Andi. You saved my life," she tells him.

Aro ducks his head and waves off her thanks. "It was nothing." I can tell he is uncomfortable with her appreciation.

"You saved the day," she says, undeterred by his humility.

I watch her, looking for any sign of lingering injury, but she seems like her old self. Feeling happy and maybe a little cooped up from being in a hospital bed for all this time.

"Aro, I want you to know how brave Lugo was that night. He sacrificed himself for me," she says.

"Thank you. That means a lot. I was responsible for him, and I should never have sent him out there. He wasn't ready," Aro says.

It's the most I've heard him speak about what happened that night. I'm glad he is talking about it. Andi has a way about her that makes people feel safe enough to open up and be vulnerable with her.

"By that logic, I would be the one responsible for the attack. I'm the one that requested an escort. I don't blame myself and I don't blame you," she says.

I can tell it's exactly what he needed to hear because his shoulders drop and a heavy sigh comes out of him.

"Let's take a walk. I've been in this bed way too long," she says and moves with ease to get out of the bed, no signs of any lingering pain.

We wander for a while through the magnificent gardens surrounding the hospital. Andi is still recuperating, so she loses her breath easily. We stop and rest at the conveniently placed benches.

"Can you believe we did it? We figured it out. No more polibots!" I say during one of our stops.

"You did. You figured it out," she corrects me.

"The first thing I do when we get back is throw those bots into the incinerator," I say.

"Oh, that can all wait. I'm not in any hurry to return to Earth," Andi says.

"You're not?" I'm surprised by her comment. I had expected her to be jumping on the first transport shuttle to get back and implement everything we have learned over the last few months.

"I trust our colleagues back on Earth to continue on without us," she says and smiles back at Aro.

41

Elowen

It's incredibly intimate to enter Aro's apartment. It feels like him the moment I step off the elevator, directly into his warm and cozy home. Soft rugs and overstuffed chairs fill the space. Shelves are stacked with pictures and books. His maximalist style is at odds with modern spartan trends.

The external wall is one giant window and a shade has been drawn, muting the bright light. I step closer to take in the view. We are hundreds of stories up and the neighboring buildings still tower over us. The view's not completely obstructed. I can still see the mountain range looming over the city in the distance.

I poke around for a quick minute before Aro appears with a fresh, fluffy towel and takes me to the bathroom. He's already turned on the water in the shower for me. Such a small gesture, but it endears me to him even more.

His shower is leagues ahead of the cramped bathtubs I've been using at the dome. It's spacious and steamy. I allow myself to linger for a while.

I start to feel guilty for how much water I use and step onto a soft bathmat. Again, I'm impressed with Aro's place. In the past I have found myself in guys' apartments that were messy and hardly habitable.

One was empty except for a bare mattress in the corner—with no sheets or blankets. Discarded empty noodle containers and torn open whisky packs littered the floor. Needless to say, I got out of there immediately. A bathmat wouldn't have even been a possibility.

Of course Aro would have a grown-up apartment. The guy who brings sunshine and confidence to every room he walks into would have a home that reflects that.

Staying here is as private as it's going to get, and I am ready to get naked. I desperately want him, and we are running out of time. I sift through his drawers and pull out one of his shirts. The maroon button-down shirt covers me all the way to mid-thigh, the sleeves well past my hands. I tug the bottom down as far as it can go, roll up the sleeves to my elbows, and inspect myself in the mirror.

I hear Aro tinkering around in the kitchen. The smell of his cooking makes me hurry to him. Aro has his back to me, cooking something on his stove. I'm impressed that he is actually cooking and we're not just having instant noodles. He's clearly enjoying himself, spinning the spatula around and adding spices with flourish. I didn't know he liked cooking. I tuck this away as another detail I will hold onto.

"That smells amazing," I tell Aro as I walk up behind him. I hug his narrow waist and peer around him to see what's cooking. It looks like stir-fry. Thick slices of meat with sautéed colorful veg in a sizzling sauce.

"I hope you like it." He turns and passes me a bowl of steaming food. I take it with me to a stool at the countertop.

My mouth waters while I blow to cool it down before taking a bite. I slowly chew the food, savoring every second.

"You're my hero. This is the first time I've had something other than noodles in months and it's amazing," I tell Aro before taking another big bite.

"I'm glad you like it. Eat up. I'm going to jump in the shower." He pulls his shirt over his head as he swaggers down the hallway. I crane my neck to watch him strip. He is exquisite. My attention returns to my food and it doesn't take long before I've finished every single bite.

Shortly after I finish my food, Aro's back and towel drying his hair. He's changed into a pair of gray sweatpants that hang low on his waist. He snags my bowl, piles on more food, fills one up for himself and sits on the stool next to me as he hands me my seconds.

"So, what's the plan?" I ask.

"You're looking at it."

"I like this plan. Real food, no shifts at the lab. A girl could get used to this." It comes out of my mouth without thinking. I want to take it back, but it's too late. The words were said, even though I know I'll be leaving soon. Even though it's the truth, I could get used to this, I shouldn't be saying it out loud.

"You could stay." It's nearly a whisper.

Aro pulls me to him and kisses my lips. He deepens the kiss while grabbing my shirt collar. I slip off my stool and take a step toward him. I find myself standing between his legs trying to get closer. I cup the back of his neck. Being here with him feels right, and I'll save all my worries about leaving for later. Right now, I just want him.

I realize I've interrupted his dinner. He's got to be starving by now. I end our kiss and climb back up onto the stool next to him. I am genuinely impressed with how quickly he eats.

"What do you think they're doing at the muradome right now?" I ask, only slightly concerned Bri has backed herself into a lie that will result in major consequences for the both of us, or that everyone at the facility will think I have a severe digestive condition.

"If Tai and Bri haven't killed each other yet, I'd say it's a pretty boring night." He smiles and takes his last bite. "Tai hasn't said a word about their little snuggle session on the couch back in the rec room."

"Bri either. I think they're in denial."

He starts cleaning up from dinner. I grab my plate to help and he snatches it back with a stern look. Next thing I know he has me by the waist and he's hoisted me up and sets me on the counter. He pushes down on my shoulders, holding me in place.

"I've got this. You stay here," he says and goes back to gathering the dirty dishes.

There's this tiny part of me that indulges in thoughts of a future here. I can easily picture myself living here in this apartment. He and I quietly going about our days and then coming together at night. Aro cooking me dinner. Us cozy on the couch together recapping our day. Traveling the planet together. I indulge in the fantasy. I'm weak when it comes to him. Every barrier I have erected between us he has systematically dismantled.

The windows past Aro grab my attention. The suns are barely over the horizon, and the sky has turned a shocking orange and blue. Aro taps a few instructions into a control pad. The window shades retract into the wall and the bright orange light fills the kitchen.

"Oh wow." I can't find the right words. Watching the sunset is another breathtaking experience. Aro comes back to me, he gets close and nudges my knees apart, bringing his body up to mine.

He puts his hands on the counter next to my hips and leans forward. I wait for a kiss that doesn't come. He watches me intently, learning every detail of my face. I savor his nearness while watching the suns sink lower and lower to the edge of the horizon. I rest my arms on his shoulders and frame his body with my bare legs. Over his shoulder, the sky changes colors as the suns continue their descent.

"Aro, turn around. You're missing the most incredible sunset."

"I'm not missing anything. This right here… is what I can't look away from." He runs his index finger down the center of my forehead and down my nose.

I pull him into me by his shoulders and kiss his gorgeous mouth. I stroke my tongue over his and squeeze his hips with my thighs. Aro quickly takes control of the kiss and grabs my ass with both hands lifting me off the counter. I wrap my legs around him and hook my ankles together. I take one last look out the window at the setting suns as Aro carries me toward his bedroom.

We make it about halfway to the bedroom when I'm pushed up against the wall, held up by Aro's hips and his mouth at my throat. Aro grips the hair at the base of my head. A breathy moan escapes my lips. Lips and teeth make their way down my neck. Aro's hard cock pushing against me sends vibrating energy to my core. The shirt I've borrowed is up to my waist and I'm completely exposed below.

Aro breaks from his kiss and looks down at me. Over the pounding of my heart, I hear a growl from deep in his chest. He peels me off the wall and carries me the rest of the way to the bedroom. It felt incredible when he pulled my hair. My fingers itch to do the same to him. Aro's got both of his hands roughly palming my ass as we approach his bed. Before we can drop, I lace my fingers through his hair and tug.

"Fuck." Aro draws the word out into three long syllables. He grinds his hips against mine and the head of his cock still inside his pants pushes against me.

Aro places me on the edge of his expansive bed. I trail my fingertips across his soft, lush sheets. His shirt comes off and for the first time I notice a black vertical tattoo traveling up his rib cage. He hooks his fingers in the waistband of his pants and pulls them down. His impressive cock springs up. Woah—this is going to be interesting. Aro closes the distance between us. When he stands at the edge of the bed, I stroke the outside of his thighs and I pull his hips toward me.

A bead of cum glistens on the tip of his dick. I look up at him from my vantage point and smile. I grab him and stroke up and down. I lick my lips and run my tongue up his shaft, then pull the crown of his cock into my mouth. A rasping breath escapes his lips and he clutches at the back of my head. I move my mouth up and down with my tongue flattened seeing how much of him I can take. I go a bit too far and gag a little. My mouth is watering because he tastes so good. With a wet mouthful of him, I look up to see his reaction. His face shows every ounce of his pleasure and his hooded eyes look down at me. I move a little faster and he pulls out of my mouth with a pop.

"This will be over before it even gets started if you keep that up." I wipe some spit off my chin with the back of my hand and scoot back on the bed to make room for him. Aro's body slides up mine and he claims me with a rough kiss. He slowly works each button on the shirt I borrowed. It feels like an eternity has passed by the time he pulls it off me.

I squeeze my arms together, pushing my breasts and nipples toward him. Aro grabs one and rubs the side of his face against my chest until his mouth is around my nipple. He draws it hard into his mouth and lightly bites it between his teeth. He kisses and licks his way over to the other side, tasting all of me. He moves back up and lightly brushes his lips against mine before he nips at my earlobe.

"Hm, you taste so good. I'm going to take my time with you." Chills spread all over my body from the feel of his lips against my ear. He groans and arches his back pushing his cock between my thighs. He bites my shoulder to help control himself. I turn his face back toward me. I want to see every expression. He kisses the palm of my hand. More chills spread over my body as he kisses the tip of each finger.

I reach down to my belly where Aro's hard cock is pushed between us. I push it down toward my pussy and work my hips against him. He closes his eyes in pure ecstasy when I use him to rub my clit. I angle him a fraction lower and grind my hips to pull him inside of me.

"We'll go slow next time," I say as I feed him into me.

My breath catches as he pushes slowly in. I've never felt so full before. "Wait wait wait." I press against his chest to hold him in place. I urge myself to relax so he can go deeper. I can feel him pulsing inside of me. He pushes deeper little by little.

"You feel so good." Aro's words urge me on and I roll my hips up to his. He sucks air between his teeth and bites his lower lip.

He keeps moving deeper and when I don't think I can take anymore he is fully inside of me. He holds still for a second before pulling back. In a fluid motion he pushes back in. He rolls his hips in and out, and I grip his shoulders with all my strength. My face drawn in with my eyebrows scrunched together. Every time he fucks into me, it pushes air out of my lungs. As our bodies move in rhythm together my breathing catches up to Aro's. I push harder and harder against him, chasing the building pressure.

Aro leans down and grabs my nipple and that's enough to send me straight over the edge. I stifle my moan into his neck as my legs shake and my clit throbs on his cock. I've never come so fast. He stills for a moment to experience my orgasm, then resumes his deep thrusts into me. He sits back onto his heels and grabs my ankles, tossing them over his shoulders. When he enters me this time the angle brings him hard against a different part of me. He leans closer again and kisses my collarbone then pushes his face into my neck while relentlessly moving in and out of me. I'm shocked to realize I'm going to come again.

Desperation takes me over and I meet every thrust with my own. This time, I hear a whiny moan come out of me when I come. Aro's movements become jerky and he pulls out of me completely. He roughly strokes his dick a few times and then a jet of cum streaks out of him. He keeps stroking and more pours out in thick ropes onto my belly. When his body is still from his release, he drops down on the bed next to me and lays on his side. A second later he jumps up and grabs a towel from the bathroom then carefully wipes away any trace of him from my belly.

I drop my head back onto the bed, close my eyes, and draw in a deep breath. My chest is pounding while I try to catch my breath. I turn my head to Aro and smile. He is completely spent. He stares back at me and without a word drags me up against his hard sweaty body. He nuzzles his face into the crook of my neck and takes in a long drag.

We lie like this for a while. Long enough to cool off and for our breathing to normalize. I can't stop smiling and he can't stop touching me. His fingers skate up and down my arms and across my back then trail down my legs. I don't even want to blink because I'll miss his face looking back at me.

"The fuse was lit the moment I saw you, and it's been heading straight towards my destruction," he says and kisses my shoulder.

"I wish things could be different, that I didn't have to leave," I say, meaning it.

"Is it selfish of me to ask you to stay?" he asks, searching my face.

My chest aches at the thought of leaving him. "I need to finish this. There is still a lot of work to do. Plus, there's something you should know about me. I'm really good at fitting in, not good at belonging," I say.

"What does that mean?" he asks.

"I can fit in just about anywhere. I am adaptable. I've never truly *belonged* somewhere. I would always be an outsider here, and that doesn't fit with who you are. Who you're going to be," I explain.

"I still have time to change your mind," he says and pulls the sheets up and snuggles deeper into me.

42

Elowen

"Elowen, wake up." I'm groggy and absolutely not ready to wake up. "Time to get up, Elowen," he says again in a singsong voice.

Aro rubs my back and speaks softly close to my ear. I growl my irritation and refuse to open my eyes. Lying flat on my stomach I blindly search for the sheets to pull over my head to hide. I could sleep for a month.

"Let me sleep."

Aro works his thumbs in a deep massage on my back, loosening all the knots.

"I take that back. Don't stop," I tell him. I hear the sheets rustle and feel the mattress shift when he gets up. "Where are you going?" I whine. Aro laughs when he returns to the bedroom.

Oil drips up and down my back, and his hand rubs in gentle circles across my skin. The oil he's using makes me slippery, assisting him with easing my sore muscles. He kneads my neck and shoulders until they're soft and relaxed. He moves down to the center of my back and the hard press of his fingers around my spine feels like heaven. I am suddenly very aware of my nakedness as he moves lower down my body.

The sheet has slipped down to my waist and Aro stops at the covering, rubbing across my lower back. His fingertips barely dip beneath the sheets and graze the top of my ass. With each pass he goes a little bit lower until he is rubbing my entire backside. He pulls down the sheet and rubs the backs of my thighs. He stops occasionally to drip more oil onto my skin and works it all over. He rubs circles all the way down each leg and then back up.

When he gets back to my ass he takes his time there. I shudder when he lightly strokes down the center of my ass and moves to the front of my body from there. He moves away from the center of me and goes back to rubbing all over. After a few more passes, his slippery fingers drag back toward the front of my body, his fingers reaching for my clit and his thumb resting between my cheeks. I can't hold still anymore and my body responds to him by lifting my hips to meet his touch.

My movement gives him access to go deeper into me. He pushes two fingers inside of me and then pulls them back out spreading my wetness. I flip over so I'm lying on my back and facing him now.

"Good morning," Aro says. I reply with a long hum in the back of my throat.

Aro drips oil down my chest and stomach. His hand moves from between my legs. He uses both hands to rub my collar bones and works his way down like he did on my back. He gets to my breasts and rubs them softly at first. His grip gets harder as my body reacts with slow rolls up and down toward him. He softens his touch again as he goes over my belly briefly before going back between my legs.

Every part of me glistens with oil. I hold onto his forearm and arch into his touch. He's worked all the tightness out of my body and it feels good to writhe against him.

Aro's fingers expertly move in and out of me while his thumb slides across my clit. He draws a whimper out of me with each pass. I reach over and grab his hard cock, moving my hand tightly up and down. Each time I reach the top of his dick, I palm the head and then slide back down all the way to the base with slow tight movements.

Aro breaks free from my touch, flips me over, and drags me back toward him. My knees dig into the edge of the bed. He takes my hips in his hands and brings me back onto his cock. He is so hard, but I am ready. He pushes all the way in against my soft core. He roughly snaps his hips and pulls out. I shift back searching for him and he enters me again. I audibly draw in a lungful of air. Aro reaches forward and grabs a shoulder with one hand, keeping his other on my hip, and proceeds to fuck me. I grab one of my nipples and tug roughly before moving down to where we are connected.

"I'm not pulling out this time," he says punctuating each word with a brutal stroke. "Don't stop," I beg, rubbing fingers along the sides of my clit. "I need..."

"Take it. It's yours." His words finish what my fingers couldn't, and I shatter apart, seeing stars.

Aro is seconds behind and when he releases inside me, every last pulse shakes my existence. He drops down, draping my back with his body. His breath coming fast in my ear. "I'm... when I'm... we're all given the shot when we enlist." He struggles to find the words. I hope it's because I have transformed him in the same way.

I already knew the males were all on contraceptives, but it's so sweet that he needed to confirm it. I kiss his cheek next to mine.

"I know."

"And over that way is the pt'Clanik ocean. There's a muradome out there with a team from Earth doing marine life studies. And past the ocean is h'Nalor." Aro points out in the distance toward the setting suns. We are the only ones on the enormous roof. He enticed me up here with the promise of another breathtaking view.

It feels like we are in a city park. The roof is covered in grass and brimming with life. It's easy to forget how far we are from the ground. The bright colors in the sky darken as the suns sink down below the horizon. After looking at the dome ceiling for months, the j'Tilak sky is much more inspiring. The high hydrogen atmosphere creates the most incredible sky. The gas scatters the light similarly to Earth's, but the magnetic fields here create vivid auroras of greens, blues, and purples across the sky. A large bright red moon is visible during the day, unlike the other two that only come out at night. It's close enough to see the deep, cratered surface.

"What's h'Nalor like?" I ask, trying my best to get the pronunciation right.

"It's mostly rainforest. The horniest plants live there," Aro says with an amused smile, waiting for a reaction.

"Don't fault my flowers for having a strong survival instinct."

"Hm, you might be right. I have some pretty strong instincts about what to do with you right now." He lowers his head towards me, like a predator going in for the kill. I've never been a more willing prey.

"What time do we need to get back to the dome?" I ask as he rubs up and down my back.

"It will be easiest to sneak back in after dark. You still worried about getting caught?" He wraps me up in his arms and holds me to him.

"I'm nervous. I don't like feeling like I'm going to get in trouble," I tell him, and for the first time the smell of him hits me. Maybe it's from being in the dome all these months, because out here in the open, the smells are incredible. He smells like fresh air and clean linen, something I didn't notice in the recycled air of the sterile muradome.

"Remember the whole 'ask forgiveness not permission'? Plus, I hate to use the royalty card, but it is effective at getting me out of trouble," he says and kisses down the side of my neck. I should argue the point that we need to get back as soon as possible, but why start being rational now?

43

Elowen

"We're almost there," Aro says softly, rousing me from sleep. I dozed off on our way back to the dome. I stretch my arms up and roll my neck. It's dark outside and I can't tell exactly where we are.

"Back to reality," I say through a yawn. The weight of our responsibilities crash back down. We've enjoyed living in an alternate universe the last two days, both of us carefully avoiding reality. It's becoming a common occurrence with Aro, something I'll desperately miss when I have to leave.

"It's not too late to turn around," he says, trying to keep the mood light.

The dome's sterile white glow reveals its location in the distance. The first time I saw the research dome, it was welcoming and full of promise. Now it's cold and uninviting, a painful reminder that I'm a guest here. I swallow hard and force a smile over at Aro, unable to think of a reason to not take him up on his offer.

"I know you feel obligated to get back to Earth and finish up the research. I think you could consider… Maybe it's possible that you…" Aro rambles and then abruptly cuts himself off.

"Aro, I wish I could stay. I love it here. But I still have a job to do."

The porter slams to a stop while I'm looking over at him. My head jerks forward.

I turn to see what made Aro stop. I strain my eyes to focus. A horde of black creatures scramble down the hill behind the dome.

"What is that?" I ask.

"Atorum."

A deafening screech pierces my ears. My hands do nothing to quiet the scream echoing in my head. Aro bangs his palm on the porter's control panel. Immediately the emergency protocol alarms blare from the dome.

"No, no, no, no," he mutters as they swarm the muradome from all angles and pile on top of each other trying to climb the sloping roof. The creatures tear giant holes, working their way in. The dome's thin roof comes apart easily with their spear-like appendages.

The cargo bay opens and porters pour out. They race around the dome, some speeding away and others positioning themselves, ready to fight off the invaders.

"Get to the base. You'll be safe there. I'll come find you," Aro says and slides the control panel over to me.

"Wait, Aro—no! I don't know what to do," I say and look helplessly at the panel in front of me.

"Don't do anything. It will take you there." He steps out and swipes his finger on the panel one last time, closing his door and sending me in the opposite direction. I bang on the plexi screaming his name as I get farther and farther from him. A giant ball of orange fire explodes, lighting Aro from behind.

He stands there, unmoving, and looks like a giant shadow. His black shape stretches and grows the father I get. The porter spins and self-corrects so I'm facing forward, ripping him from my view.

I look around the control panel. I have no idea how to operate this thing. I try swiping across the smooth surface. The panel stays blank. I'm helpless as the porter takes me farther away from Aro. Angrily, I wipe the tears streaming down my face. My throat raw from yelling for him.

Every instinct in my body tells me to turn around and go back, to help him. Rational thinking claws its way back to the surface. There is nothing I can do. He sent me to the base so he can focus on saving everyone else at the dome. My heart is pounding behind my ears and sweat trickles down my back. Aro is out there, with no protection, nothing.

"I just need to get to the base," I repeat over and over trying to reassure myself. I scan around, looking for any sign of the Atorum. I don't see anything and take a deep breath, trying to calm down. Panicking is the worst thing I can do right now. I need to stay calm. I need to think. I rub my sweaty palms on my pants and look around clear-eyed.

The porter breaks free from the forest. If memory serves, I should be getting close to the base. An alarm blares through the porter, and a red light flashes. "WARNING WARNING WARNING" lights up across the curved plexi in front of me.

All calm is out the window and I frantically look around to see what could have set off the alert. Right when I'm convinced it was a false alarm a terrifying black shape lands on the porter, slamming it into the ground and to a halt.

Its cylindrical body turns unnaturally and its eye-less face angles down. Its round mouth with rows of sharp chainsaw teeth rotate towards me. Long spikes point out in every direction. Some bend, and others straighten out. The black scales covering its body flip back and forth in waves, making a sinister click with each shift. Unable to look away from the monstrosity above me, I reach for my harness.

I fumble with the buckle. My body weight pushing on the harness makes it impossible to release. The creature searches the porter's slick surface. Its legs shift, some getting longer and some shorter as it rolls over the porter, looking for a way in.

It raises its longest limb and strikes the plexi with a bang. The porter holds and the alien tries again, attempting to stab through the barrier. Its sharp pointed leg bounces off the porter. It scrapes its claws against the glass with a piercing screech.

I finally find a grip on the harness, and I push the release button. I fall behind the seat and take a shuttering breath, finally out of sight of the Atorum. I peek around the seat and the creature senses my movement. It goes into a frenzy trying to break through. Each strike pushes the porter deeper and deeper into the ground.

A tiny fracture splinters across the surface above me. From that one break, a web of cracks radiate across the whole porter. Faint tinks and pings echo as the cracks spread. Reinvigorated with the sign of progress, the alien finally gets one jagged leg through the glass. The Atorum's leg is jammed in the hole it created, and it struggles to pull itself loose. Chest heaving, I squeeze my eyes shut, readying myself for what comes next. Time stands still while the creature works to get free.

The ground shakes with impact and a shudder runs over the porter. *Boom*. It happens again, this time closer. My teeth rattle with every impact. I can't tell where it's coming from or what it is. I squeeze my eyes shut trying to think of a plan. The next thing I know, the alien is ripped free from the porter, leaving behind its leg still embedded in the plexi, black ooze dripping down the disconnected leg onto the seat I had just been occupying.

I watch through the splintered glass and see the Atorum trapped in the Allometradon's mouth. It violently tosses the creature aside. She swings her massive tail to hit the Atorum again. She misses and smashes into the porter, fully shattering the glass around me.

Without looking back, I climb over the shards of glass and run as fast as I can towards the base. I hear the two creatures fighting behind me. The sounds of their struggle stop when the Allometradon's bellow echoes across the field. The same screech from before follows and I hear a heavy body hit the ground with the force of an earthquake. My steps falter for a fraction of a second before I can right myself and pick up speed.

I keep running, pumping my legs as fast as I possibly can. I just need to get to the base. The gate is in view. I'm so close. I'm almost there.

The menacing clicking from the Atorum is back and gets louder as it catches up to me. I don't dare turn around to see how close it is. I keep my head forward and urge my legs to move faster. I scream for help as loud as possible as I charge forward, my lungs burning. The clicking is next to my ear and right when I brace myself for impact, a bright blue beam shoots over my shoulder. A shriek is cut short when the light hits it. Black ooze explodes all over my back and I drop to my knees drawing in air between sobs.

44

Aro

A rush of adrenaline collects in my body—first in my hands and feet, then it moves to my chest as Elowen is driven away. I sent her to the safest place I could think of in that moment. *She's okay. She's safe. She is getting far from here.* I repeat those words over and over, trying to reassure myself that I did the right thing. The veins in my arms throb as blood rushes through. I roar at the painful concentration of power gathering in me. The hard plates under my skin thicken and lock into place over my torso. I relinquish control to the predator inside of me. Every cell in my body is tuned to destroy. Somehow, I have a memory of this unfamiliar power.

The heat from the explosion warms my back and I turn towards the muradome to see Atorum smashing their way in. Others lie broken and oozing on the ground from the porters' plasma cannons.

I step over a motionless black Atorum lying on its back, legs curled up into its body. I grab the largest leg and rip it off in one swift motion. I need something sharp. I check the weight of my new weapon and swing it around, loosening my shoulder muscles to ready myself for a fight. The leg whistles through the air as I slash it back and forth, ready to inflict some damage.

An Atorum drops down right in front of me. Its black scales ripple back and forth on its disgusting body. It quirks its head at me and its circular jaws creak, grinding together as the creature bares its teeth at me. It circles around me slowly, measuring me up.

I make the first move and barrel towards it. With a quick lunge, I slash with my improvised weapon. Black scum pours out from the wound as it makes one last lurch towards me. I knock it aside with another swing nearly slicing it in half. The Atorum shrieks and collapses into itself.

Another Atorum rolls towards me, spinning on its spiked legs. I take a swing and slam it into a tree. It recalibrates and comes at me again. Right before I make contact, it extends a leg and slashes my exposed side.

White hot pain radiates from my ribs. I push against the cut and my hand comes away bloody. The sight of my blood sends me into a rage. I jump into the air and come down hard on the Atorum's back, smashing it into the ground with a roar. I repeatedly stab down on the creature until it's no longer twitching.

I resume my mission to get to the dome. Plasma cannons boom all around, blasting the invaders apart with blue beams of hot light. The fire has spread to the forest canopy, lighting up the sky with an eerie orange glow. By the time I get to the cargo bay it's engulfed in flames. There's nothing there to save.

A porter slides to a stop right behind me. The door swings open and Maak has a deranged look on his face as I climb in next to him.

"Hop in—we're killing bugs," he says.

I take control of the plasma cannon as Maak spins us around. The thick blue arc clears everything in our path. Spindly legs and severed torsos fly out from the plasma cannon blast.

I watch, horrified, as three Atorum merge into one large body, and it triples in size. It approaches a smashed open porter where a Tilak soldier is trying to crawl his way out from under the wreckage. The canon is useless against the huge Atorum.

Maak turns the porter, giving me a direct line of attack. I open the door and step halfway out. I toss the alien leg above me and snatch it from the air. Holding it like a spear, I lean back and throw with all my strength. It impales the giant Atorum and pins it to the ground.

Maak speeds towards another trying to smash its way into a porter. We crash into both, pinning the disgusting bug between us and the other porter. Black ooze covers the plexi, nearly blocking our entire view.

"Dammit!" Maak says and activates the shield-cleaning blade. It spreads around the thick sludge, making it worse.

"Can you take care of that?" he asks.

"You made the mess. You clean it up."

He unbuckles and jumps out of the porter while I continue working the cannon. He rips the sleeves off his shirt and gets to work cleaning the shield. All he manages to do is spread it around more. I pick off each Atorum as they step into my narrow line of sight, until none are left.

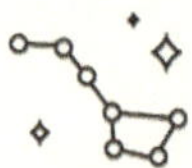

I step out and survey the damage. Smoke is still rising up from the destroyed muradome. A swarm of drones pour chemical dampeners on the growing fire. Broken trees hang at awkward angles. Puddles of black ooze splotch the landscape. I try to slow my ragged breathing, there is nothing left to kill, but I can't seem to convince myself that the threat is gone.

Nearby, Tai kicks aside the dead carcass of an Atorum as he makes his way toward me. Eyes wide, he looks me up and down.

"What the hell happened to you?" Tai asks.

Maak gives up on cleaning the shield and slaps me on the back. "Nice battleform."

Realization crashes over me: I shifted into battleform, something that hasn't happened in centuries. The awareness makes my body constrict back into its former shape. My muscles cramp painfully as they go back down to size. I look down at my shredded clothes, splattered with mire and dirt.

"You good?" he asks, looking me over for any injuries, his eyes landing on my bleeding side.

Stunned, I assess my body. "I don't know." Another realization hits me. I need to get to Elowen. I need to get to my mate.

45

Elowen

My eyes are glued to the horizon while I pace back and forth along the deck of the watchtower. I was reassured this was the best place to see anyone approaching the base after I got confirmation Bri had safely arrived with all the other evacuees. Even climbing the hundreds of zig-zagging stairs to get up here didn't tire me out.

Just stop. Calm down. He'll be here soon.

The only light in the dark sky is the faint orange glow of the fire that destroyed the dome. I watch the chaos below. Tilaks help evacuees get around and massive tankers are loaded and leave in the direction of the attack. From up here the dead Atorum and Allometradon stain the once unblemished grass.

A theory has begun to formulate in my head while I pace. The Atorum have got to be targeting humans. Between Andi, the dome, and now myself—it's the only logical conclusion.

I knock on the watchtower window, getting their attention. "Anything?" I yell through the thick glass. One guy looks up at me, shakes his head and goes back to the transparent screen he's working on.

I turn back to the empty tree line. I've bitten my nails down to nothing. I shake out my hands and resume walking, unable to stand in one place for long. Suddenly, the lights of an approaching porter flicker into view.

"Come on, Aro. Come on," I whisper.

He's got to be okay. Maybe I should have tried to turn the porter around to get him. At least there would have been something between him and the Atorum. I shake away the memory of the black leg smashing through the plexi.

Someone bangs on the glass behind me.

"He's on his way."

I take the stairs two at a time. When my feet hit the ground I bolt for the gate. I dodge porters and soldiers, trying my best to stay out of their way. I wait impatiently for the gate to open. The heavy metal creaks as it gradually opens. As the space between the two doors widens, a figure emerges. With his head hanging low and shoulders high, he forces the huge doors open.

Aro swings his head to the side. Wet hair whips off his face and he marches straight toward me.

We roughly collide, and Aro grabs my face with both hands. His eyes desperately search my face. "What happened back there?" he asks, nodding back to the wreckage.

"Sir, you should have seen her. She took on an Allometradon and an Atorum at the same time, and she's the only one that walked away," a soldier standing to the side answers for me.

A smile breaks out over his dirty face. "You're a badass."

"It was mostly luck," I tell him.

"My little dragon slayer," he says and crushes me to his chest. His tight arms hold me up. I sink into him and feel his chest pound against my cheek.

"Uck!" he says and pulls away, strings of black ooze still clinging to him.

A blue blood stain on his side is spreading.

"Aro! You're hurt," I say frantically.

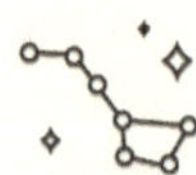

Aro drops me off at the cafeteria on his way to the med clinic. I promise to stay exactly where he put me. He frets over me for a minute, then takes off to get his side closed up.

I grab a cup of synthetic coffee and sit at one of the only empty tables. The black sludge on my back is starting to harden and itch. I watch the door, looking for any familiar faces. Tilaks file in, having returned from the dome. Some are injured. Others are covered in black but seem unharmed. Two sit down behind me and recap what happened back at the dome.

"Did you see him rip the leg off the Atorum, and then beat the other one to death with it?" one says.

"That was insane! He looked like a fucking gladiator when he threw it like a javelin and stuck that bug to the ground," the other replies.

"I lost my damn mind when he showed up like that. He was at least ten feet tall."

"Do you think the captain could teach us how to do it?"

"I hope so. I'd love to go all berserk on these things."

It hits me—they are talking about Aro. What happened out there? The conversation behind me is interrupted by a loud bang on the table, followed by another. Soon everyone in the mess hall is hitting the table with their fist in a steady thunderous beat. I look around trying to figure out what is going on.

Aro walks down the row of tables, heading straight for me. Chairs scrape the ground when everyone stands up around him, continuing their beat on the table. He slides up next to me on the bench without acknowledging the spectacle around us.

"That's quite an entrance," I say.

"Don't pay any attention to these guys. They are easily impressed."

"I overheard what you did out there. Sounds pretty impressive to me. Did I hear something about a battleform?" I ask.

"I'll explain later."

"I appreciate the humility—really, I do. But I think we can both agree that using an alien leg as a weapon is pretty fucking cool."

He grins over at me. "If that's all it took for you to finally be impressed by me, I would have done it months ago." He steals a drink of my coffee and I pretend to be offended. I savor the feeling of him against my side. I don't know what happens next, but there is one thing I have no doubts about. I have absolutely fallen in love with Aro.

"You ready to get out of here?" he asks.

"Yes, I need a shower, desperately."

"I know just the place," he says.

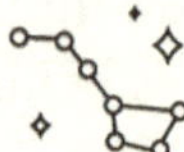

We get to the barracks where the communal shower is already in use. A half-wall blocks the lower part of their bodies. I still avert my eyes and try not to stare.

"You're done here," Aro roughly orders the two showering. They turn off their water, grab a towel, and hurry out without a word with their heads down.

"You didn't have to do that. I can wait," I tell him.

"Don't fight me on this. Get in the shower." He uses his "captain" voice on me. I'm ashamed to admit it does something for me.

"Yes, sir." I mock salute and peel off my clothes.

Aro has a shower running by the time I've gotten my boots and clothes off. I step under the water and close my eyes as it runs down my face. The shower drain turns black with the runoff from my body.

I hear the slap of bare feet on the tile behind me and turn to see Aro stepping into the shower with me. His giant wall of blue chest comes up next to me and rubs up and down my arms, scrubbing off the sticky black ooze.

"You scared the shit out of me," I tell him. "You walked straight into danger empty-handed." It was the worst feeling watching him get farther from me.

Aro never leaves anyone behind. I'm in awe of his undying loyalty to his unit. To me, he is larger than life in body and in his purpose.

"I needed to get you away from there, and there was no way I could leave my unit behind."

"I know why you did it. It still scared me to death."

"I was scared too. When I saw the wrecked porter outside the base, my soul was ripped out of my body, but I should have known that you could take care of yourself."

"You weren't the only gladiator out there tonight. I outran an Atorum."

"Gladiator?"

"That's what the boys behind me were calling you."

"You really shouldn't listen to them."

"So, what happened out there?" I ask. I wash some of the dried black tar off of his arms with soapy water. His hard muscles bunch up as I rub up and down.

"The explosions from the dome did most of the work. We destroyed the ones left behind."

"So, no beating an alien to death with a leg, or spearing anything with said leg?"

He smiles a little and shrugs, not wanting to tell me what I already know. His humility is adorable, but right now I'm craving that arrogant soldier that won me over.

"Is everyone okay?" I ask as Aro takes a squirt of shampoo and works it through my hair.

"I'm not sure. I came to you as soon as I could. We'll get the report when we go to comms," he says, concentrating on keeping the shampoo off my face while he scrubs away the remains of the mire off me.

"There you go—all better," he says and rinses my hair out. I reach my hands up to his tall shoulders, I rest my head against his chest, our bodies fused together.

He kisses the top of my head, and soothes his hands down my back, comforting me with each pass. Every touch is a reminder we are okay. That in this moment, we have each other.

He is hard against my belly as we step even closer. I spin him around and let him get the full force of the clean water.

With his back to me, I reach around and stroke his chest and hard abs, then move down to his cock. He slaps a wet hand against the tile. A low growl comes from deep in his chest. My wet body shifts over his. I move up and down with agonizingly slow strokes from behind.

He must feel me reach for myself with my free hand, because the moment I do, he turns and lifts me up. My ankles instinctively lock behind his back. The hard tile sends a shock of cold through me when my back comes against it. I push his wet hair back from his face and grind my hips against him, searching for more. The adrenaline from today morphs into desire. His lips are everywhere. I grab the back of his neck and hold him to me. I need more. I need him inside of me.

The shower door swings wide open. "Oh shit! Sorry, sorry, sir." A Tilak rambles an apology and slams the door behind him in quick retreat.

Aro mutters something under his breath as I release my legs and step back on solid ground. I pat his chest and kiss him softly.

"Let's find somewhere a little more private," I say, dragging him from the shower. I toss him a towel from the neatly piled stack. It hits his face. He drags it down his body and tucks it around his waist his erection tenting the towel.

46

Aro

The war room goes quiet when I step inside. Thirty heads turn and watch me take the empty seat next to Tai at the circular table.

"What? You act like you haven't seen a battleform before." I break the silence.

"No one has seen anything like that in centuries," Locke says from across the table.

Rialto steps into the room. The lights dim and a holographic image of j'Tilak appears. Tensions are high and we all silently wait for him to begin the briefing.

"We have learned that the Atorum were programmed to eradicate humans. The specimen that we recovered is badly decomposed. However, we have a team trying to figure out who is behind the attacks."

I think of the most outspoken anti-humans, we should have taken those protesters more seriously. We were blinded by the stupidity of it all.

Petrok steps up next to Rialto and continues. "All available units are out looking for any Atorum that might have survived. We already have eyes on the segregationist group known as HOMe, Human

Opposition Movement. For everyone's safety, the humans are required to stay on base at all times."

"I want to be the first to congratulate Captain Aro pt'Burosa. The first of our kind to summon his battleform in hundreds of years. I never thought it would happen in my lifetime," Rialto says, turning to me. Everyone around me thumps the table in unison.

I smile and wave them off like it's no big deal. I still haven't explained what this all means to Elowen. It doesn't feel right talking about it with anyone until she hears it from me.

"Thank you, sir."

"I like our chances now that battleforms are back on the table," Tai says.

I put on a convincing show of nonchalance. This is a turning point for my people. The ability to summon battleforms will alter our future. I'm aware of the significance and am humbled that fate chose me to summon this ancient power.

Elowen is my mate. She's the reason this happened. And I've never been happier. It all finally makes sense now. The moment I saw her I knew… I didn't know exactly what it was, but somehow I knew.

For the first time, I can imagine what our lives will look like. The vision of a little girl with blue skin and Elowen's big round eyes floats through my mind. I shake my head to stop that train of thought. I am getting ahead of myself.

After the briefing, I find Elowen sitting alone on a bench outside with her face turned up towards the sky. When I step in front of her and she opens her eyes to see what is blocking out the warm light, I'm rewarded with a smile.

"How did it go?" she asks, shading her face from the bright sun when I sit down next to her on the bench.

"Looks like the Atorum were programmed to target humans." She doesn't look surprised.

"Do they know why?"

"We're still figuring that part out," I tell her. The wind has dislodged a strand hair and it blows across her face. I gently tuck it back behind her ear, unable to resist the compulsion to touch her.

I scrape my hand down my face, suddenly filled with worst-case scenarios. I haven't put a lot of thought into how Elowen will react when I tell her we are mates until this moment. I just need to do it—tell her, and see what happens next.

"What's going on?" she asks. She puts her hand on my arm. The touch calms me immediately. The wind has pulled loose her hair again. This time she tucks it back herself so she can see me clearly.

"After I sent you here, I shifted into battleform. It happened because I needed to protect you, my mate."

"Woah, woah, woah. Start over. What?" she's rattled by what I said.

"During the attack, I shifted into my battleform." I say slowly. I shouldn't have just blurted it out before.

"What's a battleform?"

"It's a physical reaction to threat. It's when a Tilak's body grows, gets stronger, and is solely focused on protecting their mate. Remember what I told you about the quinstaks, and how my people used to have mates all those centuries ago?"

"And that happened to you?" she asks.

"It did. When the porter took you away, I shifted into my battleform and didn't even know it right away. It took Maak pointing it out for me to realize what happened."

"I don't see how that's possible," she says.

I start to explain the shift, "It's a biological response to stress, so—"

"Not that." She stops me. "I don't see how it's possible that you and I are mates."

"I know it sounds crazy. Different species, millions of light-years apart. But look at you and me. I've spent my life never looking at anything too closely. You've spent your life looking at things so precisely—down to the cellular level. I react, and you study and form theories and test. I break rules and you know they are there for a good reason. Of course you are my mate. You make me so much more. Balance, right?"

"Biologically—"

This time I cut her off. "It's more than that. For me. You're going to need some time. You have your process. I'll wait. See? It's already happening. I'm learning to be patient."

It feels vulnerable to give Elowen space to think about what I told her. Deep down, I know that this will all work out. I'm not worried she will reject me now, but it does feel strange to put myself completely in the palm of her hand. To give her complete and utter power over me. It's petrifying and it feels right.

47

Elowen

I watch Aro and Tai move around the mat. Like a choreographed dance with fluid and graceful movements, but also with flares of violence. Tai makes his move first. He lunges low and grabs at Aro's legs. Aro catches his arms and tosses him to the ground. Tai somersaults away before he can be pinned.

Aro snags Tai's leg and brings them both down. They grapple around and Tai slams his forehead into Aro's face with a sickening crack. Aro holds his thumb under his nose and brings it away with a dot of blood.

Aro sits back on his heels and Tai pushes up on his elbows. "If that didn't summon your battleform, I don't know what will."

"Maybe I'm just used to you fighting dirty," Aro says and wipes away more blood from his face.

Every time they say "battleform," all I hear is "mate." The word is on repeat in my head, like a song that won't stop. It still feels foreign on my lips. It'll take me a while to fully grasp what is happening. Aro made some really good points. We are opposites in so many ways, in ways that actually complement each other. Logically it doesn't make any sense. And that's what I'm struggling with. How can this scientifically even be possible? Science and the natural world rely on a foundation of order.

There are natural laws, laws that throughout time have never been broken. I don't know how being Aro's mate fits in with that cosmic order.

How do you take a human and a Tilak and pair them up forever? How does that even work? How will it work when I go back to Earth?

They've been trying to trigger Aro's battleform for hours. He struggled on his own for a while, then Tai jumped in to see if he could help. The tension was high when they first began wrestling on the mats. There seems to be more going on than just bringing out Aro's new ability. It looks like they are finally clearing the air from before. I feel a twinge of guilt, knowing I've made things more complicated for Aro.

I remind myself a few times that they wouldn't knowingly hurt each other, especially when Tai gets Aro in a headlock and his blue skin goes pale. That knot in my stomach refuses to follow directions. It won't go away no matter what I tell myself.

Bri on the other hand loves it. She's especially happy when Aro knocks Tai to the ground. I'm impressed at her ability to hold a grudge. I don't think he'll ever be able to redeem himself in her eyes. Tai has grown on me. His grumpy attitude isn't directed at anyone in particular, and I appreciate someone who doesn't pretend to be something they're not.

It's a while before Aro and Tai slow down. The deliberate stances and footwork from earlier is gone. And still nothing. Aro's frustration is evident from all the way over here.

I jump down from my spot and walk over a canteen of water and a towel when they stop for a break. Aro gratefully accepts and flashes an apologetic smile.

"I'm sorry this has taken so long."

"It's okay. It makes sense that this is something you'd need to figure out how to control."

"This is a hard seed to break," Aro says.

"You messed that up on purpose… You know it's 'tough nut to crack.'" I admitted to him a while ago that it's cute when he messes up the idioms, and now he does it on purpose to get a smile out of me. Aro tosses his sweaty towel at me, and I swat it away before it can hit my face. His grin turns my insides to mush.

"Maybe if this arrogant bastard had to work for something in his life he would know discipline," Tai jokes and grabs the canteen from Aro.

"Maybe if you hit the weight room a little harder, I'd have to actually defend myself." Aro snatches the canteen with a glint in his eye and downs the rest of the water.

"Are you saying I should stop pulling my punches?"

I can see that they're winding each other up again, and I'm over it. I want to go check on Andi and see how she's doing.

"I'm going to head out. You don't need me cringing from the sidelines every time someone lands a punch," I say.

Aro leans down and kisses me lightly. I can taste the salty sweat on his face. Surprisingly, I don't hate it.

"I'll come find you when I'm done."

"I'm going to go check on Andi," I tell Bri.

"Tell her I said hi. I'm going to stay here until someone loses consciousness," she says and laughs sadistically as the two Tilaks go back to the mats.

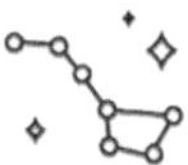

I grab my yuriOS and prop it up on the desk in our room. I link to Andi and a holographic image of her sitting up in her hospital bed projects in the room with me.

"You're looking good!" I say.

"Thanks. I feel great."

"Have they said when you can be released?"

"Not yet. They want to do some more tests. We're still waiting to see how my immune system reacts to the treatment. I'm the first human they have ever seen, so they aren't in a rush to discharge me."

"As long as they're treating you well. Think of it as an extended stay at a spa!" My suggestion gets a laugh out of her.

"I've been meaning to ask—have you heard from the EGA lately?" she asks.

"No, I haven't."

"I hadn't either until yesterday. I tried to pull up my files and the folder required a passkey for access. I reached out to the EGA and they said that they had taken possession of their 'intellectual property.'"

"That's weird." I scroll through my yuriOS to locate the files. Sure enough, a passkey is required to access my research and notes. "This can't be right. There must be some mistake."

"They were very clear that all our research is theirs and we don't have access to it anymore," Andi says.

"We're going to need that data when we get back to Earth." I continue swiping through, trying to find a way into my files.

"I'll work on getting our access back. I might know some people who can help."

I smile. I have faith she'll be able to work her connections and get us access again. This is just a misunderstanding. We were the ones that did the research. They need us.

Now that I have a few minutes to myself, I have a chance to do some other research. I want to know all the information out there about mating bonds. The biological reasons are indisputable, but the emotional or spiritual explanations aren't as conclusive.

Aro's words from days ago echo in my mind: *The universal truth that there is something beyond science, something that we don't fully understand but we feel it in our bones.* I don't know if I believe in a higher force, but I do believe in balance.

I find hundreds of stories from across the universe. I pore through each one. Some people feel complete once they accept their mate. Others say it's like finding another who shares the same soul or spirit. One culture believes mates were born from the same star. The answer is here, somewhere. I've always looked to nature for the answers. There is a purpose for everything.

I feel myself slip into a comfortable habit of "refute first, understand after." Look at things with the most objective lens possible with critical thinking and a healthy dose of skepticism at the forefront. It's what has gotten me here. I pause and repeat that same thought over in my head. *It's what has gotten me here.*

I've worked my ass off to get here professionally. I've distracted myself from feeling like an outsider by planning and plotting for the future. And I'm utterly alone. These skills have served me in one aspect of my life and nearly destroyed another.

Maybe I've returned to nature for all the answers because I'm searching for something deeper, under the surface—the roots that hold everything together.

48

Aro

The hologram lights up, projecting my father's council chambers into the briefing room. My father and his advisors flicker into view last.

"We want to congratulate you. This is a momentous occasion for our people. j'Tilak has spoken and blessed you with this power. Our world will regain balance in the face of this threat." It's difficult to tell who was speaking from the holo, but I know that voice.

It's none other than Reynauld Custos. I recognize his voice from our last meeting. He's an interesting one. His allegiances don't seem to fall to one side or another. He slithers back and forth, never making his own feelings clear. His compliment is met with skepticism.

"Thank you." I keep my remarks as brief as possible, I just want to get this over with.

"We believe it's only a matter of time before more attain battle-form. We will rely on your experience to guide us through this new era," another adds. I don't recognize the voice this time.

"All in service of j'Tilak." I give them the most bland reply I can without showing disrespect.

"Your power is an opportunity for us all. We hope that you can help us address a growing issue. We have not been satisfied with Earth's response to the Atorum threat," Syntra says. I recognize him right away as one who sides with my father.

"They have been noncommittal when we ask them about military support," Yoff says, another one who's on our side.

"We ask that you speak with the human delegation, explain to them your newfound ability, and make a few vague offers to use it for their benefit," Council member Besnik says. Besnik seems to have a good sense of strategy. I'm surprised they would come to me. I wasn't involved in the negotiations for the Apollo Treaty. I can't imagine my influence would help here.

My father has been silent this entire time. He's thoughtfully watching how I respond to their questions, not giving away his own opinions on the matter. I'm starting to understand his diplomatic approach, the way listening and watching can be just as powerful as speaking.

"It might make them friendlier to our cause if they believe you would use your battleform to their benefit," another adds before I can respond.

"Have they not honored their side of the treaty?" I ask.

"Unfortunately, there is some 'gray area.' A human concept that means they can interpret the language to their own benefit," Custos says. I don't think it's possible for anyone to sound slimier than him. Or maybe it's the bitter look on his face when he smiles. Regardless, I don't trust him.

"You're in a unique position to negotiate with our new allies. If you demonstrate your power for them, we believe they will come back to our aid," Besnik adds.

"May we ask who the honored female is that you have recognized as your mate?" Custos asks. "We assume that is the case since battleforms are triggered by matehood."

"You may not." My father finally steps in with authority. He cuts this line of questioning off, saving me from having to tell them about my human mate. Something that makes this situation even more complicated. I'm glad for more time before this gets out to the public.

The council's request has merit, but it's a flawed plan. The biggest flaw is: I can't shift into battleform at will. The unpredictability of my new ability is a problem. Until I can figure out a way to control this power, it's a hard no. My priority is simply my mate, and I won't risk putting her in the middle of this mess.

I take a minute and think about how the old Aro would tell them all to fuck off. A lot has changed in the last few months. Now I have to consider the impact my words could have. Despite what I want, I have attained battleform—and I don't know if I can control it. Or if it will ever happen again. I need a little more time to figure this out.

"I'll consider your request." I close the link and the hologram fades to nothing.

49

Elowen

The sound of a distant siren rouses me from sleep. I pull my pillow over my head to block out the sound. I feel Aro slip from the bed. Before I can register what's happening he's up and getting dressed.

"What's going on?" I ask drowsily, rubbing my eyes to wake up.

"Attack." He pulls on his pants then grabs for the nearest shirt.

I hurry to get dressed, putting on whatever is within arm's reach. Even though I technically have my own bunk, I've spent every night with Aro in his room. As captain, his quarters are an upgrade from my assigned sleeping space.

I follow him out of the room with my boots still untied and we step into pandemonium. Tilak soldiers are running in every direction. Getting dressed and arming themselves at the weapon caches throughout the base. I spot Bri standing in the center of the mayhem, not sure what to do with herself.

Aro goes straight to the command center to find out what is going on. He holds the door for me, and I slip in behind him into the dark room. A map is lit up at the front of the room. A bright orange spot on a neighboring continent identifies the location of the attack. A narrow stretch of water separates the two land masses.

"Atorum have attacked Tauros. The city is under siege. We've activated our forces to draw the fight away from the civilians," Rialto says once everyone is present.

"Departure time, 0630," Petrok announces. The map disappears and the room lights up. Everyone moves at once, going in every direction to prepare to leave.

"You'll be okay here," he says.

"No heroics. Just come back safe." It's as close as I can get to an order with him.

"I'll be back before you know it."

He leads me outside and turns sharply, pulling me into the dark alley between buildings. I'm against the wall as he steps up to me. He brackets my head with his forearm and leans in.

"I tried to tell you before—and now is the absolute worst time, but I can't leave without telling you—I love you. I felt this pull to you from the start, but the more I got to know you, how smart and funny and caring you are—how passionate you are about your work—that's when I knew that I loved you," he says looking down at me, watching my response. He pulls away slowly and puts a finger on my lips.

"Don't say anything. Whatever it is you want to say, tell me when I get back." He kisses my slack lips of surprise and steps away, leaving me against the wall, heart pounding and trying to catch my breath. I touch my fingers to my lips where he just imprinted himself on me. My heart bangs away and my stomach is tied in knots.

This must be what it feels like to be loved.

I peel myself off the wall and step back into the light. In those few moments the base emptied out. It's eerily quiet where a few moments ago it had been roaring with noise and activity. I stumble along on autopilot. So many thoughts run through my mind, making it impossible to focus and think things through.

I find Bri sitting on her bunk in the dormitory. We sit cross-legged and face each other, neither one of us saying a word. Our minds are catching up with the frantic morning.

"Aro told me he loves me." I break the silence. I have no idea how she's going to respond, she might be the most unpredictable person I know.

Bri quirks an eyebrow and I brace for the myriad of reactions that could come.

She reaches over and grabs my hand. "I'm really happy for you. And it's about freaking time!" she says and smiles.

"Am I the last to know?" I laugh a little, relieved.

"It's not like he's been trying to hide his feelings," she says.

"I don't know what it means for us long term. I don't think I can stay. I need to see this research all the way through. I can't just quit because I fell in love."

"You love him?" she leans forward, urging me to say more.

"I do. I'm not sure if that's enough though. I don't know how to make everyone happy." I've always been fine with sacrificing my own happiness, but things are more complicated now. If I stay, I'm not finishing the program I committed to. If I leave, I am leaving Aro behind. His happiness is at stake as well.

"You don't have to have all the answers," she says.

"I know. If I could have *some* answers, that would be enough."

"Love is awful. In all the stories love is happy. In reality, it's horrid. You feel sick to your stomach. You worry about everything. I don't know if everyone gets what they want in this situation. Maybe at some point you'll have to make a hard choice. But make sure you choose the one thing that you can't live without."

"Inspiring. You should write this down." I'm only partially joking. Bri is straightforward. Her words aren't soft, but they are honest.

"I'm not trying to make you feel better. I'm saying that you're normal. That these feelings are common. And other people manage to get through it and have a happy ending. You deserve that too."

"Maybe someday I can come back, after the research is done."

"You know it's not a failure if someone else on Earth finishes this. It doesn't diminish anything you did to get to this point." She sits back and watches the words land.

I take a deep breath in and think about it. I've been holding onto this narrow definition of success. I've used it as armor. Initially it kept me safe. Now it's keeping someone I love at arm's length.

50

Aro

The city's shield keeps the Atorum at bay for now, but it's only a matter of time before they breach the protective dome. Once inside, there isn't anything to stop the killing machines that are desperately trying to get in.

Our aeroglyde moves silently through the air and comes up behind the mass of swarming bugs. The plan is to maintain the element of surprise and once we are in position, it's open season on these bastards.

It will be a multi-layered assault. Porters will roll out first. They will lay down canon fire, clearing the way for my unit to come through on the ground.

I bounce back and forth between my feet, hyping myself up. I'm going to hit the ground and summon my battleform. Now's the time to put my stress theory to the test. I'm absolutely sure that once my feet hit the dirt, that power will pulse through my veins once again.

The aeroglyde rushes to the ground and lands silently. I activate my kinetic shield and jump down, feeling a rush of adrenaline coursing through me. I crack my neck and call for strength. A hum trickles through my body. The power is just dormant and needs summoning.

The porters come out blasting. Somewhere a piercing shriek draws the Atorums' attention to us. As one unit they all turn and advance on us.

This time, I throw my arms out with a roar, trying to call to that power deep inside. Still nothing. I don't have time to try again. One of the bugs lands right in front of me and turns its grotesque body in my direction. It knocks the blaster away before I can shoot. A cannon goes off behind the bug and it's incinerated right before my eyes. I look to see who saved my ass. Maak and I lock eyes before he turns the porter and continues blasting away. I grab the blaster and keep moving.

The plan is to divide the horde. Once they are split and we have a strong position, we'll crush them together, limiting their movement, and picking them off one by one.

I stalk forward, trying to gather any thread of power with each step. My boots squelch through thick black ooze already spreading on the ground. Straight ahead, an Atorum is on top of a porter smashing into the plexi. Its sharp feet try to break through the thick exterior. The porter spins and throws the Atorum off. I shoot it out of the air, its pieces rain down on the ground.

A shrill alarm goes off, bringing all the Tilaks to their knees. We cover our ears. The signal calls the Atorum off, and in a blink, they launch themselves off the ground and up into the air and out of sight.

I look around and don't see a single injured Tilak. Dead Atorum litter the ground around us. Smoke rises up from the dead ones that were hit with the plasma canon, coating everything with the smell of burnt hair. I pretend not to notice everyone watching me, probably wondering why I didn't shift into battleform.

Tai steps to my side and surveys the damage. "I was hoping to see that beast mode again."

"I wanted to give you boys the chance to kill some bugs too," I say and try to shake off the sickening feeling in my gut. I should have been able to summon it. Doubt creeps into my head. Could it have just been a one-time thing? At some point I'm going to have to explain this to everyone.

We work our way through the wreckage back to the glyder, double-checking all the carcasses on the ground. The zing of blasters goes off occasionally. Tai and I collapse on the long bench lining both sides of the hold. The air heavy with the question: why can't I attain battle-form again? Lost in thought I don't notice Maak until he's sitting next to me.

"You're welcome," he says about the Atorum he killed when I was briefly disarmed.

"I could've killed it."

"Not in that state," he says nodding at me. "What's up with that anyway?" he asks, referring to my lack of battleform.

"I honestly don't know. I thought I would be able to shift today. It just refused to come."

"It's obviously the human. Your mate was in danger before and it called to your battleform," he says.

"I hope you're wrong."

"For both of your sakes, I hope so too," he says.

"Do we need to clear the air about what happened before this all went to hell?" I ask him. We still haven't addressed him catching Elowen and I sneaking back into the dome.

"We're good. It all makes sense now," Maak says.

"In retrospect, it was a dumb thing to do. I shouldn't have taken her out of the muradome with everything else that's going on."

"Love makes people do dumb shit," he says and leaves it at that.

51

Elowen

I've been writing down everything I can remember from our research over the last few months. Everyone here on j'Tilak has been locked out of their files. It's not unusual that universities own intellectual property in situations like this. But, I have never heard of anyone ever being locked out of accessing it midway through a project.

I toss my yuriOS down and head outside for some sunlight and fresh air. I need to clear my head. Worries about the University and Aro cycle through my head. Even though the Atorum are only targeting humans, I don't like the idea of him having to fight them.

There is a tense calm at the base right now. Everyone left behind moves around quietly. We're all trying to be as silent as possible. Nothing bad would happen if I was made noise—it just feels wrong for some reason.

"There you are! We have been looking everywhere for you!" I hear a bright voice behind me and turn. Two tall, gorgeous, blue Tilak females approach me with broad smiles across their faces. The newcomers are unaware of the unspoken rule about being quiet.

"I'm Kiera, Aro's sister, and you're Elowen!" One wraps me tightly in a hug before I can even move, pinning my arms to my side while she squeezes me.

"Dear, let her go. You're going to smoosh her to death," the other says. "I'm Rameera, Aro's mom," she says kindly, taking my hands into hers. I open my mouth to formally introduce myself when Kiera starts up again.

"When we heard what happened at the muradome we had to come and meet you for ourselves," Kiera says. She looks me up and down in a friendly way. Trying to size me up.

"It's good to meet you," I tell them. "Aro isn't here though. The Atorum attacked Tauros."

"We aren't here for him. We're here for you!" Rameera clarifies.

"For me?"

"I've always wanted a sister. Now that you're Aro's mate, I have one!" Kiera says enthusiastically. I don't know how I expected his family to respond to the mate thing, but this isn't it. She doesn't seem concerned at all that I am a total stranger and human.

There is a strong family resemblance here. Kiera's beautiful eyes match her brother's, and a smile that they clearly got from their mom is permanently etched on her face. Beyond the physical characteristics, Kiera and Aro share the same intense confidence. I feel like I got swept up in a tornado and am holding on for dear life.

"There is plenty of time for that. Let's relax in our quonset. We'll keep you company until Aro gets back," Rameera says, directing us back to the main section of the base.

Someone constructed a small metal building during my walk. Rameera strides in the front door and waves me in behind her. Comfortable cushions line the edge of the open space. A few low tables are scattered throughout. One table is piled high with a variety of food.

"Where did all of this come from?" I ask, astonished that this all showed up so quickly.

"One of the benefits of being a noble house," Kiera says and pops some small berry-looking fruit into her mouth.

Rameera motions for me to sit down at one of the tables. She's tinkering around in the makeshift kitchen when a familiar smell wafts through the tent. She's making coffee. Actual coffee. My mouth starts to water. She hands me a steaming cup and I could cry from joy.

"I'm so happy to finally meet you. Aro has been very scant with any details. We decided to take matters into our own hands when Aro neglected to extend an invitation." Rameera has the same gravity around her that draws me in. It's gentler than Aro and Kiera's, but it's there. Instead of a tornado, it feels more like the soothing sounds of rain on a metal roof.

"Please, consider yourself welcome anytime, especially if you bring coffee with you," I tell both of them. I take a long, slow sip of the coffee, savoring the first taste. I settle back into my cushion and keep the mug close.

"Now that we have you all to ourselves, how much has Aro explained about matehood?" Rameera asks.

"If I know my brother, not much," Kiera says, a smile tugging at the corners of her lips. They both look at me with interest. I suck in long breath, trying to decide what to say.

"Just the basics."

"Things are done very differently here than the rest of the universe. So, I understand if it takes you a while. I remember being scared about being with Roman because of his title. I came from a little town and always felt like an outsider with all the glamorous and intelligent people surrounding him."

"Yes, that is a big part of it. I don't know anything about Aro's role and what that means for us."

"Our familial line has been a noble house since the last Tilak shifted into battleform. When Roman is ready to step down, Aro will take his place."

I try to picture what Aro would be like ruling an entire country. The image makes me smile. He will be a great leader.

"And you'd be right there next to him," she says. I'm not bothered by her presumption. It feels more like unwavering confidence.

"Even though I'm a human?" I ask.

"I can tell you that allowing outsiders to come for the first time was a controversial decision. There were those who have advocated for it for decades, and those who would stop at nothing to stay isolated. Roman took a very big risk to allow the EGA to establish research centers here. It's time we join the rest of the cosmos and some beautiful multi-species babies would do just the trick. You're Aro's mate, and the reason he was able to summon his battleform. With time, you will be celebrated," Rameera says with a wink in my direction.

"Ugh." Kiera rolls her eyes at her mom's mention of babies. It reminds me of my mom's gentle prodding about my past relationships. I can already tell they will be two peas in a pod.

"Leaders on Earth hardly have any privacy," I tell them. I pick absently at the cushion I hold in my lap.

This time Kiera responds. "You'll get some of that here as well."

"We tried to give you two a normal childhood. I know it bothered you more than Aro. He's so unfazed by most things. And you coped with your beautiful rebellious spirit." Rameera puts an arm around her daughter's shoulders.

"Every job comes with its drawbacks. We all pay a price in some way. This job happens to come with the privilege to serve our people." Rameera's devotion to pt'Clanik is admirable.

"There is some freedom within the job as well. I've always loved traveling and seeing other cultures and ways of life. I act as an ambassador. Since you're a biologist, I imagine you could spend your time on… biologist stuff," Kiera offers up in the most endearing way. Another thing she has in common with her brother.

"Aro has told me a little about how delicate this ecosystem is. From the moment I stepped outside of the muradome, I immediately knew I would do anything for this world. To be in a position to actually do that is beyond my wildest dreams."

"Elowen, you would be able to do something no one else has ever done. You could be the one person to show that outsiders could love and protect j'Tilak just as much as we do," Rameera says.

I can tell they're trying to put all my worries to rest. Their support means a lot to me. Although I miss Aro and can't wait for him to get back, I'm glad to have this time with his mom and sister.

"Okay, Mom—I think we've said enough. She's going to feel like we are giving her the hard sell," Kiera says.

I hold onto the warm mug like an anchor.

52

Elowen

"Come check this out." Kiera invites me over with a pat on the seat next to her. I sit down next to her, the three of us huddled together as Kiera flips through images on a yuriOS.

"Look! Heto!" Kiera exclaims when she comes to a picture of a white, fluffy animal. It's her, as a child, standing next to a waist-high rabbit with floppy ears. "I loved him so much!" She gushes over the image of her pet.

"That thing was a menace. It left droppings all over the house that your father would always seem to step in." Rameera sounds less nostalgic about the animal.

"He's cute," I tell Kiera.

She flips through a few pictures of Aro and Kiera smiling brightly with their arms around each other, posing in front of a beautiful home surrounded by tall trees. The farther she swipes, the younger everyone appears. She pauses her scanning on a picture of Aro as a young teenager, tall and gangly. "Has he told you how I used to beat him up?" Kiera asks.

"Actually, he has. Although I didn't fully believe him until now." I snicker at the image. "He told me it took an entire battalion to teach him how to defend himself." I peek over at Kiera. She looks proud of herself.

"He was such a softy he would always let me take the upper hand, even though he was always bigger and stronger than me," Kiera says.

"Aro has always been our bright light. That's what his name means and it's suited him from the day he was born." Rameera has a soft far-away look in her eyes.

"And Kiera means dark one. I've been proud to carry that mantle from the day I was born."

"My parents named me Elowen after a type of tree back on Earth. Not as eloquent as 'light and dark one,'" I tell them.

"I was quite captivated by the little trees on Earth. They were so cute and dainty." Rameera always has a nice comment about Earth on hand. I can tell she is making an effort to connect with me. She is just being kind. There is no comparison between Earth and j'Tilak. This place is superior in every possible way.

"What is light without the darkness? As a child, Kiera was always ferocious about any perceived injustice. Especially toward Aro. One year, Aro came home to visit during his basic training. During his absence Kiera had grown up and Aro became the ferocious one. Aro glared at anyone she brought home. He was utterly intimidating."

"Remember that time I didn't speak to Dad for 3EMs because he was mean to Aro?" Kiera laughs at the memory.

"You were so determined to give him the silent treatment. I thought you'd never forgive him," Rameera adds.

"There was only one time that my father raised his voice at Aro, and I would still be holding the grudge if Aro didn't tell me to drop it," Kiera tells me.

I suspect I already know the origins of this story. That moment when his father accused him of avoiding his responsibilities stuck with him. A new understanding of that story hits me. It was a king urging a prince to grow up. My heart breaks a tiny bit for that young lanky kid with a smile too big for his face. He's got a tough outer shell, but the more I get to know him, the more I see how deeply he feels things.

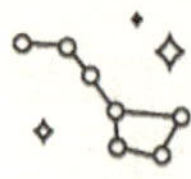

"Look who finally showed up!" Aro says as he steps off the aeroglyder.

"I'm not here for you. I thought we should ignore your desperate attempt at getting attention," Kiera says back to Aro.

"I hope they haven't scared you off," he says and pulls me into his side.

"How did it go out there?" I ask.

"Tauros is safe. We were able to get there in time," he says without going into detail.

"Were you able to…" I trail off, not wanting to say the words in front of everyone. He has been so private about his struggle to summon his battleform.

"No. We can talk about that later," he says and kisses the top of my head as we walk to the barracks.

53

Elowen

"Aro, get your ass out of bed."

I jerk awake to the sound of yelling and banging on the door. I sit straight up and look around trying to figure out where all the noise is coming from.

"I'm up, I'm up. Fuck." Aro rubs his eyes and eases me back down to the bed. Making no effort to actually get up.

"I hate morning people," I tell him.

"You grumbled when I woke you up, and I made it quite pleasant. Kiera has a much different approach." Aro sighs and pulls me closer.

"I'm scared to see what happens next if we don't get up," I say.

Aro tightly holds our sheets in place. "You can't give in to her demands. If she catches a hint of weakness, it's over. I'll keep you safe."

His face is inches away and I can't resist kissing him. His sleepy eyes are incredibly sexy. His hair is tousled, and he's warm and inviting. I tug on his lower lip to open his mouth, deepening the kiss. Aro rolls on top of me, pinning me to the bed. He drags his hand up the top of my thigh under my shirt. He grabs my breast and grinds his hips into me. His hard cock pushes between my legs with only his sweatpants between us. I'm pulling at his waistband when I hear Kiera at the door again.

"Aro, if you aren't in the gym in three minutes I will hack my way through the door and drag you out," Kiera yells against the closed door and kicks it before she turns and walks back down the hallway.

"Kiera is about to learn a very important lesson about respecting others' privacy." Aro grinds into me again undeterred.

"Let's get up. I'd like to be wearing pants the second time I see your sister." This time I'm successful in my attempt to get out of bed. Aro watches me as I pull on my clothes.

"I'm really getting tired of all of these interruptions," he says bitterly and swings his legs onto the floor.

"Twice. It's happened twice," I say and pull my hair back into a high ponytail and laugh.

"Two times too many."

Pouting Aro is cute.

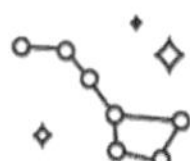

"There is a really easy way we can test that theory," I say. Kiera, Bri, Tai, and I have all been in the gym for hours while Aro tries to summon his battleform.

"No, absolutely not. I'm not doing anything that puts you in danger, just so I can test my ability," Aro says.

"It's not a bad idea. The more you shift, the easier it will be," Kiera says, unintimidated by her brother's glare.

"It's a terrible idea," he says.

"Tai could take me out. We'll hide out in the forest for a bit, and you can come find us." Kiera and I seem to be the only ones who like this plan. Everyone else avoids eye contact with me when I look for support.

"I said no." Aro seethes. His voice echoes through the empty gym.

"I'm also invested in helping you figure this out," I say stepping up to him.

I give him my best power pose—my "you aren't the only badass around here" hands-on-my-hips stance.

His eyes darken. Oh shit—this backfired. He doesn't look mad anymore. He's turned on, and he's looking at me with different intentions now. This conversation is heading in one direction. One that won't resolve the issue at hand.

Tai, Bri and Kiera slink away into the background as the tension rises between Aro and I. They pretend to be focused on something out of the way.

"You know it's more than that. It's not safe out there," he says pointing to beyond the base walls.

"Tai can take care of me. Or he won't and you can come save the day. Be the knight in shining armor and swoop in."

I return the smolder and walk my fingers up his chest and stretch up to kiss the underside of his jaw.

He grinds his teeth together and huffs out a breath. I scoot closer to him, bringing our bodies together.

"You play dirty," he says, finally looking down at me.

"This is important." My breath hitches when he leans down and runs his hands down my backside.

"Nothing is more important than your safety. The answer is still no," he says with a cocked eyebrow. I sway on my feet when he steps back, putting distance between us again.

"What's your brilliant plan then, since you won't try my idea?" I say, not giving up.

"I'll keep trying here with Tai."

"It's not working. You're wasting time. There could be another attack any minute," I plead.

"I'll think about it."

I squeak with happiness and jump up to him, hooking my legs around his waist.

"It's not a yes," he says, clarifying.

"It's not a no either," I say and kiss him.

"I'll think of another way. I just don't want to argue with you anymore."

I get down from him and stand up pressed against him. "You left before I could tell you something yesterday."

"What did you want to say?" he asks quietly, his voice thick.

"I love you, too."

"You can't just say that because I let you win an argument," he says. That lighthearted, arrogant Aro is back for a moment. I realize how much I missed that part of him since the world fell apart.

"I do—I love you. Thank you for giving me some time to figure out the mate thing. I needed a little time to sort that out. I did some research."

"I wouldn't expect anything less," Aro says with a smile.

"And I want you to know that if there were anyone in the entire universe I would want to be my mate, it would be you. You are everything. You are loyal, and kind, and funny, and you are always thinking of how you can solve everyone else's problems. You listen and you make me feel seen. You are always saying how incredible I am, but you need to know how incredible you are." I watch a smile stretch across his face.

"It's about time. I've been waiting for you to finally realize it. I'm glad you're catching up," he says. He scoops me up into a hug and spins us around.

"Be quiet and kiss me, you arrogant ass."

54

Aro

"Where the fuck is she?" I bellow at Bri from across the mess hall. Every head in the room whips toward me. She's sitting alone holding a coffee cup and slowly stands and starts walking towards me.

I need to find my mate, right now.

"I don't know," she says. She tamps down her hands and looks around the room to see who's watching. Everyone else has gone back to what they were doing to avoid getting caught in the crossfire.

Elowen wasn't in our room when I went to get her for dinner and she's not with Bri.

"You tell me right now if she left the base." My throat constricts.

"I don't know where she is. I was also looking for her a while ago." I can't tell if Bri sounds concerned because of my reaction or for Elowen's safety.

"Is she with Kiera?" I ask.

"How would I know?"

I level her with a look. If Elowen was planning something, Bri would definitely know about it.

"I haven't seen either of them," she says.

I stomp away before I say something I'll regret later. My feet carry me to transpo and an empty charging deck. All I know is blood pounding in my ears and rage.

My surroundings blur. I hear a distant roar and feel a burn in my throat.

Metal buckles under my fists and I'm running through the field outside the base. I toss a porter aside like a child's toy as I gain speed. It sails through the air and smashes into a tree, sending broken glass and splintered wood into the air.

Brush scrapes against my legs and snags on my ripped clothes. Sturdy branches bend and snap as I rush through them with unwavering focus. A sick satisfaction courses through my veins at the sight of the destruction in my wake.

I smash through trees and rocks trying to find her. I am so angry that they went through with this plan, after I specifically said no.

I stop in my tracks and take in a deep hard breath, searching for Elowen's familiar smell. Real panic hits my veins when I don't pick up her scent. I look for signs of Atorum instead. This can't be happening. She has to be here somewhere.

1807 Incoming message from Elowen Carson

Elowen: I'm okay. Come back to the barracks when you're ready.

Anger and relief slowly spread across me. I look down at my unfamiliar hands. My shredded clothes hang loose from my body. My breathing is loud and hoarse. I turn back to the base and retrace my path of destruction. My oversized footprints deep in the dirt. A crew is already repairing the gate I burst through in my rage to find my mate. My nostrils flare when I pick up her scent.

She's waiting for me in our room.

"Aro, just listen for a minute, please," she says pacing back and forth.

Even though I shifted back, I can still feel the thrum of power through my body. "Explain," I say and clench my jaw.

"You didn't want me to be in danger. And I've been completely safe this whole time."

"You tricked me into thinking you'd left." I finished for her.

"I did. I wanted to know if you would shift by thinking I was in danger. That you could somehow figure out how to summon the change, from a perceived threat." She takes a step towards me. "I'm sorry I scared you. I didn't see any other way." Another step closer.

Even though I am angry, each step she takes brings my heart rate down. My breathing slows and my head clears.

"Where's Kiera? I'm going to kill her," I say.

"Leave her out of it. This is between you and me," she says another step closer, now standing within arm's length. But I don't reach out to her.

A breath rattles in my chest. "Are you afraid of me now?" I ask. I didn't realize until now that I was worried that my battleform would change the way she looked at me.

"Never. I know you would never hurt me, in any form," she says and moves closer, bringing her body up against mine. Showing me that she isn't scared to be close to me.

"I never want to see fear in your eyes when you look at me."

"You won't," she reassures me.

"Don't do that again. We make these decisions together."

"I have something important that you need to hear," she says.

My jaw ticks, preparing to hear something I won't like.

"Your battleform is really hot." She puts my hands on her hips and arches against me. I can't resist the urge to flex a little when she touches my arms. The look in her eyes melts away any lingering anger.

She pulls the torn shirt from my shoulders and lets it fall. She twists our bodies around and closes the door behind her without taking her eyes off me.

She pulls my loose-hanging pants down from my hips. My cock got hard the moment she looked at me with those eyes. I reach up and grab her thick hair in my fist and pull her head up to meet my gaze. Her soft gasp makes my cock twitch.

"You're still in trouble," I say against her lips before I roughly take her mouth with mine.

"I know," she says and shudders against me when I drag my teeth down her throat. I pull at the snaps on her coveralls, exposing her soft creamy skin. I rip the two sides apart and her clothes fall into a pile at her feet.

"You owe me a new pair of coveralls," she says and bites at my lower lip.

I rip away her underwear next. "And underwear!" she shrieks. "It's hard to find clothes in my size." I smack her ass with a loud crack. A red mark appears—and it's fucked up how hard that makes me.

"You can borrow my shirts." I sit on the edge of the bed and pull her down to straddle me. She arches her body, and I see stars.

"You don't want me running around the base in just your shirt," she says and grinds harder.

"Why are you still talking?" I ask before biting down softly on her nipple that she shoved in my face. She gasps. I chuckle at my ability to make her lose words.

I scoot us back and lay flat on my back. She shifts up and slowly lowers herself onto my dick. She is so wet I slide into her and sigh as she takes all of me. She whimpers softly when she reaches the bottom.

I grab her hips and lift her back up. She nearly comes off of me before I slam her back down. She meets every thrust. I could die a happy Tilak watching her bounce up and down on my cock. My fingers dent into her soft rounded hips when I lift her up.

Her head is thrown back, exposing her long neck. I reach up and grasp her throat gently, feeling the tight cords of her neck flex.

She leans forward and uses my chest for leverage. I reach down and position my thumb at her clit. Every time she drops down, she drags my thumb through her, pushing on that sensitive place. She speeds up. When she comes, she takes me with her.

Our legs are tangled together. Everything feels right in the world with her next to me.

"You make me feel like I've discovered something that I never knew existed," I tell her. "And now that I know it…"

"There is no unknowing it," she finishes for me.

55

Aro

"The attack on Tauros is a major escalation. We have notified our new allies and we expect Earth will be activating their forces. Today we prepare for their imminent arrival," Rialto announces, kicking off our briefing with news we've all been expecting.

"Today, Aro will be leading you through the process of integrating their forces with our own," Petrok says.

"Aro, the floor is yours."

"When the human forces get here, I'm going to need you all to be focused and on your best behavior. I know you aren't used to it, so start practicing now. There is no ETA, but we expect an announcement anytime. We want to be prepared. This is an important transition. We need to establish jurisdiction immediately. The last thing we want is a bunch of humans showing up thinking they are in charge."

"You already fucked that up. We already know Elowen owns your ass," Viktor says from the back of the room. A few snicker at the comment.

"For your sake, I hope you fuck better than you talk trash." The room turns their laughter toward Viktor.

"Your mom wasn't complaining last night." Everyone's in hysterics at Viktor's comeback.

218

"We're calling the shots. We have a strong presence on the ground. We anticipate they will be providing a wide cover outside the atmosphere. This way we have a wide band of safety should any more Atorum show up to pick a fight," Tai jumps in, trying to keep us all in line.

"All coordination will go through central command. This is an evolving situation. I ask that you all show flexibility as we navigate this new relationship."

"I heard someone was flexible in the shower the other day!" Bennet jumps into the fray.

"That's all you got—after such a nice and easy setup?" I say.

"You know who else is nice and easy?" Bennet shouts.

"Bennet, I'm surprised you can even talk. You look like you stuck your dick in a light socket with that haircut. I might be easy, but all you fuckers know I'm not nice." Before Bennet can respond, Tai steps up and nudges me away from the podium. I take the hint and rein it in.

"Tai's going to walk you all through the comms protocols." I hand the podium over to Tai. He brings up the new chain of command, showing how we're going to work with our new allies.

Petrok pops his head through the door and waves me over. I follow him into Rialto's office. He closes the door securely and nods to Rialto.

"We heard from Earth," Petrok says somberly.

"They aren't coming," Rialto says.

56

Elowen

"They aren't coming," Aro says.

My mind goes blank. That can't be right. I drop down onto our bed, trying to make sense of what Aro just told me.

"I don't understand. The treaty says…" My voice trails off while I try to figure out why Earth wouldn't be coming to support j'Tilak.

"They made it clear they have what they need from us, and they have honored their side of the treaty by temporarily being on standby following the initial attack," Aro explains. Pacing around the room, he shoves his hair back out of his face.

"It's just a matter of time before the Atorum attack again."

"The noble houses are still trying to negotiate the terms. Apparently some language in the treaty is vague."

"And we're just supposed to sit and wait until there's another attack?"

"It's not looking good. We've decided to begin evacuations."

"What can we do? Can I convince them to come? They might listen to me," I offer.

"My father's advisors asked me to appeal to Earth. To see if my new ability would be enough to get them to act," Aro says.

"That sounds like a bad idea. It's still too unpredictable."

"I'd be putting myself in the middle of this mess. I don't want to be used as a tool for either planet. It also has the risk of getting you involved," he says quietly.

"You think they would use me to get to you?" I ask. He sits down next to me on the bed.

"That's exactly what I think. They wouldn't hesitate to put you in danger if it meant I summoned my battleform." I can hear the stress in his voice. I take some of the blame for this. In a way, Aro is having to choose between me and doing everything possible to help his people.

Wait—it's not my fault. It's not Aro's fault. It's the EGA that has put us in this impossible situation. If they would do what's right and honor the treaty, we wouldn't be in this situation.

There is a sour taste of betrayal in my mouth. I came here for the good of humanity, and this is how they say "thank you." The thought of returning to Earth makes me sick to my stomach.

"We'll figure it out," I tell him and climb into his lap, wrapping my arms around his broad back.

"You know that I'll do anything to protect you," he says against my hair, holding me to him.

"I will too," I say and rest my head against his hard chest.

57

Aro

"We finalized evacuation plans. The shuttle will be ready in two days." Tai's words feel like a stab in the gut. He waited to drop this news until most of the fight was worked out of me.

"We're running out of time," Tai says reluctantly.

We've been training for hours. I haven't been focused, but he has taken it easy on me. He's stopped himself when he could have taken me down, more than once.

I'm resentful that after everything Elowen and I have been through, she's being ripped away from me. I still haven't given up hope that there is some way to keep Elowen here. The thought of being away from her feels like I've cut off a part of my own body.

We sit between bouts, both of us dripping in sweat. My yuriOS lights up with a link request. I slide my finger towards my palm and a holographic image of my father appears, hovering over my upturned wrist.

"Is your base prepared for the evacuations?" he asks.

"Yes. Everything is ready."

"Are you ready to—" I stop him from finishing that sentence. I don't even want to hear the words.

"No. I'm going to ask Elowen to stay. She will be safe here at the base until we have some answers about who is behind this." I know I sound like a petulant child, but I can't let her go. We belong together.

"Aro, you can't keep her locked up here. It's not fair to her," he says with care.

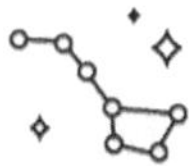

I'm tired. Tai and I trained until the early hours of the morning. When I finally climb into bed next to Elowen, I can't sleep. I lie listening to her soft breathing while my mind continues to race. It feels like I'm getting farther from being able to summon my new ability.

<h1 style="text-align:center">58</h1>

Elowen

"I'm not leaving," Bri announces as she strides into my room.

"Is that an option?" I ask. She and I are scheduled to be on the shuttle tomorrow. The notice we received didn't look voluntary. I've been dragging myself around today, not letting myself dwell on what is going to happen tomorrow.

"I don't care. I'm staying. Fuck Earth. I can't believe they would turn their backs on this place. I'm not going." She says what I've been thinking for the last few days. The idea of returning to Earth makes me sick. It seems our research is enough, and my presence isn't as essential as I had believed. Even if they did need me, I'd loathe myself for the rest of my life if I went back and abandoned j'Tilak and Aro. Especially Aro.

I've been playing out a scenario in my head where I leave temporarily, then figure out a way back once it's safe. If we all leave, the Atorum will cease their attacks, but we'll never know who is responsible. Another small idea I've been toying with in my head keeps cropping back up. I shove it back down. There are about a million different reasons why it's a bad idea.

"What are you going to do? Hide in the bathroom when it's time to leave?" I ask.

"Something like that," she says.

"Evacuating doesn't mean you have to return to Earth. Just hang out on some random planet for a while. Then you can come back," I suggest, hinting at what I've been mulling over.

"They will never let us back if we leave. Humans are public enemy number one now. If we leave, it's forever," she says plainly.

My stomach drops. She's right. Why would they let us come back? We will be shipped off to Earth, regardless of what we want. I've been waiting to tell Aro my plan. I've changed my mind about wanting to go to Earth. I go back to another tiny little seed of an idea, the one that I've been brushing off and refusing to consider.

Aro walks in the room with a smile that doesn't reach his eyes. Something is up, and I don't think I'm going to like it.

Bri excuses herself. She can also tell that something is happening, and she doesn't want to stick around for it. I wish I could hide as well. I sense bad news coming, and I don't think I can take any more.

"I'm finally ready to face reality. This entire time, with you and me—you've been telling me that you'll be returning to Earth. I'm finally ready to accept it," he says gravely.

"Aro, I want to stay." I force the words past the lump in my throat.

"Elowen, you're needed back on Earth. Your research is too important," he continues, hardly looking at me.

"They don't need me. They cut me off from my research. They've tossed me aside."

"They do need you. And I need you to be safe. So, I want you to leave tomorrow," he says. He finally drags his eyes over to mine. It feels like my chest has been ripped open. He's been unwavering in wanting me to stay. Until now.

"If I stay, you can shift into battleform. You can end this," I say.

"No," he says.

"If I leave you won't be able to shift. The Atorum will leave if there aren't any humans here. You'll never find out who was behind all this," I say, trying to get through to him.

"Then that's the risk I take. Because I refuse to put you in danger. I want you to leave," he says, unaffected by my begging.

"Aro, no. I love you. I'm not going to leave," I say, resolute in my decision.

"You don't have a choice. You will be on that shuttle tomorrow morning."

Tears pool in my eyes. "Aro, please don't make me go. I can help. This is my place, here with you." A single giant tear escapes my eyes and drips down my face.

"This isn't your world. You belong on Earth," he says, his voice cold and hard.

"That's bullshit and you know it," I say, not wanting to believe him.

"The shuttle leaves tomorrow at 0600, and if you aren't on it, I will personally load you onto a transport and send you back to Earth." He stands up and walks out of the room without a backward look in my direction.

I lie on our bed all night, numb and waiting for Aro to return. He doesn't. By morning I'm desperate and grab my yuriOS.

Outgoing message from Elowen Carson
Elowen: I need your help.

59

Aro

The ground vibrates as the engines roar to life. I look up from the central command systems and watch the lander slowly rise up from the ground and hover for a minute while the landing gear retracts.

I hate myself right now. I am a coward and avoided Elowen all night. If I saw her again, I would have given into any demand she made. I wouldn't have been capable of saying no to anything she asked of me.

The lander rises higher and higher. The suns burn my eyes as I watch it ascend.

The hurt in her eyes was evident when I told her she had to leave. Just a few months ago, the idea of her staying here would have made me the happiest Tilak in the universe. Now, I've been ripped apart. I feel like I'm drowning.

This pain is what is going to fuel me. Now that she is gone and safely tucked away, I can face what will happen next.

The briefings are all the same. We are doomed. The Atorum haven't left and are currently advancing on the base.

Tai walks into central command without a word. His hair is a mess and the lines on his face are deeper. Maybe tired? Maybe sad?

"I found Bri hiding in a cleaning bot closet. She tried to avoid evacuation," he says.

"You weren't on escort duty. How did you know she didn't board?" I ask, suspecting I know the answer already.

"I was just making sure she followed orders. She is stubborn, and she hasn't made her feelings about Earth a secret since they pulled out of the treaty. Not too hard to predict she would try to stay," he says.

"How did Elowen do?" he asks.

"I don't know, I didn't see her off," I say without looking away from the screen ahead of me. I can't bear to look at him right now.

"What did you do?" It's a question that sounds more like an accusation.

"Last night, I told her she had to leave. I told her she didn't belong here and that I would personally load her on a shipping transport if she tried to stay behind." I swallow the bile that has risen up into my throat.

"Wow. I didn't take you for a coward. That might not even be a strong enough word for what you did," he says.

"I know. I needed to say something to make her leave."

"Are you going to try and fix this?" he asks.

"I don't know that she'll even give me a chance to explain. I avoided her all night and she left without saying goodbye."

"I was right. It's so much worse than coward."

"I know."

"At least I had the balls to look Bri in the eye while I dragged her onto the lander," he says. That does make me look up. It's the closest he's ever come to admitting his feelings for Bri.

"She'll never forgive me. She told me about twenty times," he says.

"It doesn't matter if they forgive us. They're gone, for good."

"You need to pull yourself together. The fight isn't done. For some reason, the Atorum haven't stopped yet."

"I'll fight," I say and leave the room. I can't be around anyone right now, even my best friend.

I move through the quiet base. Everyone moves around without saying a word. Even the bots are quiet, knowing what a somber day it is. I skirt around the quonset my family has been living in for the last few days. I'm not in the mood to deal with their prying questions. My feet take me to our room without me realizing it.

The room is perfectly clean. It's like she was never here. I sink down onto the bed and drag her pillow over my face to inhale her scent, the only thing left of her. Taking it deep into my lungs.

I lie there, unmoving, questioning everything, doubting myself for probably the first time in my life. This is what it feels like—a lifetime of unfaltering arrogance has finally caught up with me.

I drag in every breath, knowing that this last reminder of her will disappear over time. Soon it will all be gone.

60

Elowen

I don't believe a word Aro said. If it didn't hurt so badly, I would laugh at how cliché it is. I remember the first time I saw this trope in a vid when I was a little girl.

A boy had a pet wolf he couldn't keep any longer, I can't remember exactly why. Maybe the wolf acted out… Regardless, the boy chased the wolf off, saying horrible and hurtful things. When the confused wolf finally ran off, the boy fell to his knees and cried. My mom comforted me while I cried along with the boy in the vid.

I was so confused. How could the boy be so cruel to his beloved wolf? None of it made sense at the time. She soothed my hair down and explained that sometimes people will say things they don't mean so they can save those they love.

I know what Aro was trying to do. The hurt deep down in my chest is from him not coming back, not saying goodbye and not seeing me onto the lander. That part stings the most.

It's not long before my yuriOS lights up with a link request from Aro. I quickly decline. I'm not ready to speak with him yet. It's better if he doesn't know what I'm up to right now.

For days I've been trying to think of anything I can do to help j'Tilak. I hoped that I could appeal to Earth, that as a human I could convince them to come to our aid. Part of me knows it wouldn't have done anything.

Earth made a calculated decision. They had all the research they needed, research I worked day and night to give them. In my naïveté it never occurred to me to hold back on sending the information over. They play politics when so many lives are at stake.

Betrayal isn't strong enough to describe what I feel right now. I'm appalled and full of rage. It's not right and I refuse to be complicit. They happily took the research to help themselves and abandoned their allies when they needed them the most.

My mind kept coming up blank on any other option, until last night. While I lay there waiting for Aro to come back to our room, that tiny little seed of a plan that I'd been brushing away took root in my head.

"I brought you some noodles. They're probably cold," Maak says as he slinks into his room.

"Thanks. I'll eat later. I'm not hungry. My stomach is in knots," I tell him.

He drops the bowl of noodles on his desk in the corner and turns the chair to face me as he sits down.

"You should eat. It might be a while before I can get away to feed you again."

"You're probably wondering why I asked you for help," I say, guessing at his motivations for sitting down to talk with me. It's not a secret that Maak has kept his distance from me and Aro since he caught us coming back into the dome that night.

"I am," he admits.

"I knew you would help me stay. I also know that regardless of what you think of me, you want what's best for your world. And I respect that," I say.

"You know he will kill me if he ever finds out that I helped you stay."

"Another risk we all take in service of j'Tilak. You and I both know that if I evacuated the Atorum would just go away and we would never know who was responsible for this."

"What's the strategy here? How long do you think you can hide in my room before you get caught?"

"I'm still trying to figure that part out. I've got plan A, and if that doesn't work, we'll resort to plan B."

"Do I want to know either one?" he asks.

"It's probably for the best if you don't." I grab the bowl of noodles he smuggled in for me and take a small bite. Maybe it's the conversation, or the confirmation that I'm eating—Maak turns to leave.

Before reaching the door he turns and says, "Whatever it is you're thinking. I hope it works. We can only fight them off for so long."

I do too.

61

Aro

As I suspected, she declined my link. And I deserve it. I was horrible and she is completely justified in never wanting to speak with me again.

Suddenly our room feels suffocating and I need to get out. Somewhere I can think about anything else. I head back to central command. The mission briefing will be starting soon. I might as well get there early.

I'm hardly paying attention while Rialto and Petrok go through the procedure. Our sentinels have detected the Atorum presence approaching our base. We're preparing for the worst.

"The Atorum have adapted to our defenses. Each time they have attacked, they have learned our methods, making each following assault that much more difficult for us to fend off."

"We stay on the defensive this time. Crews are erecting battlements as we speak. Our only objective is to survive," Petrok says gravely.

I go through the motions of what is required of me. None of it feels real. It's not enough to stay busy. My thoughts always return to her. I've given up on summoning my battleform. It's a small comfort that Elowen is safe, but it also means there is no hope in me shifting again.

Tai hasn't given up. He keeps sending me messages trying to get me to train with him one last time. I ignore all his attempts at reaching me.

The alarm blares, warning of the Atorum's arrival. It's time. They're here. I make my way to the battlement hoping the necessary adrenaline shows up. If I can't summon my battleform, I'll at least need that rush to keep me fighting.

The defensive structures are impressive. Plasma cannons have been mounted along the entire wall, ready for an attack from any direction. I take my place, closest to where they will attack.

The swarm of Atorum creeps out of the forest, heading straight for us. That all-too-familiar shriek pieces our ears.

They writhe and shift as they stack up on each other. Some climb up the shielded walls. Plasma cannons fire off, blasting them apart. When one group explodes into pieces, more bugs pour in to replace them. They just keep coming.

Their attack on Tauros has taught them well. Glittering cracks form along the barrier shield. They breach the shield faster than I thought possible. Cannons fire off in rapid succession aimed at where they make progress. I ready myself to fight.

The cracks in the shield splinter out. One deep crack spikes its way across the entire length of the shield. It's enough for an Atorum to squeeze through. The first is killed instantly, followed by a trickle of them squirming through the crack. The break widens and the Atorum pour in. We can't keep up with the relentless onslaught.

An Atorum drops down and lands on the battlement not far from me. I rush at it and blast it apart easily. Three more take its place. I'm quick with the blaster and destroy those three as well. The base is covered in black sludge, and every Tilak is fighting these monstrous creatures.

I watch one Tilak be overtaken by a horde of bugs. He's dragged down as they swarm over him. I charge at the pile and reload my blaster canister while I pull the bugs off the fallen Tilak. He's covered in mire, which holds him down to the ground.

I try one last time to summon my battleform. A ripple of power runs through my veins, but it's not enough to bring about the change.

A sonic boom waves over the base. The ground surrounding us buckles from the pressure. Where did that come from? I search for the source of the noise. Atorum all around us shudder to the ground and curl up on their backs, dead.

I run back up the battlement, desperate to see what happened. A second blast echoes through the base. The Atorum that survived the first blast fall to the ground.

A sleek Na'Lorskan warship slowly passes over, temporarily blocking out the sun before it lowers to the ground in front of the base.

I race down the stairs and hit the ground running for the gate. Using all my strength I push open the gate, slowly at first then gaining momentum. I squeeze through the opening as soon as I can.

A short Na'Lorskan female walks down a gangplank towards me. She smiles as I skid to a stop in front of her.

"You must be Aro," she says, a wide toothy smile across her tiny mouth.

62

Elowen

The walls in Maak's room shudder from the sonic boom Priya warned me about. I steady the bowl of cold noodles on the table. The world may be coming to an end, but Maak would never forgive me if I messed up his room. I hold my breath and wait. I'm under strict orders to not come out until after a second blast.

My head has been full of worst-case scenarios all day. She promised she would get here as soon as possible. Plan A is a simple one—really only two things need to go right. But a lot can still go wrong. Priya's got to show up on time and her new weapon needs to do what she thinks it's capable of. Emphasis on "thinks." It's never been used before.

I take a few calming breaths and channel the confidence Aro so easily radiates. Everything is going to be fine. My plan will work, and we will figure out exactly who's responsible.

I slide the dresser away from the door once the room stops shaking for the second time. The furniture wouldn't have kept the Atorum out, but it gave me a false sense of security, and I'll take what I can get.

The halls are deathly quiet. Outside, the aftermath of the attack steals the breath from my lungs. I make my way through rubble, dodging medbots as they zoom in every direction checking the soldiers and administering aid. I duck as one speeds over me nearly taking my head off. It would be pretty ironic if I got taken out by a freaking medbot at this point.

I search for Aro among those upright and helping the injured. His confidence has rubbed off on me because in my mind it's not even a possibility he could be one of the fallen. I see him in the distance, his back to me. There is no mistaking my mate, even from here. I break into a run, jumping over dead bugs with an athletic ability I didn't know I had.

Priya sees me first and points a long slender finger in my direction. He spins around and stands frozen in place. I don't slow down when I get close. Instead I launch myself into the air and knock him to the ground. I grab both sides of his head and search his face for any sign of injury.

"You saved us," he says quietly, staring up at me in awe.

"I saved us." I smile down at him.

"You were supposed to evacuate," he says numbly.

"I'm more of an ask-forgiveness-not-permission type." I quote him from that first time he made me spicy noodles.

"Do you hate me?" he asks hesitantly.

"I know what you were trying to do. You can't scare me off. I'm here, with you, where I belong." I lean down and kiss him with everything I have left in me. He crushes me against him.

"How did you do it?" he pulls away, breathless from our kiss.

"I know people," I say and smile up at Priya. "You made it just in time," I tell her.

63

Aro

"He's dead. I'm going to kill him. And then I'm going to invent a way to reanimate his body, and I'll kill him again," I say after Elowen tells me how she managed to avoid being evacuated.

"It was the right thing to do," Elowen says and climbs up onto my lap. I dragged her to our room, wanting some privacy while I got answers.

"He should have never allowed you to stay. He disobeyed orders, and put you in danger," I tell her. The fight is already leaving my body as she kisses along my jawline.

"If I had been evacuated, who was going to save your ass?" she says.

I grip her waist and pull her closer. I still need the reassurance of her touch to remind me she's here.

"Maak only did what I asked him to do."

"I don't know why you didn't just evacuate and then contact Priya from the shuttle," I say, nuzzling into her neck, softening against her touches.

"There was always Plan B if she didn't get here in time," she says.

"And what exactly was Plan B?" I close my eyes, knowing I'm not going to like what she says next.

"I was going to help you summon your battleform," she says between kisses.

She would have sacrificed herself for j'Tilak, for our home. Conflicting feelings battle inside me.

"Promise me you won't kill Maak," Elowen says, forcing my head up so we are eye to eye.

When I don't answer she says again, "Promise me." This time she's more forceful.

"I promise," I grind out between clenched teeth. "Where did Priya come from?"

"I ran into her on my way here. She's one of my oldest friends, and I called in a favor. I reached out last night and barely got the words out before she was on her way."

"I can't believe that you did this. I should be angry. I should be livid… I'm just so fucking proud," I tell her. "I'm so sorry for what I said. I'm sorry for being such a coward and hiding from you."

"I know why you did it. I understand, but don't do that shit again." Her smile takes the sting out of her words.

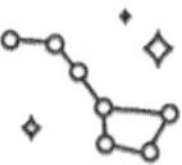

The least damaged Atorum is dragged into the medical tent. It's already starting to deteriorate and ends up in pieces by the time it's on the table. Elowen suits up and approaches the bug. She nervously wipes away the sweat collecting on her brow.

"Here goes nothing," she says and makes a long incision along the hard exoskeleton. Black mire leaks out from the cut and collects on the table. She pushes aside the organs to get to its central nervous system, where we'll find the data we need. We'll finally know who's responsible. She locates the ventral nerve and gently pulls it loose from the connective tissue.

Elowen carefully lays the long cord down on the table next to the Atorum's body and slices off a thin sample from the nerves. Her hand shakes when she places it in the flow cytometer. The sample is sucked up into this machine that looks like any other cabinet along the walls.

She explained to me that behind the closed panels, the cells are dropped single file through a laser that will analyze each individually. The room is silent except for the quiet whir of the machinery while it runs the diagnostic.

I look over at Elowen while we wait, both of us anxious for the results. I jump a little from the harmless chirp that indicates the report is ready. I swipe the control panel, expanding it so we can read the results together.

"Reynauld Custos," Elowen says, not recognizing the name.

"Motherfucker," I mumble.

64

Aro

My father and I wait near the gates for his council to arrive. We have spent the last two days strategizing, down to the last detail. If we do this right, Custos will implicate anyone else that worked with him.

We don't have to wait long. The porters file in one after the other in rapid succession. The overdressed Tilaks look out of place at the base and stand out like a sore thumb. I remind myself to check with Elowen to see if that's the right way to use that term. Their long robes are likely touching dust for the first time. Rialto and Petrok join us, ready to take a tour of the damage caused by the Atorum.

After a brisk welcome, we lead them all to the battlements so they can see the sheer scale of destruction. From up here, there is no denying how grave the situation had become.

I take note of who stands near Custos, who whispers under their breath into his ear, and who avoids looking directly at the scene below. Custos is the only one who keeps their gaze fixed on the distance rather than looking down.

Next, Rialto leads to the war room. I can tell Custos is uncomfortable. He shifts in his seat and drums his fingers against the hard table. His eyes are darting around like he's looking for a quick exit. A holographic image of an Atorum comes up in the center of the room.

"Now that we are all familiar with the devastation these creatures are capable of—a human scientist was able to determine who is responsible for all of this." My father hesitates to continue and looks over the room. Everyone looks around anxiously except Custos, who sits with a deadly calm, watching me with black eyes that betray nothing.

"Reynauld, this is your one chance to explain your actions. After this you will be held accountable for what you have done, and I will no longer entertain anything you have to say," my father says ominously. The room is deathly silent and everyone turns to him.

Custos clears his throat and with narrowed eyes says, "Have you seen what they did to their own planet? They would have destroyed ours as well! I did this in service of j'Tilak." His calm cracks as he bangs his fist on the table.

He looks around at all the other advisors, trying to determine if anyone agrees with him. Everyone looks back with disgust.

"They are not trustworthy! They have already broken their commitment to come to our aid! I just wanted to get them off the planet. No one needed to get hurt," he pleads. His argument gets no foothold with the others.

"Aid that we requested because of you!" I snap. I get a sharp look from my father. This is the part where we are supposed to stay quiet and let him dig his own grave.

"You have to know I did this for our people," he says, trying again to get someone—anyone—on his side. "Fine. When the humans destroy us, you'll have no one to blame but yourselves." His tone turns sharp when he realizes no one is going to take his side.

I look at my father in a silent request to speak. I have a few things that need to be said. He nods, silently granting me permission.

"We are faced with an opportunity to join our world with the rest of the universe. Yes, this opportunity will come with challenges, challenges that will make us stronger and better. The balance of our world is always shifting, and there will be repercussions. We will find a new balance in our world. And when that equilibrium shifts, we can give into the fear of that change, or we can face it—head on. I trust in our world, and our people, that we can face that fear. We have so much to offer the rest of the universe. We can open our world in a way that aligns with who we are and be a source of inspiration and strength."

I think I forgot to breathe during my monologue. I pause and drag in a breath. The suspicion that this threat came from our own people has been sitting heavy on my shoulders for a long time.

"I had to take a hard look at who we are, and who we want to be. I've never been so sure of anything in my life. My vision for our future is not isolating from everyone else—hoarding our way of life and resources. It's not just coexistence, but learning from each other and creating something new."

"Now that the immediate threat to the humans has been resolved, I want to discuss allowing them back." My father sets the trap. He wants to know who will use the opportunity to keep j'Tilak free of humans.

"They're already gone. We can go back to how things were before," Custos cuts in.

"As far as I'm concerned, our allies are always welcome back," Besnik says, choosing her words carefully.

"Only our allies?" My father asks for clarification.

"Um… What I meant to say… You know, the humans," she trips over her words trying to align with what she thinks my father wants to hear.

"I will personally welcome them back," another says from across the table.

All, except Custos, nod in agreement. I'm satisfied he's alone in this. Petrok drags Custos to his feet. He doesn't put up a fight. He knows he gambled and lost.

With Custos gone, the Council falls easily into their habit of long-winded discussions. My father gives them all a chance to speak their minds about Custos and the future of our world.

I'd like to take some of the credit for setting the tone because they are speaking more passionately about the future than I have ever heard before. It's still boring as fuck, but I stay focused on what everyone has to say. It's going to take more than one impassioned speech to get this done, but I'm committed to making it happen.

My father stops me on our way out. "Aro, I've never been more proud—as a father and leader of this house. You've made us all proud today."

For the first time in my life, my father thumps his chest, honoring me.

65

Elowen

I look out over Bihar from the roof of our building. The city is gold and shining as the suns dip down towards the horizon. I come up here almost every day to watch the sunset. Part of me still can't believe this is my life. If this is a dream, I never want to wake up.

Something brushes up against my ankles while I watch the sky, drawing my attention to my feet. A small yellow blossom creeps its way across the rooftop garden in search of its new home. I kneel down on the soft ground and watch it roll and sway, taking a meandering path away from me.

A shadow appears from behind and Aro sinks down onto his knees next to me. The sight of him still makes my heart beat faster.

"How did it go?" I ask. He spent the day with his father and the remaining group of loyal advisors. One of many meetings that will change the course of history for our home.

"More of the same. We're working on a long-term settlement plan," he says and sits more comfortably on the ground next to me.

"When does Bri get back?" I ask. I've been missing her these last few weeks. And it's been surprisingly hard to get a hold of her.

"Tai's working on it."

"Look at us—you making plans for the future, and me just sitting up here living in the moment. Who'd have thought?"

He pulls me onto his lap, my favorite place to be in the universe. I lean back onto his chest and watch the yellow flower find its spot. It nestles into the soil and then slowly unfurls its roots and beds down.

"Ah, look, she found a place to put roots down," Aro says.

"She did."

The End.

UNTANGLED

01

Bri

I pull off my boots for the millionth time and dump out the sand. It was a struggle to get up this dune. I'm drenched in sweat when I look back down at where I started the climb. My wrecked escape pod is nestled between dunes. It's hot. I'm sweaty. And there is sand, everywhere. Everywhere, everywhere.

The console was dead by the time I came to. I woke up in the dark escape pod with a pounding headache. I swiped my hand across the panel and blindly searched for toggles or buttons to initiate a reboot. My fingers eventually snagged on the emergency survival pack under the cockpit. I pulled the portable respirator out of the pack and secured the face mask as tightly as I could. I turned on the air supply and shoved the canister for it back into the bag.

The bitter air flooded into my nose. It was gross but at least it would keep me from suffocating if this planet didn't have a suitable atmosphere for my puny human lungs. Fortunately I didn't need the respirator for long. The moment the hatch opened it flashed green indicating the atmosphere was safe.

From up here, there are dunes in every direction except one, so that is exactly where I will be heading. To the north? south? Who the hell knows what direction? But it's flat and the cracked ground riddled with dried up-bushes looks better than digging my way through more sand.

This is all Tai's fault. If he would've just minded his own damn business I wouldn't be here right now. Wherever the fuck here is. Scalding sand surrounds me and is currently sticking to every part of my body. I hate sand. I hate it so much. I don't even like the beach.

The only redeeming quality of the beach is the water and it's absolutely my luck that I've crashed on a planet covered in sand with no water in sight. There are no waves crashing against the shore making me forget the itch of the sand in my underwear. No cold-water lapping at my feet, just the rough grains between my toes already causing blisters. And there is a distinct lack of ice-cold beverages with tiny umbrellas to quench my thirst.

What I wouldn't do for one of those drinks right now. I'd order a pink one, with a slice of fruit or pretty flower on the rim. The kind of drink I tromped through the sand to deliver to some rich asshole laying on a lounger every summer.

Fuck the beach and fuck this place.

I put my boots back on and cinch them tight. It won't keep the sand out, but hopefully I won't have to stop so often to empty them. I rifle through my pack one last time, taking inventory of what I've got to keep me alive until I can find help.

The contents haven't changed the last three times I've checked. I just need a tiny bit of reassurance that I'm not going to be baked alive out here. I've got a week's worth of nutritional gel packs.

"Hello, my old friend," I say as I open one up.

I've got my air supply canister, my dead yuriOS datapad, a few dozen hydration packs, a foil blanket, liquid sutures, and a tiny translator patch. Whoever thought to include that did me a solid. I don't feel like playing charades to get myself out of here if no one speaks universal language.

I step down on the opposite side of the dune, heading towards my salvation—solid ground. My foot sinks down into the sand, and before I can catch myself, I'm rolling ass over tea kettle down the hot sand. I land with a thud at the bottom of the dune. It's just as solid as I had hoped—but it knocked the air out of my lungs. Now I've got a face full of sand and a swollen ankle, but at least I've made it down.

"That's one way to do it." The delirium has already started to kick in. First, I talked to the gel packs. Now, I'm talking to myself. It's not been long since I woke up in the wrecked pod, and I'm just one volley-ball away from full-blown insanity.

I tighten the straps of the pack and trudge forward. My shirt is drenched down my back. It pours down my legs and my socks absorb most of it. Two thoughts flash at the same time: Did I pee myself? Or did I just destroy the only fuel I've got to keep me alive?

"Fuck!" My yell is absorbed by the hot ground. I drop to my knees and flip the pack open. Most of the hydration packs broke along with half of the nutritional gels. I slurp the oozing gel off my fingers, try-ing to get anything I can from the ruined supplies. I wish I had peed myself. Something I've never thought before. Wow, context really is everything.

I lean back on my heels and take a steady breath. Now is not the time to freak out. I need to remain calm and focused. Losing it now could be the difference between life or death. And I refuse—absolutely refuse—to be taken out by a goddamn oceanless beach.

I pull the pack back on and start walking. I'm just going to think of this as a little pleasure hike. It's going to be a hilarious story I can tell over cocktails, regaling a crowd with my survival skills. Whenever I'm in these terrible situations I play this game. I picture myself later retelling the story that I'm currently in. I think of ways to make it funny and maybe even embellish a tiny bit to up the stakes.

The terror at realizing I've lost half of my supplies is nothing com-pared to the horror that ripples through my body when I realize that my shirt and pants are bone dry in no time at all. That was quick. And it is not a good sign. I need to find help, quickly. I need to pick up the pace. I dig deep into that stubborn part of me that refuses to give up.

The toe on my good side catches a rock and I'm pitched through the air again, landing on my face. Again.

"Jesus titty-fucking Christ."

I push off the ground and resist the urge to start listing my ail-ments. That won't do me any good. I'm fine. This is going to make one hell of a story someday.

ACKNOWLEDGEMENTS

If you've made it this far, there are a few things you need to know about Uprooted. There is no way this book could have gotten to you without the love and support of some amazing women (and one man).

Rachel, your loving hands gave me the courage to take this on. You folded me into your beautiful world and I'm forever changed.

Cynthia, you helped me find my own way. You looked at a messy first draft of a brand-new writer and saw potential. Not only did you help me build this world, you gave me the tools to build so many more.

Sandi, you brought so much joy to this book. When other writers are in editing hell, I was having the time of my life. Your laugh lights up the entire universe. You're a rock star and I am the founding member of your fan club.

Catherine, your relentless confidence in me came at just the right moment. Having you in my corner has been such a gift.

Brandon, thank you for building a life with me. Your love and stability has given me the freedom to be creative and take chances. You nudged me to start this whole thing, so you only have yourself to blame.

Last but not least, I want to thank Snoop Dogg, just kidding... I want to thank me. I want to thank me for believing in me. I want to thank me for doing all this hard work. I want to thank me for having no days off. I want to thank me for never quitting. I want to thank me for always being a giver and trying to give more than I receive. I want to thank me for trying to do more right than wrong. I want to thank me for being me at all times.